FOUR CONTEMPORARY
ROMANCE NOVELLAS

Sleigh Bells Ring

Sandra D. Bricker, Barbara J. Scott,
Lynette Sowell, Lenora Worth

GILEAD
PUBLISHING
Wheaton, IL

Sleigh Bells Ring
Published by Gilead Publishing, Wheaton, IL 60187
www.gileadpublishing.com

ISBN: 978-1-68370-007-4 (print)
ISBN: 978-1-68370-011-1 (eBook)

All I Want for Christmas © 2016 by Sandra D. Bricker
Her Old Kentucky Home © 2016 by Lynette Sowell
I'll Be Home for Christmas © 2016 by Barbara J. Scott
Please Come Home for Christmas © 2016 by Lenora Worth

Lynette Sowell is represented by MacGregor Literary, Inc. Barbara Scott is represented by the literary agency of WordServe Literary (www.wordserveliterary.com).

Editors: Barbara J. Scott and Sandra D. Bricker
Cover and Interior Designer: Larry Taylor

Printed in the United States of America

Contents

All I Want for Christmas

by Sandra D. Bricker

Dear Jo-Jo,

If you're reading this letter, my attorney has finally located you. The last address I had for you was no good, so they hired an investigator to track you down and let you know about my fate. It seems you girls have scattered in every different direction, but I wanted you all to know that the horse farm is legally yours now. Not that it belonged to anyone else since the day your beautiful mom came to stay.

I wish we could have spent some time together before the cancer got ahold of me—just one of the many regrets I have these days. Baby, I hope you've been able to find a little forgiveness for your old man over the years. I wasn't the best father—or any kind of father, really—but I've always loved you. I pray you know that, and I'm truly sorry for all the years we lost.

Tuck

[Love] always protects, always trusts, always hopes, always perseveres. Love never fails.

—1 Corinthians 13:7–8

CHAPTER ONE

Joanna had intended to sleep in past seven, especially now that she had the option—an unusual occurrence for a Thursday morning except for her recent state of unemployment. But her internal clock had gone off at ten minutes before the hour just to irritate her. The voices in her head simply refused to shut up, and she finally surrendered and climbed out from under the multiple quilts layered over her.

She padded to the kitchenette in bare feet, still wearing her drawstring, pink-flannel pants and long-sleeved Henley. She pressed a folded paper towel into the brew basket and spooned some coffee into it before running water into the carafe. By the time she produced a mug from one of the hooks under the shelf, the fragrance of freshly brewing coffee tickled her nose. After filling her mug, she noticed a few grounds floating around in the cup and scooped them out with the back of the spoon before stirring in the creamer. She nearly dropped the spoon when someone pounded on her door three times.

Joanna squinted at the clock. "It's not even eight o'clock in the morning," she bellowed as she made her way across the room. Peering through the peephole, she grimaced at the distorted image of a young twentysomething with wire-rimmed glasses. The collar of his coat stood upright against the wind howling through the narrow passageway. After a moment, he thumped his gloved fist against the door again, twice this time.

Joanna left the security chain in place and unlocked two deadbolts and the doorknob. She pulled the door back a few inches and looked out through the opening.

"What do you want? My husband is sleeping," she fibbed.

The guy narrowed his eyes for a few beats before answering. "Miss

Tucker? Joanna Tucker?"

"Who wants to know?"

The hiss of the wind through the outdoor passageway turned to a roar, and all of his sandy hair blew to one side of his head. His small frame nearly toppled over.

"I'm Stephen Sample," he shouted. "I work for Hanks and Stern."

"I'm sorry. Who?"

"The Law Offices of Hanks and Stern."

She glanced over at the overflowing, metal bowl on the table next to the door, the place where she dropped all of the bills and unopened collection notices awaiting her attention. She thought she remembered a logo bearing those names on at least one of the envelopes in the bowl. Or maybe two of them. There wasn't a handwritten address in the lot of them—just various business fonts spelling out Ms. JOANNA TUCKER. Or in the case of Fort Wayne Medical Center's invoice, JOANNE ROSE TACKER. It seemed nothing ever came to her mailbox anymore without metaphoric extended hands and raised palms, seeking funds she simply didn't have.

"We've been trying to make contact with you on behalf of Robert Tucker."

Joanna's entire body froze, more from the mention of the name than the frigid winter wind slithering in through the small opening. "I don't know anyone by that name," she lied and started to push the door shut.

"Ms. Tucker," he objected, pressing his palm against the door so he could slip his business card through. "Please. Can I come inside and speak to you? Five minutes, and I'll be out the door again." When she didn't reply, he added, "It's really cold out here."

"Wait there," she snapped and closed the door. She studied the card as she rushed to the bathroom. She grabbed the plaid, flannel robe from the back of the door and slipped into it, burying the man's card in the pocket as she returned to snow-boy waiting outside. "Five minutes," she told him as she belted the robe. "No more than that."

"Thank you." Panting, he hurried inside, brushing the snow from his thick hair. "This weather is ridiculous."

It's winter. And we live in Indiana. It's not all that surprising, is it?

"I just made some coffee." She padded over to grab a second mug. "How do you take it? I have creamer but no sugar."

"Black is fine. Just something to warm me up would be great."

Joanna set the cup on the small table and nodded toward the second chair. He sat, wrapping his now-ungloved hands around the mug for warmth. She retrieved her own coffee and folded one leg beneath her before lowering into the chair across from him.

"What's your name again?" She clutched the warmth close to her face.

"Stephen Sample." His hand left the coffee long enough to produce an envelope from the inside pocket of his coat, and he slid it across the tabletop toward her. "Robert Tucker retained our firm . . ."

Again, her father's name stopped her from breathing. As the young guy nattered on, she opened the envelope and retrieved a small packet of papers. On top, a crisp letter of introduction on embossed letterhead bearing the name of the law firm.

Dear Ms. Tucker:

On behalf of your father, Robert Tucker, we would like to inform—

"—and I'm sorry to say . . . it was cancer."

Stephen Sample took a slow, clueless sip from his coffee as Joanna's heart lurched against her chest, and she jerked her head up to look at him. "I'm sorry. What did you say? He's dead? The father I hardly knew I still had . . . is *dead?*"

"Yes, ma'am."

"How?" she stammered. "What was wrong with him? What kind of cancer?"

Stephen Sample set his coffee mug on the table. "Lung."

Sudden memories of cherry pipe tobacco swirled through her mind, and Joanna swallowed all of the other thoughts so that she could ask just one question. "How long did he know?"

"A month, possibly. Six weeks at the outside."

Her voice softened. "And how long have *you* known?"

"We've been trying to make contact with you for quite some time.

We've sent at least four letters. And we couldn't find a current phone number . . ."

Joanna glanced again at the metal bowl near the door. Why hadn't she opened one of the letters? She'd never imagined that correspondence from the Law Offices of So-and-So could have been anything except a series of collection notices. She never dreamed . . .

". . . so I finally decided to try stopping by this address on my way in to the office to see if I could make contact in person."

"How did you even find me?"

The young man belched out a chuckle and shook his head. "It sure wasn't easy, I'll tell you that."

She took a sip of coffee and slowly swallowed it. "What do you want with me? I mean, if he's already gone. Is this some sort of notification thing then?"

"There's a letter there from him." He pointed to the papers she held. "The second page, right after the one from the firm."

Joanna turned the first page facedown on the table. The next—a short, handwritten note on lined, yellow paper—caused her vision to blur. No mistaking it. Tuck's handwriting. She blinked several times to bring the words into focus.

The final line of his note choked her: *I'm truly sorry for all the years we lost.*

The years they'd *lost?* How about the years he'd stolen when he walked out the door and never came back? All the birthdays he'd missed—hers and the ones of her three older sisters. She'd spent so many years watching out the window in the hope that he might happen by to give his youngest daughter a birthday hug.

And what was this addition at the bottom of the note? A Scripture verse? Oh, that was rich. Biblical reference from the guy who lived off his wife's faith instead of developing some of his own.

"My darling, my faith won't do your soul any good," she remembered her mother telling him one Sunday morning as the rest of his family assembled in the great room. "Come to church with us."

"Say a prayer for your old man, will you, Jo-Jo?" he'd asked as he tugged her toward him and finished buttoning her coat.

"Sure, Daddy. But I wish you'd come with us. Just once."

Forcing back her tears, Joanna sniffed as she packaged the paperwork together again and folded it back into the envelope.

"Have you contacted my sisters?"

"Our investigators are still trying to reach Isabella."

"Amy and Sophia already know then?" She swallowed her dismay with a gulp of air.

"I believe so, yes."

Joanna narrowed her eyes and stared at the door over the slope of Stephen Sample's shoulder. Why wouldn't either of them have called her? Sure, they didn't talk all that often, but being told that their father had died certainly warranted a special effort. And what about Jed? Why hadn't he or his mother let her know? Jed Weatherly couldn't pick up and dial a phone?

"If you can help us to get in touch with Isabella—"

"She travels a lot," Joanna muttered. Then, when the young man's curious stare poked her, she shook her head. "I'm sorry. I'll call her today and tell her to look for your correspondence."

"Excellent. Then if she'll just call our offices—"

"I'm sure she will."

He sat there for what seemed like forever before he finally stood and put on his gloves. "Well, thank you for seeing me. And for the coffee." Glancing at the envelope on the table, he added, "You have my card. And there's also contact information inside. Have a nice day, Miss Tucker."

A nice day? This guy had just broken the news that Tuck was dead and then wished her a nice day?

After she bolted the door behind him, Joanna stalked to the table and stood over the envelope for several heartbeats before grabbing her half cup of coffee and heading straight back to bed.

"Jedediah? Are you listening to me?"

Jed's neck snapped as he jerked toward his mother. "Sorry. What did you say?"

"Would you like a little more stew before you head home?"

He'd nearly forgotten where he was. He glanced up at his mother standing on the other side of the island and sighed. "Oh. No thanks, Mom. I've had plenty. It was great."

Sarah walked toward him and placed her hand on his shoulder. "Did you hear back from any of the girls?"

Jed ran a hand over the stubble on his cheek and sighed. "I've probably called Jo-Jo's number a dozen times since Tuck passed. But I haven't been able to catch her, and there's no voice mail on her phone. I don't even know if I have the right number anymore because her emails are bouncing back." He groaned and ran his hands through his hair. "I just hope the lawyer in Fort Wayne has better luck than I did."

"It's a shame they all four missed out on attending the services." Sarah picked up the empty stoneware bowl in front of him. "I have to believe they'd have come to the old coot's funeral if they'd known."

"I can't speak for the others," Jed told her, "but Jo-Jo would have been here. I'm convinced of that."

"It's late in the day. She should be home from work by now, don't you think?"

"Depends. I don't even know what she's doing these days," he replied.

Sarah picked up Jed's cell phone from the counter and handed it to him. "Why not give her another try."

Jed searched his contacts for Joanna's number and clicked on it. Once again, a string of unanswered rings with no voice-mail pick-up.

"Nah," he commented before disconnecting and tucking the phone into the pocket of his denim shirt. "I'm headed home for the night. Anything need doing around here before I go?"

"You could kiss your mama."

He chuckled and planted a kiss on her cheek. "Thanks for the grub."

"Anytime."

Jed slipped into the double-breasted, dark-brown peacoat he'd discarded on the chair and buttoned it on his way to the door. "I'm due over at the Triple Z before nine in the morning. I should be back by early afternoon."

"I'm going over to Josie Emerson's around ten so we can cook up a week's worth of meals and drive them out to the Barrett clan. Todd's on his own now with those six kids of his."

Jed cringed and shook his head at the thought. "Be careful heading out there, Mom. The road washed out last week, and they're rebuilding the retaining wall on the east side."

"Yes, Son. I've been out to Todd's place twice since Miranda's funeral."

He knew better than to play the overprotective son with his independent mother. Still, it never seemed to stop him. He kissed her cheek a second time before turning up the collar of his coat and heading out into the bitter cold.

The November chill clocked at twenty-one degrees on the oversized thermometer on the outside wall, and the stones beneath his boots crunched out the noisy soundtrack of his departure. He dug the key ring out of the pocket of his jeans before he crossed the front porch that used to be the converted bunkhouse where he'd grown up. Now . . . his private sanctuary. *Home.*

He poked the key into the deadbolt and groaned in relief when he crossed the threshold and pushed the door shut behind him.

Jed removed his gloves and stuffed them into the pocket of his coat, which he hung on the steel rack. Sliding an armful of logs out of the top shelf of the built-in, he carried them over to the fireplace and sat on the stone hearth. Once he'd stoked the fire into a full blaze, Jed ambled over to the leather sofa and dropped onto it. Propping his boots on the arm, he folded a throw pillow, jammed it into the curve at the back of his neck, and closed his eyes.

"Long day," he muttered just as sleep whirled in like a sudden storm and carried him away.

CHAPTER TWO

Joanna glanced at the dashboard clock: 1:42 a.m. The last leg of her trek from Fort Wayne had taken longer than anticipated. Under the cover of darkness, she found it difficult to discern whether time had taken a toll on the house, but she leaned forward and surveyed her old Kentucky home through the frosted windshield.

She removed the keys from the ignition and grabbed her purse and bulging overnight bag from the passenger seat before climbing out of the car. Joanna hesitated at the front door before inserting the battered, gold key into the lock and gingerly turning it. The gargantuan thermometer still graced the porch wall, and its reading of eighteen degrees sent a shiver up her half-frozen spine. She took care to enter as quietly as possible, assuming Sarah Weatherly still occupied the house. Of course, she couldn't be sure.

Joanna flipped on the crystal-based lamp on the table by the door, and its white light flooded the room as nostalgia deluged her emotions. Some of the furniture seemed new, and the nubby rugs that used to cover the aged, gray, French oak floors had been replaced by prettier ones . . . but the place looked very much the same. She didn't know why that surprised her, really.

She inched toward the hub of the main floor—the kitchen—and could almost hear the clamor of four children and their mother moving around the island, packing school lunches, and arguing over who got the last green apple in the bowl. She ran two fingers along the edge of the black marble countertop . . . the curved edge of the massive farm sink . . . touched the gray, brick backsplash behind it . . . twisted the brushed-nickel knob on the drawer. Someone had finally repaired it at some point, she realized. It didn't come off in her hand.

"Joanna? Is that you, Sweet Pea?"

She reeled at the unexpected intrusion to her reminiscence and looked into the aged face of Sarah Weatherly. Sarah had always been lovely, and the years had repaid her countless kindnesses. A few more wrinkles around the eyes and mouth, a slight sag at the jowls, considerably whiter hair, but time had been obliging and gracious.

"Sarah. I'm so sorry to wake you. I meant to arrive much earlier in the evening, but—"

"Nonsense. This is your home. You come and go at any time you see fit."

Joanna sighed. "Thank you."

"Did you drive all the way from Indiana? You must be exhausted. Are you hungry?"

The truth was . . . Joanna was famished. She hadn't eaten since grabbing two tacos at a drive-thru before crossing over into Ohio. "A little. But you go back to bed. I can find something on my own."

Sarah ignored the suggestion and shuffled toward the refrigerator. "Jedediah and I had stew for supper. There's plenty left over."

Jedediah.

The mere mention of his name pinched a corner of her heart that Joanna had all but forgotten. Her first crush. How she'd followed that boy around like a big-eyed puppy! And when her sisters filtered away to start their own lives and Joanna considered doing the same, she didn't have to wonder what to do about the homestead. Jed had loved the place almost as much as she had for most of his life.

Jed's father had come to work managing the ranch before she could even remember, bringing along his lovely wife, Sarah, and their young son, just six years older than Joanna. Tuck and his buddies had converted the original bunkhouse into a small home for them. By the time Mr. Weatherly passed away, Tuck was off somewhere in the Middle East and Jed took over where his dad left off.

Joanna was only twelve years old when eighteen-year-old Jed stepped into his dad's shoes. His first act had been to work with Marlena, Joanna's mother, to fulfill her longtime dream and add the presence of a *rescue ranch* of sorts, a haven for former racehorses to retire or be adopted out for non-racing purposes. To offset the cost of their care, Jed devised a plan so kids could come and ride them or take lessons and get an afternoon of a genuine ranch-like experience.

The clank of the bowl as Sarah set it on the kitchen island brought Joanna back to the moment. The savory fragrance of beef stew and warmed biscuits drew her to the counter-height stool in front of it, and she sat down as Sarah folded a paper napkin.

"I can warm some more if this isn't enough to curb your hunger." She placed the napkin next to the bowl and set a spoon on it.

"This will be plenty, Sarah. Thank you."

"Sweet tea?"

Joanna smiled, wondering how long it had been since she'd been offered a glass of sweet tea. "Absolutely. Please."

Sarah's slippers scuffed as she walked to the row of glossy white cabinets and pulled open the one with a shiny glass insert and retrieved a glass. As she poured, Joanna dunked a biscuit into her bowl to sop up some of the gravy. She moaned with pleasure at her first bite.

"This is delicious, Sarah."

"Thank you, Sweet Pea," Sarah said as she delivered the tea. Joanna had forgotten that Sarah had always called her by that name. It flooded her heart with warm comfort.

After a couple of bites, Joanna decided to broach the topic of the heart-thumping, attractive elephant in the room. "So you said you had dinner with Jed. How's he doing?" She wondered if her attempt at sounding casual had clanked as off-key to Sarah as it had to her.

"Oh, he's just dandy. Tired as all git-out though. He took a job out at the Triple Z on the outskirts of town after your daddy passed to help with the expenses 'round here until the lawyers could get a line on one of you girls."

He's covering the upkeep himself?

"Why didn't he call one of us?" Joanna asked.

"He tried. But your voice mail never picked up, and your emails started bouncin'."

"Ohh."

In an effort to make ends meet, she'd given up her landline months ago, and then her cable and Internet. Then she'd lost her job.

"Did you get any of his emails, honey?"

"No. I changed Internet providers and got a new email address. I should have called one of you to check on things. I don't know why I didn't do that."

Sarah walked over to her and rubbed her arm briskly. "Listen . . . Your daddy passed peacefully. I'm guessing you probably wondered about that. He fell asleep right over there in that club chair he loved so much." Joanna glanced at the worn leather chair, imagining her father sitting there, all six-plus feet of him stretched out. An imposing figure when looking down at one of his four daughters . . . but somehow, when he curved into the right side of that chair, he looked as approachable and cozy as a sleepy old hound. "Matt was with him. I hope that brings you some comfort."

Joanna lifted one shoulder in an attempt at a shrug. "That's good at least."

But it didn't feel good at all. Sure, she supposed it was great that Tuck died in a quiet way. But . . . *Tuck died.* Without one of his four daughters by his side. Or even speaking to him. Fort Wayne was just a little over four hours—and yet an entire lifetime—away from that club chair where her father had taken his last breath. She wondered if that final breath had been tainted with resentment. A sense of abandonment. *Loneliness.*

The thought of him feeling lonely just about killed her. Six feet four inches of imposing confidence—that was how she remembered Robert J. Tucker. But in his last moments, had her self-assured father wavered at all? Had he been frightened?

"Joanna," Sarah interrupted her thoughts with a honey-dipped drawl. "Are you all right, honey?" Joanna hadn't realized she'd been crying until Sarah wiped the tears from her cheek with the corner of her napkin. "You're fretting about your daddy, aren't you?"

Joanna sniffed back the emotion, aware of the increasing heat radiating across her cheeks. "I just hope he didn't hate us for leaving him alone."

"Ah, Sweet Pea, your daddy loved y'all with his whole heart," Sarah crooned.

Joanna turned and looked into Sarah's pretty blue eyes. "He wasn't . . . scared?"

"Scared? No, he wasn't scared. Your daddy knew where he was headed, and he wasn't frightened of that at all."

Joanna narrowed her eyes as she considered that thought. Her mother had deep, abiding faith for all her life, but *Tuck?* She didn't ever remember hearing one word about faith in God from her father.

"Can I get you anything else to eat?"

"No, that was really good."

"Let's get you settled in your own room then, shall we?"

Sarah extended a hand and Joanna took it, picking up her purse and bag before following the older woman down the hall to the buttery yellow bedroom behind the last door on the right.

"While you get ready for bed, I'll just take this quilt—" Joanna watched as Sarah yanked the covering off the closer of the two double beds with the familiar ornate iron headboards. "—and put it into the dryer for a few minutes so it's nice and cozy for you to slip under and get a good night's sleep."

"Sarah, you don't have to—"

"Don't be silly. I'll be back straightaway." Sarah reached the doorway and then turned around. Dropping the mound on the foot of the bed, she tugged the embroidered cases from the pillows. "I'll just put these in there, too, and add a little lavender so they'll be warm and fragrant for you."

Joanna shook her head and chuckled. "Well. Thank you."

After Sarah had gone, Joanna set her bag and purse on the bed against the window—Bella's bed. Joanna and Bella had such good years together, sharing this bedroom. Sarah used to help her mom keep house, and she'd changed the linens on those beds hundreds of times. Maybe more. But tonight was different somehow. It had been so long since anyone had looked after Joanna in that way.

In the dryer? With lavender?

Her eyes misted over with tears before she even recognized the emotions hitting her. She unzipped her bag and tugged out the pajamas she'd rolled and pushed in just that morning.

As she changed, Joanna's focus went to the light-gray floorboards covered by the dark-gray area rug with large, loopy, pink flowers around the border. The edges were somewhat tattered in places, but she didn't much care because that rug represented the sweet memory of shopping alone with her mother—something that hardly ever happened, the two of them alone without the other girls—for a rug to cover the cold floors of her and Bella's bedroom. They'd driven all the way into Lexington that day and stopped at the food court for a hot fudge sundae before heading back. More tears spilled just as Sarah returned.

The woman who had been like a second mother to her tossed the warm quilt and pillowcases on the bed and sat beside Joanna. "Coming home after a long time away is always emotional, isn't it?"

Joanna could only nod, and she dropped her head to Sarah's shoulder.

The sunrise called her name that morning, and despite the frigid thirty-degree temperature encouraging her to remain inside, Joanna wrapped herself in the bed quilt, brewed a cup of coffee in the Keurig on the counter—*no need for a paper-towel filter!*—and tucked her thick-socked feet into her boots before stepping outside.

Resting the cup on the wide armrest of the redwood chair, she tucked her legs beneath her and set out to enjoy the vibrant blues, pinks, and oranges of the Kentucky sky coming alive for the day. She'd all but forgotten the beauty of the place sprawled out before her. Sipping the steaming hot coffee, she basked in the unexpected joy of coming home.

Home.

The word echoed inside her as one of the horses whinnied in the stable. Joanna grinned. After she dressed and had breakfast, she determined to take a walk down the hillside and check out the farm's four-legged guests. She wondered how many of the stalls were filled these days.

"What on the Lord's beautiful, green earth—?"

Joanna's head jerked toward the voice, her heart pounding, hands trembling at the sound of it. She nearly dropped her coffee as Jed Weatherly stomped up the steps and leaned one hip against the wood banister, his light-brown eyes flashing and the dimples caving in on both cheeks.

"Jo-Jo?"

She took a moment to purposefully breathe before she smiled at him. "Hi, Jed."

He shook his head and stared at the scuffed tips of his boots, and she noticed the sun streaks in his dark-brown hair before he looked up and made the connection again. Those gold-flecked eyes of his had always done her in.

"You are the last thing I expected to see bundled up on the porch at the crack of dawn today. You're a sight for these sore eyes. Get up out of that chair, girl, and give me some sugar."

Pulse thundering, Joanna rose from the chair and set her cup on the arm. Pulling the quilt snugly around her, she casually put one foot in front of the other while screaming inwardly. *It's Jed! It's Jed!*

When she reached him, he hauled her into a bear hug and rocked her back and forth. "I can't believe you're here. This old place has sure missed you, girl."

But have YOU missed me?

He gently pushed her away, holding her a couple of feet from him as he looked into her eyes. It felt like an electrical connection to Joanna, one that had been fired up and waiting for years to be plugged in again. The intensity was almost too much for her.

"I tried to reach you about Tuck," he said in earnest, pulling her back to reality. "I'm real sorry."

"It's my fault. I should have contacted you with my new information. I learned to put thoughts of this place behind me . . ."

"Well, you're here now. C'mon and let's get inside and have some breakfast before the second string comes in."

The second string. She'd forgotten the term inherited from Tuck that referred to the ranch hands.

Joanna picked up her coffee mug and headed through the door as he opened it. He trailed her inside.

"Whoa, that sure smells good," he called out to Sarah, who was flipping pancakes on the griddle. "Look what I found hanging around on the front porch, Mom."

"Yes, I see that. I found her myself in the kitchen in the middle of the night." Sarah looked up at Joanna and grinned. "We had quite a nice time catching up, didn't we, Sweet Pea?"

"We did. I'm like one of those old raccoons. She fed me, so I stuck around."

Jed and Sarah laughed in perfect harmony, and it warmed her heart. Joanna set her cup in the sink and asked Sarah, "Do I have time to get dressed?"

"About fifteen minutes and it's on the table."

"I'll be back in ten."

She hurried off down the hall, wondering how in the world she could transform into someone else entirely—someone Jed might notice and be attracted to—in just ten minutes. She imagined that with her hair unbrushed, her face scrubbed clean, wearing winter boots and a bed quilt, there wasn't much there to inspire the attraction of a man as beautiful as Jed Weatherly. But oh, how she'd loved him once upon a time. And how she'd dreamt of the day when he might notice the *woman* burgeoning inside of her.

Why hadn't she thought of Jed when she chose the few items she'd pack for her trip to the horse farm? Everything she might have worn to look more ... *What? Womanly?* ... had been tossed into cardboard boxes and moved to a friend's basement with the rest of her possessions for safekeeping before leaving Indiana. That irritable landlord of hers would have deposited all her belongings in a dumpster when he stormed the gates to evict her, of that Joanna was certain.

After slipping into jeans and a taupe, cable-knit sweater, she tamed her wild hair into a loose braid that fell forward over one shoulder. She smoothed a little tinted moisturizer over her face, curled her eyelashes, and applied pale-pink lip gloss. While poking small, hooped earrings into her ears, she suddenly wondered if Jed had a woman in his life these days. After all, she'd been gone a long time. Maybe he was *married!* Maybe she was braiding her hair and wearing earrings for a married man. In fact, perhaps a gorgeous blonde wife with a big bustline and tiny little feet waited for him at the house, wearing an apron, and—

"Stop it!" she muttered through clenched teeth. "Stop it right now."

Joanna glared at her reflection and shook the train wreck of thought from her mind. When she finally closed the bedroom door and headed down the hall toward the kitchen, a new mission occupied her thoughts: *Check for a wedding ring.*

"Perfect timing," Sarah announced, but her voice sounded like a dull hum behind the light-brown eyes that momentarily waylaid Joanna. And then came the ultimate obstacle—those sunken dimples on either side of his smile—that took over where the gold flecks left off. "Go ahead and doctor your coffee the way you like it while I dish up some breakfast."

What had she said? *Something about coffee . . .*

Jed slid the tray bearing cream and sugar containers toward her. "Oh. Okay."

As he removed his ring-free hand, her unbridled glee forced Joanna to grin like an idiot.

"You look happy this morning." Jed took the stool next to her at the island. "Glad to be home?"

She gave a noncommittal nod as she concentrated on stirring cream into her coffee, silently thanking God for evaporating all thoughts of the imaginary, apron-wearing blonde who had occupied his kitchen for a few dreadful moments.

Sarah set a plate down in front of her, and Joanna gasped at the sight of it. Two large pancakes, an egg—sunny-side up—a mound of home fries, two sausage links, several orange sections, and two large strawberries. "I don't think I've had this much food over an *entire day*, much less for breakfast."

Jed chuckled as his mother set a plate in front of him, even more heavily laden. "Food is love in my family, Jo-Jo. Don't you remember that?"

She smiled. "I could have come back to find you pushing five hundred pounds and too fat to sit in a saddle."

"It takes a lot of willpower to keep that from happening."

"Hush now," Sarah said, her back to them as she rinsed a dish in the sink. "Say a prayer over your food and eat your breakfast."

Jed and Joanna exchanged grins. Jed bowed his head and spoke a blessing before they dug in.

"Speaking of family," Joanna said, wiping egg from the corner of her mouth, "how's your cousin? Sarah said he was here with Tuck. Is he still a soldier boy?"

Sarah clicked her tongue several times, shaking her head. "Matthew would not tolerate being called a soldier, Sweet Pea. He's a Marine through and through, just like your daddy."

The reference tweaked her heart. Jed's cousin Matt had always admired Tuck so much, and about thirty seconds after his eighteenth birthday he'd enlisted.

"Matt took care of Tuck for months after he got sick," Jed told her.

The fork froze in the air a few inches from her mouth. "He did?"

"Matthew trained as a navy corpsman and then as a medic in the Marines," Sarah chimed in. "When he came home, he went back to school for his R.N. degree. Since Tuck had been discharged because of his condition, Matt stayed here at the house for a while. He worked closely with the doctors to make sure Tuck had everything he needed."

Why didn't I know this?

"That's . . . surprising," she admitted. "And very sweet. So where is he now?"

"He moved into a small place not too far away," Sarah said, sipping her tea.

Conversation flowed smoothly as Sarah and Jed caught her up on life in Bluegrass Crossing. Before she knew it, Joanna had consumed every speck of food on her plate.

CHAPTER THREE

Joanna stopped as one long nose poked over the stall door. She placed a halved apple on her flat palm and held it out to the gray mare, who chomped it happily.

"That's Lucinda," Jed said as Joanna stroked the horse's neck. "She has some calcification in her knees that prevents anything more than light riding. We've been using her as a therapy horse. She gets requested more than any of the others on property."

A cocoa gelding caught her attention from the next stall, sniffing the air and extending his neck over the door. "I have a little something for you, too."

"Stanley," Jed told her. "He's a showman from down Louisville way. He's still being rehabbed, but he'll be ready for riding lessons—and hopefully adoption—in the next month or so."

Joanna fed him a carrot and tickled the bridge of his nose with two fingers. "Any familiar faces left over from my days here? I don't guess Sally's still alive."

"Sorry."

Her heart dropped a little. She'd learned to jump on Sally, a dark-brown quarter horse. The two of them had won three medals together, and Joanna had considered Sally her best friend for most of her adolescence.

"But do you remember Maranatha?" he continued.

The memory pushed a wide smile across her face. "The Morgan my mom loved to ride."

"Mari's grandson is down at the end there." He pointed out the last stall on the opposite side of the barn. "Big Red looks just like her. About sixteen hands tall, beautiful auburn coat."

Joanna hurried to the stall and peered over the door. Dark-chocolate eyes met hers, and the shiny, copper-red horse stalked straight for her.

"What's your fancy, Big Red? Carrot, apple, or sugar?"

She placed two sugar cubes on her palm and offered them to him. He lapped them up without hesitation, then looked back for something more.

"No need to be a pig about it," she teased, and she extended a long, fat carrot on the flat of her hand, which he then devoured. Jed stepped next to her, and Joanna sighed. "He's gorgeous."

"A little temperamental like his grandmother, but a beauty."

Joanna rubbed the Morgan's neck before making her way past the rest of the stalls, handing out snacks and snuggles and soft greetings.

Jed walked along beside her in silence until he observed, "You're in your element here, Jo-Jo."

"It feels like another life in some ways." She twisted the end of the plastic bread bag she'd used for the stable treats. "And still, it's like I never left."

"What's Indiana been like for you? I've wondered about your life there."

"It wasn't much of a life." She chuckled at the admission. "I mean, I kind of bounced around a lot. I loved my last job, but I was laid off just before getting the news about Tuck."

"What were you doing? At the job you loved."

"I started out as a receptionist, just answering phones and taking messages. But it evolved into more of an overall administrative thing, and I felt like I was really finding my niche, you know?"

"Running the place." He nodded with a mock-serious expression. "I can see where that would be a good fit for a bossy little thing like you."

She nudged his rib with her elbow and laughed. "You've hardly changed a bit, you know that?"

"You either."

As they reached the open door of the stable, Jed grabbed the collar of her coat, pulling gently until she faced him. He had nearly a foot of height on her, and as he gazed down, his normally light-brown eyes churned, stormy and dark.

"You remember the day you kissed me in this barn, Jo-Jo?"

She chuckled and looked away, but he used one finger to nudge her face back toward him until their eyes met again.

"I remember." Her voice came out raspy.

"You couldn't have been twelve years old."

"I was fourteen."

He thought it over, then nodded. "That would have made me twenty."

She pressed her lips together and shrugged. "Sounds about right."

"You said something like, 'I won't always be just a kid to you, Jedediah Weatherly.'"

Joanna remembered like it was yesterday.

"And then you wrapped those skinny arms of yours around my neck and planted one on me."

"After which, you shoved me away and told me to go on home."

"Did I?" he asked.

"Yes. So I did."

"I seem to recall you hated me a little bit after that for a very long time."

She sighed. "I didn't hate you. Not ever."

"No?"

Their gazes locked for a long and meaningful moment before she spoke. "No."

"You were right about one thing."

"What's that?"

"You sure don't seem like a little kid to me now."

"I grew up."

Jed lifted her braid and stroked it. "I'll say you did."

Joanna wondered if anyone's heart ever spontaneously combusted out of nothing but nearness to someone like this. If not, she figured she might be a first for the medical books.

Suddenly, a little afraid of her own feelings, she pulled away from him, lifted her chin, and stomped back toward the house.

"Hey, wait up!" Jed called, jogging to catch up to Joanna. She seemed to make it a point not to slow down in the least, so he mimicked her stride and caught up to her. "I didn't mean to make you uncomfortable back there."

"You didn't."

"Liar."

She giggled softly before lowering her head, watching the ground intently as they strolled toward the house.

"All I meant to say is that you've . . . changed." When she glanced over at him, he laughed and slipped his arm around her shoulders, drawing her close. "In a good way, Jo-Jo. Don't get your dander up."

"I'm not," she objected. "You just reminded me of one of my most embarrassing life moments, Jed. Hey, don't you know anything about women?"

"I thought I did," he said with a laugh. "Guess not."

"Nope. Not so much."

When he released his hold on her, Joanna slipped her arm through his. After a stretch of silence, she nodded toward his small house in the distance. "You still living down there?"

"Yup. Did some work on it last year, too? It's looking pretty good."

"What kind of work?"

"Upgraded the appliances in the kitchen, added some new tile work."

Joanna halted. "You know, Jed, Sarah told me you were working out at the Triple Z to make money for upkeep around here. Why would you do that?"

"The leftover inheritance from Tuck's folks kept the place going pretty good for a while, but all three of the ranch hands who stuck around took pay cuts to help out. Then the taxes came due before Tuck died, Jo-Jo. One of the outbuildings all but fell apart, and there was a massive leak in one of the back bedrooms of the main house. I couldn't reach you or your sisters; Tuck was gone. I had to do something. We'll get some help in a few weeks when we can take those thoroughbreds to auction. They should bring enough to keep things going for a while."

She sighed and looked hard into his eyes. "I'm so sorry. I hope you've kept a log of your expenditures. We all just went our own ways and put this place behind us, didn't we? When we heard our father had come home to the horse farm, we just figured . . ."

Jed stroked the sleeve of her coat. "It wasn't like the old life was calling any of you back here."

"No. Not at all."

"I get it," he reassured her. "But you're here now. Any chance the others will join you?"

"I doubt it." She looped her arm through his again as they walked on. "I wish they would, if only for one last Christmas hurrah, you know?"

"You're planning to sell the place then."

"I'm not bringing that up to my sisters just yet. We can discuss that if—*when*—they come back at Christmas. But I think we almost have to. You said yourself the place isn't self-sustaining."

"Still. I'd sure hate to see it sold."

Joanna looked up at him with understanding in her striking, greenish eyes. "You've lived here more years than I ever did, haven't you? I guess it's home to you and Sarah as much as—or even more than—it is to any of us."

"Yeah," he said, surveying the land with a wistful sigh. "No denying it feels like home." With a sharp inhale, he added, "But there's been some interest in the land. The Realtor's name is Dan, and he volunteers with the rescues sometimes."

The idea of moving on left a hollow feeling beneath his ribs. Oh sure, he could probably find another job somewhere, maybe even a permanent thing out at the Triple Z . . . but still. Leave this place?

"Thanks, Jed." She placed her free hand over the other one locked onto his arm and leaned into him as they walked. "I suddenly feel like it might be a hard good-bye. For me, at least."

For us all.

As they neared the house, the front door opened and the three ranch hands filed out.

"Hey, Jed," Gil shouted, and the others waved at him.

"Second string has had their grub," Jed announced, returning their waves. "Time to go over the day's chores and get out to the Triple Z."

"I just hate it that you're working two jobs, Jed."

"Nah. It might open the door for a new gig if this one dries up." He tried to sound lighthearted for her sake, despite not feeling it.

"I'll go help Sarah with the cleanup," she said, dropping her arm from his. "Will I see you later?"

"Probably. And Mom's got some plans to cook for a family in need today. Maybe you'll want to go along."

"I think I'd like to stick close to *h-home*," she said. Jed couldn't help noticing how she tripped over the word. "Maybe Skype with my sisters and catch them up."

Jed planted a kiss on her cheek. "It's likely I'll see you for supper."

Was it his imagination or had her porcelain face flushed with pink?

"Okay." She lowered her head as she released his arm and headed toward the main house.

"Hey, Jo-Jo?"

She stopped and turned back to look at him, both eyebrows arched and those hazel-green eyes of hers flashing. "Yeah?"

"I'm glad you're home."

"Thanks, Jed," she replied.

He wished she'd said, "Me, too," but she hadn't. He watched as she widened the gap between them, wondering how long she planned to stick around . . . whether she'd find herself happy to be home again . . . and just how long such a shift in thinking might take for the likes of Joanna Tucker.

CHAPTER FOUR

"Jo-Jo. You got *bangs!*"

Joanna fingered her long bangs and chuckled. "Yeah. A girl I worked with thought it was a good idea. She went to hairdressing school before switching to sales, and one Friday night she talked me into letting her cut my hair."

"It looks good."

"They're always in my eyes."

"You could trim them shorter. They look really good on you."

"They bug me."

Bella laughed, and the sound of it rang against Joanna's heart like church bells chiming somewhere in the distance. Familiar and sweet. So much of what she needed just then.

Joanna leaned closer to the computer screen and touched Bella's virtual face, traced her shoulder-length brown hair with one finger. "I miss you so much."

"I miss you, too. Why don't you come up to Chicago for a visit? Maybe spend Christmas with me. I don't have another trip scheduled until after the first of the year, and we could have so much fun together. What do you think?"

She sighed. "I would *love* to spend Christmas with you. But I have an even better idea."

"Why do those words still make me shudder a little?"

"Come to Kentucky," Joanna blurted. "We need to decide what to do with this place. Did you know Jed has been working a second job to keep things going for us? Anyway, wouldn't it be nice to spend Christmas here together while we make that decision?"

"What, all of us?"

"Why not? We could dig out those holiday treasure boxes of Mom's and really do it up right. Relive all the traditions she loved. Bake some snickerdoodles and those little butter cookies with the gun that makes them into shapes. Remember those?"

"You know Amy and Soph will have nothing to do with this hare-brained idea of yours, right?"

"If I can convince them, will you come?"

Bella stared at her through the screen, a blank expression on her pretty face.

"Or even if I can't convince Amy and Sophie, won't you come, Isabella? Please?"

"Jo-Jo—"

"C'mon. I need you."

"Why can't you come to Chicago instead? You can need me here as well as there."

"If I tell them you're coming, won't Amy and Sophie be more likely to join us?" Before Bella could answer, an idea sparked and Joanna gasped. "I know. I'll bring them in now."

"Jo-Jo—"

"Hang on, hang on. I'm calling Soph." She opened the Skype menu and clicked on the plus sign, then on Sophie's number.

When her sister didn't respond, she tried Amy. Joanna's heart dropped slightly when there was no answer there either.

"It's just as well," Bella told her. "They're never going to—"

"Remember what Mom used to say?" Joanna interrupted. "Life and death are in the power of the tongue. Don't you speak those negative predictions like you always do. Give me a chance to bring them around. Try and think positive about it, would you?"

"Oh, I'm pretty positive they—"

"Stop," Joanna exclaimed, but she couldn't suppress the chuckles that rolled out of her. "Stop it right now."

"Fine." Bella tossed her hands in surrender. "You just go right on believing, little sis. But I think you're going to be very disappointed."

"No, I'm not. You'll see. We deserve one more family Christmas here, don't we, Bella? Mom would *so* love that."

"You're impossible." Bella shook her head.

"But that's why you love me." Jo-Jo grinned.

"Nooo. I love you *in spite of* your impossibleness. Don't get that twisted."

"Tomato, tomahto. I'll call them on my cell later today, and I'll let you know when to arrive."

Bella shook her head and smiled. "Impossible."

Joanna waved at her. "Talk to you soon. I love you."

Her older sister sighed. "I love you, too."

The instant Joanna shut down her laptop, she scurried out of the bedroom on the steam of pure adrenaline. She headed straight down the hall and up the wide staircase that led to the attic loft that had once been the girls' magnificent playroom. The Victorian dollhouse she and Bella had received the Christmas Joanna was eight caught her eye immediately. It still sat on the low, trestle table with a plank top and distressed black finish. Her mother had loved that table so much.

The antique key still protruded from the narrow drawer on the front, but the once-shiny purple tassel dangling from it had seen better days. Joanna approached it with apprehension, turned the key until it clicked, and pulled open the drawer. A messy stack of weathered photographs filled the drawer to overflowing.

She gathered them with both hands and went over to the faded-green settee by the window to look through them. Yellow beams of sunlight turned bluish and green through the filter of the floral pattern of stained glass set into the window frame. She remembered the top photograph as if it had been taken just a month ago. Sophie and Bella lounging under the Christmas tree in those matching flannel nightgowns their mother had made for all four girls. Red-and-green plaid with starched white cuffs and Peter Pan collars. Her neck itched a little at the memory.

She laid the picture facedown beside her on the settee. The next one gripped her throat like a vice. Her beautiful mother leaning onto the outstretched arm of her husband, Tuck, her pregnant belly fat with their youngest—Joanna. She turned that one over atop the other and methodically went through the entire stack.

When she'd finished, Joanna crouched low and peered through the kitchen window of the dollhouse. The teeny table was still meticulously set with Lilliputian china and glassware. The imaginary occupants used to gather there to enjoy hypothetical holiday meals of roast goose, mincemeat pies, and plum pudding borrowed from the writings of Charles Dickens, or sometimes they ate chestnut soup, smoked salmon, and herb-roasted chicken on loan from a Parisian menu Bella had read about in one of her books.

"You girls used to love that precious dollhouse," Sarah said from the top of the stairs, startling Joanna. "I'm sorry. Did I scare you?"

"I didn't hear you on the stairs." She straightened.

"Doing a little remembering?"

"I came up here to dig out my mother's Christmas boxes, but I was hijacked."

"A lot of nostalgia in this house for you." Sarah pulled open the first of four low doors built into the side wall of the sloping roof. "I think the Christmas boxes are in this one."

The small woman nearly disappeared inside. "Are you planning to do a little decorating for the holidays?"

"I'm hoping to convince my sisters to come back and spend Christmas. It might be our last time here with all of us together."

Sarah dragged a large box through the opening and scuffed it across the floor before retreating inside for another. Joanna spotted the marking on the side of the tattered box, written in thick, black marker in her mother's loopy cursive hand.

Ornaments.

Sarah pushed a hefty plastic tub toward her, and Joanna tugged it the rest of the way until it rested at her feet. "Wreaths, stockings, and snowmen," Sarah read aloud, tapping her finger on the identification written on masking tape across the lid.

"The snowmen." Joanna excitedly popped the lid from the tub and grinned down at the large cotton-ball snowman with a top hat and an orange-glitter, carrot-shaped nose. "Mister Henderson!" She removed the snowman and stood him on the table against the storage wall. "Amy made him."

"I remember he had a place of honor each year on the ledge of the front window," Sarah reminisced. "Wasn't there a second one like it?"

"Yeah, the one Sophie and Bella made fell apart a long time ago. They didn't use enough glue."

"And you? Did you make a snowman, too?"

"We had to throw him away. I thought it was a genius idea to make him out of Styrofoam and cover him in glitter. But Mom was still cleaning up glitter the next September, so we couldn't put him out again." Joanna dug through the bin in search of— "Oh, look!" she gasped, gingerly removing another snowman from captivity, this one more beautiful than the others, and she cradled it in her arm. "Mom bought this one at the Christmas bazaar in town."

Sarah moved toward her and ran her finger over the sparkly wreath hanging around the neck of the decoration made from crocheted, white yarn interlaced with metallic-silver threads. "It's lovely."

"Do you know where Mom's recipes might be?" Joanna asked. "And what about her cookie gun? I want to make snickerdoodles and those little colored ones in different shapes."

"There's an old, wooden box with a broken hinge in the kitchen cabinet. I think I saw recipe cards in there."

Joanna tenderly transitioned the snowman from her arms to the round table. "It's going to be the best Christmas any of us have had in years. I just know it."

Sarah softly stroked Joanna's hair. "I hope so, Sweet Pea."

"I'll tell ya, Jed, we'd be lucky to have you on a full-time basis here at the Triple Z," Randy told him as they loaded the bed of his truck with bales of hay. "If you'd have accepted and become my barn manager back when I offered, there wouldn't have been any more discussion. But Caleb's working out pretty good, and I don't have another opening for you. I'm sorry about that."

"I understand." A bit disappointed, Jed heaved another bale into the bed, followed by another. Yanking the blue-print kerchief from his back pocket, he wiped his forehead. "I never could have imagined moving on from Tuck's place, but things have changed since he passed."

"His girls gonna put the place up on the block?"

"Looks that way."

"Leaves you and your mama with an uncertain future, I s'pose."

"It sure does. But you know me. I know there's a road all laid out. Just need to find the trail."

"I'll keep my ear to the ground." Randy tossed another bale into the truck. "You're a good man. Any horse farm in the region'd be lucky to have ya."

"Appreciate that."

"But nobody ever made money turnin' a place like that into an old folks' home for a buncha horses, did they, Jed?"

"Getting rich never was something Marlena Tucker gave much thought to. My old man seemed to think she could keep things on an even keel though."

"Lot's changed in this region since your old man's days."

"Sure enough."

Despite his preoccupation on the ride home with the mental checklist of the tasks that awaited him, it wasn't any one of the hundred line items, or even the hot meal primed and ready, that drew him. No, over and above the growl of his hungry stomach, the crux of his thoughts orbited a solid nucleus of dark, wavy hair and embers flickering inside greenish eyes.

A fragrance that whisked Jed straight back to childhood assaulted him even before he opened the front door of the main house. He paused with his hand on the knob, breathing in the essence of his mother's cooking, wondering whether he should knock first. After all, they weren't the only ones around anymore. Before he made the decision, it was made for him. His mother opened the door.

"You comin' in or do you plan on standing out there on the front porch all night?" She shot him a teasing smile.

Jed kissed her cheek as he passed. "What do I smell?"

"Roasted rosemary chicken," she replied, pushing the door shut behind him, "glazed carrots, mashed potatoes, and gravy."

"That's it? Slacking on the job?" he joked. "Nothing for dessert?"

"Nothing for you. The rest of us are having warm apple crisp with vanilla ice cream."

He looked around the great room and into the kitchen. "Jo-Jo's not here?"

Sarah grinned at him and nodded toward the hall. "Upstairs. Why don't you go tell her we've got about ten minutes until we eat?"

Grateful for the mission, Jed took the stairs two at a time. When he reached the top, he spotted Joanna sitting cross-legged in the middle of the floor, surrounded by what looked like an eruption of Christmas boxes and bins. When she looked up, a smile spread across her entire beautiful face and set her eyes ablaze.

"Well, look at you," he said.

"Hi, Jed. How was your day?"

"Long. How about yours?"

"Not long enough. I came looking for a few Christmas decorations, and I've been trapped here in this sea of memories ever since."

"So can I deduce from this Christmas extravaganza that you reached your sisters and suckered them into coming back for the holidays?"

She lifted one eyebrow into a perfect arch. "Well, Sophie turned me down flat. But Bella will probably come in time for Christmas, and I may or may not have used a bit of a dirty trick to reel Amy in."

"What'd you do?"

"I had a conversation with my nephew Timothy and told him what an amazing time he would have if they came up from Louisiana. I might have even *promised* him the chance of a white Christmas." She cringed, and Jed laughed at her. "Just *the chance.*"

"Shame on you."

"I know. Toying with a seven-year-old like that." She tipped her head to the side. "But all's fair in love and family Christmases, right?"

"I'm not sure that's how the saying goes."

"Sure it is."

"Jedediah?" Sarah called from the bottom of the stairs. "Are you bringing Joanna down for supper?"

He grinned at her. "I forgot. My mother has dinner on the table. You coming down?"

She nodded and extended her hand. "Help me up? I've been in the same position for hours. At this point, I don't even know if my legs will straighten."

Jed wrapped his hand around her wrist and eased Joanna to her feet. She stretched her limbs, and just before they headed for the stairs, his cell phone hummed. The screen told him the call originated from the Triple Z.

"Go on down," he said. "This is my *other boss*. I'll be right with you."

Joanna descended the stairs, and Jed answered the call. "Hello?"

"Jed, Randy here."

"What's up?"

"I was thinking about our conversation this morning, and I made a call to a buddy of mine. He has a working ranch out in Montana. Couple hundred horses, a thousand head of cattle. Looks like he might have a spot for you out there if you're up for a move. Is that something you might want to pursue?"

Jed hesitated, taking an instant to enjoy the harmony of laughter coming from Joanna and his mother in the kitchen.

"I'd like to hear more about the details," he replied. "What can you tell me about it?"

"I'll text you his number. He's waiting for your call over the next day or two."

"Thanks, Randy. Seriously, I appreciate it."

"Sure thing. See you in the morning?"

"I'll be there."

CHAPTER FIVE

"Pastor Tobin, it's so good to see you," Joanna heard Sarah say downstairs. "Let me make you a quick cup of coffee, and then I'll go and see if Joanna is up and moving around yet."

Joanna grinned. Not only was she up and moving, but she'd been dressed for hours. In fact, she'd already had her first two cups of coffee and gone for an extended walk down to the stable to spread some love in the guise of apples, sugar cubes, and carrots.

"I'm up here, Sarah."

"Sweet Pea, can you come downstairs for a moment?"

"On my way."

Joanna wound the cord around the button on the front of the leather journal in her hands and set it on the settee before standing.

Pastor Tobin. As she descended the stairs, she couldn't help but wonder who this Pastor Tobin was, and more curiously, why he wanted to see Joanna. She thought perhaps she might recognize him, but as she emerged from the hall and entered the kitchen, the luminous smile of the man across the island from Sarah sparked no familiarity at all.

"Oh good," Sarah said as she hurried over and took Joanna's hand. Leading her to the other side of the island, she added, "Joanna, this is Reverend Lucas Tobin. Pastor, meet Joanna Tucker, the youngest of Tuck and Marlena's daughters."

"It's a pleasure," he said. "There's no mistaking it. I see both of them in you right off."

Joanna reached out to shake his hand. "You knew my parents?"

"Yes." Then he corrected himself. "Well, I knew your father. But I've seen many a photograph of your mother. You have her countenance."

That seemed like a high compliment. Joanna was just seventeen when her mother was killed by a drunk driver on the interstate, but the woman's radiant glow had remained with her in all the years since then . . . and with everyone else who ever knew her, too.

"Thank you," she told the reverend. "How did you know Tuck?"

"He was a member of my church for several years."

Joanna had trouble concealing her astonishment, but the line of Scripture at the end of his note to her scrolled across her mind. "Tuck went to church?"

"Indeed. He was an active member, in fact."

She glanced at Sarah for confirmation. "That's . . . surprising. My mother had deep faith, but Tuck never really seemed to *share it*."

"No. He came to faith in Christ after he returned from overseas and retired here in Bluegrass Crossing."

"I didn't know." Joanna fought against the ridiculous urge to cry as her expression broke and both corners of her mouth turned down involuntarily. What was happening to her emotions?

"Tuck spoke of you girls often. In fact, we prayed together on more than one occasion that he would be able to reconnect and make amends."

Her stomach soured at the words, and the threatening tears turned desert-dry in an instant. She couldn't help wondering how a man might go about *making amends* with the daughters he abandoned, leaving them in the care of the wife who adored him, who never allowed a bad word to be spoken about him, who struggled to keep his family's homestead afloat without a lick of support from him, or even so much as a word.

"Well, that would have been . . . *interesting*." The pastor's somewhat surprised expression checked her heart. "I mean, I can't imagine how he might have accomplished that after everything. But it would have been interesting to hear what he had to say."

Sarah reached over and squeezed Joanna's wrist. "Your daddy loved you girls very much."

"All evidence to the contrary," she muttered.

Pastor Tobin took a sip of coffee before setting it in front of him and wrapping both hands around it. "Tuck was a changed man in his later life."

She wasn't sure how to respond, so she didn't.

"I hope you don't mind me stopping by to meet you," he continued. "Sarah's son, Jed, mentioned you'd come home, and I just wanted to look in and see if there's anything I can do for you. And to invite you to visit one of our services while you're here."

"Well, I appreciate the invitation, but I'm not really the churchgoing type." It struck her how disappointed her mother would have been at hearing those words . . . and how much like her father she sounded. "I mean, I believe in God and everything, but—"

"No, I thought you might find some value in meeting the people in Tuck's life before his death. In hearing what kind of man he'd become."

"Oh."

She considered his words for several seconds and decided to follow what her mother had advised more than a few times in her adolescence. *Always choose to be courteous, Joanna. You'll find life will go much easier once you learn you don't have to share every thought you have the very moment you have it.*

"I appreciate that, Pastor. Thank you for thinking of it."

"Maybe you can come along with Jed on Sunday."

"Jed?" Joanna looked to Sarah, who smiled at her.

"Jed is an elder at Pastor Tobin's church," Sarah said.

An elder. "What is that, exactly? Like a preacher or something?" She held back the spontaneous chuckle threatening to pop out of her.

The pastor grinned. "Our board of elders helps govern the church. Jed is a peacekeeper and prayer warrior by nature, and he's brought those qualities to his leadership role. We're blessed to have him."

"I know he feels like he's the one who is blessed to serve," Sarah added.

Pastor Tobin handed Joanna a business card. "Here's the information on the times and location. I hope you'll pay us a visit one Sunday, Joanna. I think you'll find it very enlightening." He took one more sip of coffee before standing and putting on his overcoat. "It was a pleasure to meet you."

"You, too," she said, not entirely sure if she meant it.

Sarah walked the man to the front door while Joanna remained standing in the kitchen, replaying his visit.

"That was nice, wasn't it?" Sarah said when she returned.

"Mm," Joanna replied, not sure what else to say.

"I'm so sorry I didn't know you were upstairs during breakfast. But didn't you hear the ruckus of all the boys here?"

"I was probably at the stable. I've only been upstairs for the last hour or so."

"Have you made any headway with finding the Christmas decorations you wanted?"

She nodded. "Yes, but I also came across some non-Christmas treasures. Some photographs and my mother's diary." She sniffed and shook her head. "I didn't even know she kept a diary."

"Oh, how lovely," Sarah exclaimed. "How was it, reading what she'd written?"

"I only got started, really. But just seeing her familiar handwriting, hearing her voice through the words on the pages—it makes me feel close to her again."

"Of course it does," Sarah said and kissed the top of her head. "Can I make you some breakfast? I have some waffle batter in the refrigerator. Maybe a nice, warm cinnamon waffle and some eggs?"

Joanna chuckled. "How is anyone around this place under four hundred pounds with you on the job, Sarah?"

"I feed them and Jed keeps them active." She smiled. "It all balances out."

"Well, a waffle doesn't sound so bad."

"I'll have something on a plate for you in fifteen minutes or less."

"I'll just make another cup of coffee and keep you company while you work to make me fatter."

The afternoon air had grown colder than it had been in recent days. Granted, the calendar had moved Kentucky closer to the winter season, but Thanksgiving had barely passed. It seemed a little early to Jed for this type of cold—the kind with a bite, the kind that turned the barely-there stubble left on his face into crops of tiny, sharp, frozen blades.

He hadn't intended to have dinner with his mom that night, but instead of going straight home as planned, he steered his black F-150 pickup to the main house and parked there. In addition to wanting to make a sweep of the place in preparation of what might come with sub-zero wind chills over the next few nights, he figured he may as well have a conversation with Sarah about the new developments of the day.

Jed pulled the Stetson low on his forehead and pushed his way through a headwind to the front door.

"Jedediah, I didn't know you were coming," his mother said when she looked up from the stove. "Joanna and I decided on a pretty simple supper. Nothing too substantial. But I have leftovers from last night's chicken if you'd like."

"Whatever you're having is fine with me." He kissed her cheek. "Where's Jo-Jo?"

"She's in her room, trying to reach one of her sisters on her computer screen."

"Have any of them agreed to come for Christmas? She seems really set on that idea."

"I know she is. I hope she won't be too disappointed if they don't come."

"I'm glad we have a few minutes alone, Mom." Jed tugged off his gloves and pushed them into his coat pocket before he removed it and draped it over the back of Tuck's leather club chair in the great room. He rested his hat on its crown before turning back toward her. "I had an interesting phone call today."

"Oh?" she said, stirring something in the large, cast-iron pot on the stove.

"I don't think the girls will have much choice but to sell this place after the first of the year, and it got me to thinking about where you and I will land when that happens."

"I'm sure our Lord has it all in hand, Son."

"I agree." He smiled. "I spoke to Randy about getting hired on full-time at the Triple Z, but he's already filled that barn manager position and doesn't have anything else to offer."

"Oh, honey, I'm sorry to hear that. I know you've enjoyed your time working with him."

"Well, he has a friend with a horse and cattle ranch about twenty times the size of the Triple Z, and he gave his buddy a call to tell him about me."

"Wasn't that nice?"

"It was." He swallowed the hesitation that had haunted him all day. "So the guy . . . made me an offer."

Sarah tapped the wooden spoon on the inside of the pot before setting it into the spoon rest. "Jedediah, that's wonderful. Is it something to get you excited and out of bed in the morning like this place does?"

"I think it could be. And the thing is, room and board are included. And a place for you, too, if you're interested."

"For *me?*" She chuckled. "You don't need to bring your mother in as a package deal. You just find somewhere that will make you happy, and that will make me happy. The good Lord will take care of me."

"The thing is, Mom, I couldn't really take this job unless you want to come along."

Her eyes glazed with curiosity. "Why ever not?"

"It's in Montana."

"Montana! You're moving to *Montana?*"

"Who's moving to Montana?" Joanna asked as she joined them, and both Jed and Sarah appeared startled.

"Jedediah has been offered a position at a ranch out there," Sarah revealed.

The look on Joanna's face puzzled Jed. He couldn't read much of anything from her reaction. She remained oddly silent for a good stretch of time. Finally . . .

"That's a relief," she said with a lopsided smile. Then she glided past Jed and moved next to Sarah, picking up the spoon and stirring the mystery contents of the pot. "I hate the idea of blindsiding you—I mean, *uprooting* you—with the sale of this place and you having nowhere to turn. You spent so much of your time and energy mopping up Tuck's troubles."

"Well, I haven't made any decisions yet." Jed sighed and tucked his hands into his back pockets. "I thought I'd see how things shake out here. Unless you already feel like you don't need me."

"Oh no," she said on a bubbling laugh. "We need you. At least until my sisters arrive and we make some decisions."

"So your sisters are coming?" Sarah asked. "All three?"

"I don't really know yet. Bella will come. I know she will. And Sophie said this morning she'd think about it."

"Wouldn't it be lovely to have all four Tucker girls here to celebrate the Christmas holiday, Jedediah?"

"That it would," he answered.

"It would make your mama and daddy so happy," Sarah told Joanna, "to know this old place sang again with their family's laughter. *It's a family homestead*, that's what your daddy used to say."

Jed didn't hold out much hope for Joanna's sisters deciding to forget the past and fly into town just to spend some time at the horse farm—Tuck's *family* ranch. And that reality made his heart sink a little on Joanna's behalf.

When their eyes met, Jed thought he detected a mist of emotion in Joanna's. One side of her mouth lifted in a crooked little smile again, but she didn't break the connection of their gaze as she said softly, "Montana. The other side of the world. What about your mother? She'd hardly ever see you."

"I was kind of hoping she'd come with me."

Joanna turned to Sarah and exclaimed, "You're leaving, too?"

The older woman slid her arm around Joanna's shoulder and smiled. "Nothing's been decided yet, Sweet Pea. No one's going anywhere just now."

Jed watched Joanna lower her gaze, and her shoulders rose and fell with a silent sigh.

"What're you two cooking, anyway?" he asked. "It smells pretty good. Mind if I stick around?"

"Of course not. You know better than to ask," his mother said. "It's chicken and dumplings. Joanna and I found it in her mother's recipe box this afternoon, and we just happened to have all the ingredients we needed."

"There's a freeze moving in tonight," he said. "I'm going to refresh the batteries in the lanterns and radio now in case we lose power, and I'll check the exterior water pipes after supper."

Sarah nodded. "Good thinking. We'll need to leave the water running in the sinks tonight, too. Don't want the pipes to burst."

CHAPTER SIX

Joanna's coat was a tight fit over the double portion of sweaters she'd stuffed into it, and Sarah had provided a pair of fleece-lined work gloves to slip on over her much-thinner pink ones. The thermometer on the outside wall had dropped to single digits by the time they finished dinner, and when she stepped outside, the wind whipped across the porch with such strength that she could hardly stand against it.

"It's pretty early in the season for these temperatures," Jed told her as he crouched and felt around the hose bib attached to the side of the house. "On Thanksgiving Day, we were all wearing our jackets unzipped. This turn sure doesn't bode well for the kind of winter we might see by Christmas."

"What about the horses?" she asked. "Has the stable been winterized?"

"We did some work out there just a few weeks back." He stood, then bit the fingertip of his glove to pull it from his hand so he could reach into his pocket for his cell phone. "I'll send the boys down to blanket the horses who need it. We wouldn't normally do that so early in the season, but I think the weather report warrants it for a night or two. Let's pray the power stays on. I don't want to lose heat down there."

Joanna took the opportunity to watch him while Jed typed in a text with his thumb, his hat pulled down low and the collar of his coat flipped upright. She could hardly get a good look at him, except for those striking eyes of his, narrowed as he focused on the screen in his hand. When he finished, he tucked the phone away and replaced his glove before glancing at her.

"I wonder what we'd ever have done around this place without you," she said.

"Been doing it a long time."

A random memory flickered out of nowhere, and Joanna grinned. "Remember the night of the autumn hayride, Jed? When you took Becky Whitlow down to the stable so you could make out with her?"

It appeared to take a moment for him to connect to the name, but when he did he flashed a sly smile at her. "I recollect that was my senior year. And you hadn't even started high school yet. You like to scared the sense right out of Becky and me when you fell out of the hayloft trying to spy on us."

A flush of embarrassment washed over Joanna as the wind scratched her cheeks. She dug her double-gloved hands into the pockets of her coat. "I wanted to get a closer look."

"At what exactly?"

She sighed. "I don't know. I wanted to see how you held her, how you moved in for the kiss. I hadn't seen a lot of kissing just yet—"

"Not counting Amy and Tim." He chuckled.

"Yeah, not counting them. But I was . . . curious."

Jed grabbed the lapels of Joanna's coat and lifted them around her face to keep her warm. "Did you get all the information you needed before falling twenty feet into a stack of hay?"

Oh, I fell far more than out of a hayloft that night, she mused as their gazes remained locked. *I fell so hard for you on that hayride, and you didn't even know I existed.*

"You were far too young back then to be thinking about how I planted one on some girl's lips."

"I suppose you're right."

"Didn't stop you from wondering though, did it, Jo-Jo?"

She grinned. "Nope."

"You still wondering? About my technique and all?"

"It may have crossed my mind. Now and then."

"Permission to demonstrate?"

Joanna's heart pounded so hard that her pulse beat like a bass drum in both ears. "I suppose." She sounded far more casual than she felt. "For the sake of resolving any unanswered questions."

Tightening his grip on her lapels and strengthening the lock on their gazes, he stepped closer and drew Joanna toward him slowly. Her frozen lips tingled in anticipation, and she trembled—either from expectancy or from the arctic wind; she couldn't be sure which. When she thought Jed's lips might finally touch hers, as his strong hands took hold of her shoulders and Joanna's eyes fluttered shut, she sighed through her nose—an exhale twenty years in the making. The oddest sensation came over her. It felt like *falling*. Not out of a hayloft this time, but into a similar emotional abyss. A real kiss from Jed Weatherly would be well worth the wait, she felt certain.

The sweet sensation of falling turned to one swift *thud!* as Jed kissed the top of her head and chuckled as he released her.

Sarah had large mugs of hot cocoa waiting for them when they returned, delighting Joanna when she topped them with sputtering mounds of whipped cream and shavings of dark chocolate.

"You two enjoy your cocoa," she said, replacing the can of whipped cream into the refrigerator door. "There's a hot bath and another chapter of a good book with my name all over them."

She kissed each of their cheeks and headed for the hallway. Just as she reached it, she turned back and shot them a very serious expression. "I'm just two doors down, you know. Voices carry in this old cathedral."

"Yes, mother," Jed joked.

"Don't forget it."

"Goodnight, Sarah." Joanna chuckled.

"I'll be awake for a while yet," she reminded them.

By the time her bedroom door clicked shut, Joanna turned back to find Jed crouched at the fireplace, stoking the blaze with an iron poker before tossing two more logs inside. She fetched their hot chocolates, set the mugs on the coffee table in front of the oversized leather sofa, and folded one leg beneath her as she fell into the cushions.

They remained silent, each of them nursing their warm beverages by the glow of a crackling fire and dim yellow lamplight. Joanna wiped a rogue dollop of cream from her nose before blowing into the cup several times. Still, the cocoa burned her tongue at first sip.

"So," she said, once she'd recovered. "Montana?"

"That's where the offer is."

"It's so far away."

"Beautiful country though."

"Have you already been?" She set her mug on the table to give it time to cool.

"Once. One of a couple of bonding trips my dad took me on."

"How old were you then?"

"Eight? Before he came to work here. We went to Glacier National Park and did some hiking and fishing, saw some spectacular mountain ranges."

Joanna smiled. "I remember you and your dad being very close."

"We were. I wish we'd had longer."

Mornings with her mama in the adjacent kitchen skittered across her mind. "I know what you mean."

Jed hadn't taken a single day off since he'd gone to work at the Triple Z, a fact which helped to eliminate all traces of guilt that morning when he phoned Randy to say he needed to take one now. On his way out the door the night before, Joanna had turned on the charm when she asked if he might be free to search the property for a tall Christmas tree with her. In the spirit of wasting no time—and giving her no time in which to reconsider the request—he'd agreed. "How about tomorrow? We'll make a day of it, if you want. Maybe go into town for some lunch afterward."

Even though they'd decided he would stop by around eleven to pick her up, Jed had gone out to the stable at seven that morning to prepare the horses and wagon for their ride. He'd showered, shaved, and dressed, and had been tapping his boot on the leg of the coffee table for half an hour or more. He was on his third cup of coffee and second blueberry muffin, which he'd poached from the kitchen before leaving the main house after midnight. His mom had more than a dozen of them under the glass dome on the counter in preparation of first- and second-string breakfasts the next morning, and he'd told Joanna he figured she wouldn't miss a few, knowing full well she ran a tight ship and counted every one. But clear thinking had been eradicated by the brown sugar crumble on the top of those muffins.

The clock on the dash read 10:57 as he pulled his truck in front of the house, and the thermometer on the porch hovered just above twenty degrees when he walked through the door a few minutes later.

"You said *around* eleven," Joanna joked when she saw him. "It's one minute till."

"And your point?"

"No point. Just an observation."

"So I'm punctual." He removed her coat from the peg on the wall and held it for her. "Ready to go?"

"No greeting for your mother?" Sarah asked from the kitchen.

He smiled at her as Joanna shrugged into the sleeves of her coat. "Kiss your mother," she said, producing soft pink gloves and a matching beanie from her pockets.

Jed closed the gap between them and wrapped his arms around his mom and squeezed. "Good morning, Mother."

"Good morning, Son. Enjoy those muffins, did you?"

"Very much. I didn't think you'd mind."

"Why would I? I tend to feed you most mornings anyway, don't I?"

"And they were delicious." He kissed her cheek. "We're going for a ride to shop the property for a Christmas tree. And we'll probably have lunch at the Bluegrass Bistro in town—maybe get back here late in the afternoon to set up the tree."

"You know, you can buy a tree from the Monty family's grove out off the State Road," she announced to them both. "That's much warmer than saddling up horses and going out into the cold on a day like this."

"But, Sarah," Joanna objected as she tamed her wild waves by tugging the beanie onto her head, "it wouldn't be the same as cutting it down right here on the ranch like we used to."

Sarah and Jed exchanged suppressed smiles. "All right then," Jed's mother said. "I'll have everything ready for tree-trimming upon your return."

Joanna beamed. "Thank you so much."

"Bundle up," she called to them as they headed out the door. "It's going to be very cold again today."

Jed reached around and turned Joanna's collar upright. "Shall we drive to the stable?"

"Oh no." She produced a dark-pink, infinity scarf with flashes of metallic silver in it. Pulling it over her beanie-compressed head like a hood, she turned and grinned at him. "Let's walk. This is exciting, isn't it?"

Jed smiled at her exuberance. He'd forgotten that childlike quality Joanna had displayed from youth. She'd always been the one in the room to raise everyone's spirits, always the first to see the brighter side of a near-impossible situation. But that joyful naiveté had all but disappeared after her mother's death, and he'd seen no signs of it through the time she'd announced her plans to leave the horse farm and search for something else—in Indiana, of all places.

"Anything new from your sisters?" he asked as they headed for the stable, the ground crunching beneath their boots.

"I spoke to Sophie this morning. I pulled the *come-see-Matt* card in hopes that reminding her of your cousin's presence might entice her. But she didn't make any promises. Amy's avoiding the conversation altogether, although it looks like I do have her son on my side. And Bella . . . now she's making noises about David wanting them to spend Christmas with his family, but I'm not buying it. She's wanted to break up with him for months now. She has no intention of spending Christmas with him and his family. She's just trying to make excuses."

"They've been together a long time, haven't they? Maybe she's had second thoughts about the split."

Joanna sighed noisily. "Personally, I think she's a fool. David is the sweetest guy on the planet for putting up with her nonsense. She's crazy to think about turning him loose."

"To each their own." But for Joanna's sake, he hoped at least Isabella would make the trek back home. The two of them had always been so close. Joanna would need Bella's support when it came time to say good-bye to the old homestead.

They reached the stable, and Jed yanked back the wide door. A couple of long noses protruded over stall doors to greet them.

"I didn't realize before," she said as they entered. "This barn really needs a few coats of paint."

"As soon as spring rears its beautiful head, the guys will be on that."

She clucked softly. "I guess I didn't need to tell you, did I? You're on the ball with everything around here."

"I want you to tell me," he said seriously. "We'll make it a team effort to get you top dollar for the place."

She touched his sleeve, and he turned to look at her. "Thank you, Jed. I'm so grateful for you."

He covered her gloved hand with his own and nodded. "Ready to ride?"

"More than."

"I thought we could hitch up the wagon to—"

"Oh no. I'd really like to go on horseback, if you don't mind."

"Once we find the right tree and cut it down, it'll be easier to—"

"Can't we just rope it to one of the horses like we used to, and let them drag it home?" She looked up at him with those hopeful eyes. "I know it probably seems silly to you, but I want to do it the way we did when we were still a *family*."

Jed sighed. "Let's saddle up then. I'll be your family today."

She squeezed his arm. "Jed, you've always been my family. You know that."

He hadn't known. But it soothed his heart to hear her say it.

CHAPTER SEVEN

O n the ridge over there," Joanna called over her shoulder, and Jed laughed.

Joanna had been leading the way ever since they left the stable. Jed wasn't about to ask her to slow down or to let on how challenging it was to catch up to her. She'd said she hadn't been in the saddle since leaving the farm, but no one would know it to look at her. That Morgan she'd chosen to ride—Maranatha's grandson, Big Red—was in his element, too, as his rider gave enthusiastic permission to let loose into a full gallop. Those two were a perfect match.

"Over here," Joanna called out into the cold, and by the time Jed reached the top of the ridge, she'd climbed down and led Big Red by the reins toward a cluster of evergreens. "What about that one over there? I noticed it right off."

Jed dismounted and removed the metal tape measure from his pocket. "That's gotta be twenty feet tall, Jo-Jo. And so bushy, we won't be able to get it in the front door."

"We couldn't trim it?"

Rather than trying to reason with her, he simply moved to a smaller tree a dozen yards back and extended the tape measure upward. "This one's more like it," he said. "Fifteen feet, with a few feet to spare at the base. What do you think?"

He expected a bit of push back. Instead, Joanna answered with a straightforward decisiveness that astonished him. "Yep. That's the one. Where's the axe?"

She'd vetoed his intent to haul a chainsaw along when they were setting out that morning. "Do you know how much longer it will take with an axe?" he pointed out, but she'd stood her ground.

"Tuck used an axe. I want to do it like we did when I was little."

He'd had his doubts, but Joanna held her own out there amidst the pines, giving a play-by-play as if Jed was her student in the art of safely cutting down a Christmas tree. She took the axe from him.

"Cut a notch on one side," she said, whacking the tree. "Now one on the other side. Now the first horizontal cut—" This chop pushed a strange and noisy groan out of her that seemed to originate beneath her ribs and move on the steam of raw emotion.

Jed stepped closer and tried to remove the axe from her hand, but her grip remained tight. "It's my turn," he told her. Joanna maintained her grip, and Jed gently peeled one finger away, and then another. "This is a team sport, remember?"

When she finally let go, she seemed to cave in, and tears spilled unexpectedly down her flushed face. He wondered at first whether she'd been hurt. Maybe the axe had slipped. He tossed the thing aside, and it fell to the ground as he pressed her hand into his palm and splayed her fingers to investigate.

"Does this hurt?"

"What?" She sniffled. "No, I'm fine."

But the whimper that followed told a different story. Before he could inquire further, Joanna pushed herself into his arms and collapsed against him, sobbing.

"Jo-Jo." He wrapped her firmly in his arms. "What is it?"

"I can't believe . . . he's really . . . *gone* . . ." she managed. "Again."

"Who?" *What a stupid question.* "Tuck?"

She hadn't seen or spoken to her father in forever. Still, he supposed grief knew no logic or reason. In his own experience, grief was just . . . *grief*.

"I know it probably sounds stupid to you." Her words muffled against his coat. "But I'm just so *angry* with him." Wrapping her arms tightly around his neck, she added, "He stole so much from me. From all of us, really. From my mother most of all."

Jed stroked the sparkly scarf that had fallen from the top of her head and slouched at her neck. "I know," he whispered.

But did he really? Jed wasn't sure.

She pulled back and looked up at him with weepy eyes, their color turning a bright emerald green in the sunlight. "My sisters have all these memories of him. Things they got to do together, places they went with him when we were a family. But I was the *youngest*. By the time we could really start making memories together, Tuck was gone. Fighting for his country instead of for his family. For *me*."

Jed wiped away a stream of tears from her cheek with the thumb of his glove. "I'm so sorry, Jo-Jo."

"The only memory I have to hold onto is this hazy recollection of riding out here on horseback, just me and Tuck, and cutting down a tree. We dragged it back, and my mother—who was like another kid at Christmastime—waited at the house with my sisters, making hot chocolate, with Bing Crosby singing on the stereo . . . and . . ." She buckled under the emotion and fell back into his arms. She almost shouted her next words. "All he left me was *Christmas*, Jed." She thumped her fist against his shoulder. "Is it really so much to ask of my sisters that they give that to me just one more time?"

"No." He hugged her to his chest. "It's not too much to ask."

Right there and then, Jed determined to find a way to reach out to every one of her three sisters and make sure they knew what was at stake for Joanna. They were coming home to Bluegrass Crossing for one more Christmas if he had to drag each one of them back like that tree they were cutting down for the great room in the main house.

Joanna had never been to the Bluegrass Bistro before, but she knew its setting well. When she was a kid, the beautiful antebellum estate had been a home on the historic registry. It had since been rezoned and turned into a commercial site with the name *Wentworth* on the sign out front.

The circular drive in front of the three-story, stately, columned brick building forked off in one direction, and Jed steered his truck around the side of the building. A hostess led them past framed photographs of Kentucky Derby winners, and Joanna paused at one of them: Dirk Mallard, the jockey who rode the Tuckers' final entry in the Derby. Standing next to that winning stallion, Dirk's broad smile showed the two shiny gold teeth that used to fascinate Joanna.

"Remember him?" Jed asked as he stood behind her.

"Of course."

"Dirk went to my church for years. Passed away recently. The same cancer as Tuck."

Her heart wrenched slightly at the thought.

The hostess circled back for them and noticed the picture that had caught their eye. "Oh, that was Dirk Mallard," she said. "He was a local Derby winner from right here in Bluegrass Crossing. The horse farm he represented really used to be something back in the day. I don't think they're around anymore." With a shrug, she added, "Right this way."

Joanna shot Jed a grimace before following. When they reached the table, she told him, "I met your pastor, by the way. He came and invited me to church."

"My mom mentioned. Is that something you're interested in?"

"Maybe. At some point."

He nodded, relieving her of her coat before pulling out her chair. "I understand. You just let me know when you're ready, and you can come with me if you'd like."

Once he sat across from her, Joanna smiled. "Why are you always so nice to me?"

"I'm a nice guy," he said. "It's just how I roll."

She chuckled at his response, and the amusement brought unexpected relief to her soul.

"They're known for their homemade soups here," he said, opening his menu. "I'm partial to the broccoli cheese."

And I'm partial to you, she thought as she unfolded a second menu.

"Broccoli." She wrinkled her nose, and Jed laughed.

"You've never gotten over your aversion to broccoli?"

"I think I'll try the vegetable beef."

After an hour of amiable conversation combined with warm bowls of soup, thick grilled-cheese sandwiches, and glasses of sweet tea, Jed paid the check while Joanna made a quick stop in the ladies' room. The late afternoon sky had darkened prematurely, and the wind brought with it a bitter punch.

When they drove away from the old mansion, her cache of excitement mounted again as fat snowflakes fluttered from the sky just when the truck emerged from the old covered bridge and turned toward home.

Emotion bubbled up from within her as she cried out, "Jed, it's snowing!"

He grumbled out an attempt at sharing her enthusiasm, but unconvincingly.

Before they reached the house, Joanna spotted a strange glow on the horizon. "What is that?" she asked as Jed steered them around the curve. When the house came into full view—fully outlined in large, colorful bulbs of red, green, and white—Joanna gasped, slapping her hand over her mouth, her eyes so wide at the sight that they burned. "How did—Jed, did you do this?"

He smiled at her. "I might have made a phone call while you were in the restroom. The guys and my mom did the rest."

On the other side of the front window, another glow drew her attention. "And what's that?"

When Jed drove up to the porch, the heavy wooden door whooshed open, and Sarah stood there smiling at them, wearing a kelly-green sweater. Soft strains of "White Christmas" wafted toward them from the inside of the house, delivered in the distinct stylings of Bing Crosby.

"Sarah, what's going on in there?"

"I thought I'd check the strands of lights for the tree you cut down," she replied with a broad grin. "The boys came up from the bunkhouse to help with the rest. I've got some hot cocoa simmering on the stove, and all the decorations are lined up in boxes in front of the fireplace, waiting for you."

Joanna whirled around. Jed stood a few steps behind her, his face illuminated by his Cheshire cat smile, and she rushed toward him so eagerly that she almost knocked him right over.

He opened his arms, his laughter melodic, and lifted her straight off her feet. "I think you deserve another happy Christmas here," he growled into her ear. "It's been far too long."

"Oh, Jed, thank you. Thank you so much."

And without further consideration—or even one thought about the fact that his mother stood there watching them from the doorway— Joanna wrapped her arms around Jed's neck and planted several quick kisses on both cheeks. She felt his entire body turn rigid as he slowly, carefully lowered her to the ground, and set her on her feet again. When they parted, she looked up into his eyes and sighed.

"Thank you," she whispered hoarsely.

"Oh," he said, grinning and shaking his head, "you are very welcome. Thank *you*."

CHAPTER EIGHT

I think it's lovely that you're crusading on behalf of my sister, Jed," Bella crooned over the phone, "but David's really committed to the idea of spending the holiday with his family. Maybe I could make it after the first of the year."

"Jed, it's so nice to hear from you," Sophie exclaimed a few minutes later. "I know how Jo-Jo can be, believe me. She's a dog with a bone. But really, I can't see any reason to come back there and relive memories that were dead and buried with our mother."

Later still, Amy sighed. "I've already spoken to Joanna about this, Jed. I have no interest. She'll just have to understand and move on like the rest of us."

He'd gone to all the trouble of pilfering Joanna's cell phone, sneaking off to the bathroom to transfer the three phone numbers into his contact list, and waiting impatiently for the next day so he could make those calls. And this is what he got for his trouble: excuses, selfishness, and closed minds.

He inhaled sharply, swallowing his irritation as best he could. "Listen, Amy. I understand. But you three have a lot more history to draw from. Joanna was so young. All she has left to cling to are a few happy Christmas memories. She's cut down a tree and decorated it, pulled out the carols your mom used to play. And she's lit up like that tree, by the way, just thinking about having you all together one more time. You're going to deny her this? When one last Christmas as a family is all she's asking? It's not much, if you really think about—"

"I'm sorry, Jed. I think your heart is in the right place. But there's a lot you don't understand. And why are you championing this cause for her anyway? Did Joanna put you up to this?"

"No." He pinched the bridge of his nose and sighed. "It just seemed like the right thing to do to let you ladies know that your youngest sister is suffering here. She needs you. *All three of you.*"

"And we're there for her in any way we can be, Jedediah. Just not in this."

On the walk to the main house a while later, Jed replayed those conversations until his brain ached. He hoped he'd at least given Amy a cordial good-bye before hanging up, but he couldn't really be sure. In fact, he felt pretty certain that, in his frustration, he may have hung up on her.

"Just in time," Sarah called out when he opened the front door. "Do you need to wash up?"

He stood in the kitchen doorway, a frown on his face, and nodded. As he headed for the hallway bathroom, he heard the *jingle-thump-thump-jingle* of someone—presumably Jo-Jo, but sounding very Santa-like making her way down the loft stairs. When she appeared around the corner, a thick red velvet strap of jingling bells hung around her neck as she carried two boxes and several glossy shopping bags. She gasped as she nearly slammed straight into him.

"Here," he said, taking the boxes out of her arms. "What have you got there? I'd have thought every ornament, snowman, and wreath had made its way to the tree already."

"I found our stockings! I want to hang them on the mantle."

"And you're jingling."

"Oh." She giggled as she shook the bells hanging around her neck. "We used to hang these on the sleigh on Christmas Eve. Do you remember?"

He smiled. "I do."

She jingled the strap enthusiastically, clanking the bells. "Tuck used to say . . .," she said, tensing her face to imitate him, "Whenever a sleigh bell rings, one of my little girls gets their wish."

Jed remembered Tuck saying that very thing many times. A take on the classic movie, *It's a Wonderful Life* . . . every time a bell rings, an angel gets its wings. He smiled at Joanna and nodded at the bags left in her hand. "You've been shopping, I see."

"I wanted to show them to you and your mom. You'll never believe what I found at a little shop in town today. I got one for each of us."

Each sister? The sisters who won't be coming home for Christmas? Jed's heartbeat thumped at the mere thought of Joanna's probable disappointment.

"Matching flannel nightgowns—red-and-green plaid—almost just like the ones Mom gave us way back when." She giggled. "Amy will just *hate them!*"

The delight in her voice at challenging her oldest sister resonated with him. He hoped the pajamas hadn't been too expensive. And that she'd saved the receipt.

He dropped the boxes on Tuck's chair as Joanna produced one of the ugly—err, *nostalgic?*—nightgowns from the bag.

"Look at these, Sarah." She held the nightgown in front of her and swung her body from side to side like a Christmas bell. "I got one for each of us to wear. Aren't they fun?"

"They'll certainly put everyone in the mood for remembering," Jed's mother said.

Jed's heart ached for her. She'd always been the encourager, just one of so many good qualities.

"Jo-Jo, listen," he began, pausing as he considered how to say it. "If they *don't* come for Christmas—"

"Don't even say that. They will, Jed. I just know it."

"How about some supper?" Sarah interjected. "Stuffed peppers and homemade French bread with garlic butter. Let's sit down, shall we?"

Jed and Joanna took their usual spots on one side of the island, and Sarah set savory, fragrant plates in front of them. When she took a stool on the short side of the counter, she arched a brow at her son. "Why don't you pray over our meal, Jedediah."

Jed snatched Joanna's hand from where it rested in her lap, then took his mother's outstretched one and bowed his head. "Father, we thank you for this food and ask your blessing over the hands that prepared it, and over all of us as we enjoy it. We also ask—" He hesitated for an instant before continuing. "—that you would answer Joanna's prayers.

Bring the Tucker girls home for Christmas. In the precious name of Jesus, we pray."

"Amen!" Joanna declared, and Sarah echoed her enthusiastic sentiment.

———

Sarah loaded the dishwasher as Jed wiped the island countertop. He intermittently glanced at Joanna as she applied adhesive hooks to the mantle and draped red stockings from them, singing along with Bing's "It's Beginning to Look a Lot Like Christmas" the whole time. His heart hurt for the joy in her, the same joy that would surely be decimated very soon by the harsh blade of reality.

A flicker of guilt scorched him. Hadn't he prayed for God to bring her sisters home for Christmas? Maybe it was *his* faith that needed an attitude adjustment, not Joanna's.

"Have you thought about telling her?" his mother whispered, and Jed jumped. He hadn't heard her approach.

"That her sisters aren't really coming?"

"Oh, no. There's plenty of time for that. I mean about your feelings."

He glared at her. "What feelings?"

"The ones of *love* . . . that you have for *her*."

Jed's heart pummeled the inside of his chest. "What are you talking about?"

"I'm your mother. I've noticed."

"Mom—"

"Jedediah. Tell her."

He stalked toward Joanna, shaking his head. "Can I help you with that?"

"I'm just about finished."

Shiny silver embroidery spelled out each of the Tucker sisters' names. But until that moment, he hadn't seen the outer two stockings. MOM on one side, DAD on the other. She was really into the reliving-the-past thing, wasn't she?

After straightening the stockings and the garland running along the edge of the mantle for the third—or maybe fourth—time, she stood back and admired her work. "It looks beautiful, right?"

"It does."

"Just like when my mom used to decorate. My sisters are going to love it."

Jed placed an arm around Joanna's waist and led her over to the sofa. Instead of sitting next to him, she moved to Tuck's chair and sank into it, grinning as she rubbed the leather arms with both hands.

"I can almost smell that awful pipe tobacco of his when I sit here."

Before Jed had the chance to reply, his mother stepped behind the chair and wrapped her arms around Joanna's shoulders. "You've done a beautiful job over the last few days, Sweet Pea. This place looks so festive."

"Thank you, Sarah."

Peering at Jed over the top of Joanna's head, she told them, "I'm going to my room to call Matthew. He's been on my mind all day."

Jed nodded, and Joanna patted Sarah's hand and thanked her again for all her help. Once she'd gone, Joanna pushed out of the chair and plopped next to Jed on the couch.

"I've been thinking about it," she said. "And I'd like to go to church with you on Sunday, if you don't mind."

"Happy to have you. Mind if I ask what changed your mind?"

She lifted one shoulder in a gentle shrug. "Maybe it's all the decorations or Bing Crosby on the stereo, or maybe even just the vibe of this house." She paused and swallowed hard. When she looked back at him, her greenish eyes teemed with tears. "That's not it. It's my mother. I've been reading her diary and thinking about how strong her faith was. It was never just *words* for her. Jesus was as much a part of her everyday life as my sisters and I were. She had a *living faith*, if that makes any sense. It's been making me feel like I'm . . . *missing* something. Anyway, I think I'd also like to go to your church to meet the people who knew Tuck when he found that kind of faith. If he did."

"Oh, he did."

"That's good, right?" She sniffed back her tears. "It means . . . he's with my mom, doesn't it?"

"It does."

Joanna moved closer and dropped her head to Jed's shoulder. "It makes me happy to think of it like . . . he finally came home to her. She waited such a long time for that."

Jed touched her chin with two fingers and angled her head toward him. He gazed into her eyes for several beats. He had no idea what it would mean for them going forward. His heart pounded so hard at the thought that he suspected it might explode, yet Jed knew the time had come to say the words.

"I love you, Jo-Jo," he confessed as they parted.

And Joanna . . . *burst into laughter.*

When she saw his expression, she covered her mouth. "Oh, I'm sorry. It's not funny. It's just—*a relief.* I love you, too, Jed."

"Just listen to this one last passage," Joanna told Bella's image on the computer screen. She opened the leather-bound journal to the page she'd marked with the ribbon.

"I can't believe you found that. I've wondered over the years what ever happened to Mom's diary."

"Here it is. Listen to this." Joanna shifted the leg folded beneath her before reading: *I heard from Tuck today. A picture postcard from Istanbul—a lovely photo of a harbor there called the Golden Horn—and just a few sentences scribbled on the back. "En route back to Kabul," he wrote. "I don't know what awaits us, but I want you to know I'm sorry for disappointing you. So many sorries for so many disappointments. Tuck."*

"Well, that was something, I guess," Bella interrupted. "Tossing a few apologies at her before he maybe got killed in Afghanistan."

"There's more. She writes, *It might not seem like anything to the average onlooker. But I know, for Tuck, that was a milestone. I continue to pray he'll come home to us one day, Lord. Until then, my life revolves around our four stunning girls. Through them, I am fulfilled and happy."*

Bella's hand went to her heart, her facial expression crumpled, and she looked away from the screen.

"Oh. And Bell? Did I mention to you that Jed Weatherly says he loves me?"

Bella jerked back toward the screen, her mouth hanging open. "I'm sorry. What did you say?"

"Yeah." She suppressed the smile that threatened. "Jed's in love with me. And it only took twenty-some years for him to come around. Honestly, I don't know what took him so long."

Bella broke into a guffaw, and the two of them shared belly laughs.

"Jo-Jo, listen. I have to go," she said once she recovered. "I have that conference call with my boss in ten. But first, I know I don't have to ask you if you love him back because . . . well, it's Jed."

Joanna shrugged. "Yeah. But I do. I really do still love him. With all my heart."

"Any idea what you two are going to do about it?"

"I wish I knew. He's been offered a job in Montana, so there may not be anything left we *can* do."

"You'll figure it out together."

"Hey, Bell?"

"Yeah."

"Please come for Christmas."

"Jo-Jo—"

"Really, I almost don't even care if Soph and Amy come now. I'm so sick of begging them. But *please*, Bella. You and me. Come and spend Christmas with me on the horse farm. Just say you'll think about it."

After several moments of silence, Bella nodded. "I'll think about it. But I'm not promising anything."

Once she disconnected from Skype and closed her laptop, Joanna went to the mirror hanging behind the large, mahogany dresser. She fixed her hair and applied some lip gloss, then changed into the thick, black sweater she'd found in her mother's still-untouched dresser. With her hair loose, she looked more like her mom than she'd ever noticed before. Others had remarked on it often, but she finally saw it. And it made her smile.

Despite the inclination to hurry off to her destination, Joanna hesitated, then sat on the corner of her bed. After a moment, she bowed her head and closed her eyes.

"Jesus," she whispered, then she sighed, not sure how to phrase everything that trudged around her heart. "Jesus," she repeated. "My mother really loved you, didn't she? And Pastor Tobin says Tuck eventually shared her feelings. Is that true?"

She didn't suppose Tuck—or Sarah and Jed as well—would have said so if it wasn't the truth.

"I think I'm glad about that," she murmured. "But at the same time, I don't guess I can just crouch down under that umbrella to try and get in on it, can I? I mean—if you're interested—I'd like to know you better *myself*."

Her eyes flew open at the words. She hadn't really intended to say that, exactly. But what *had* she meant to say?

"I feel like you've been trying to tell me something," she told the closed bedroom door. "Like you're calling me to something different. Something . . . *higher*. Is that the case? Are you asking me to come closer? To get to know you?"

After a moment's thought, Joanna slid impulsively from the side of the bed and landed on her knees. As she bowed her head, tears pushed against her clamped eyes and forced their way out in streams.

"I remember the Sunday school lessons," she whispered. "But it's different now. I feel you in my heart, pulling me toward you. I just want you to know . . . I *believe*. I know you're my God. I want to follow you. Tuck may have failed me as a father, but you haven't, have you? Maybe you've just been waiting for me to wise up and see these things. But I'm here now. If you'll have me. Just tell me somehow what to do, what comes next."

An hour later, after she'd confessed a lifetime of doubt, rebellion, and independence, Joanna stood, dried her eyes, and slipped out to the great room. On her way out the door, she slid into her coat, tugged her pink gloves into place, and pulled the beanie over her head. Halfway down the drive, she looked back at the incandescent holiday tree filling the window and followed the trail of colorful lights outlining the large house. A peculiar sense of joy squeezed her heart. She still loved this place so much.

When she reached Jed's front door, Joanna stood there before knocking. Had she made a mistake in coming? Would her words come out in a jumble, or did she have time to lasso them into some semblance of order?

Jed opened the door at her first soft rap. "Jo-Jo. What are you doing here?"

"Are you taking that job in Montana, Jed?"

"Hello to you, too."

"Do you think there's any chance we could bring this place to life again? I mean, if you stuck around and helped me. Do we have a shot at that?"

"Would you like to come in?"

She dropped her head and groaned. "Did I make it up in my head or did you actually tell me you *love me*? I mean, I know you told me you did, and I'm happy about it because I really love you, too. You already knew that though, didn't you?"

"I—"

She recognized the landslide of words as they slid into a full-on avalanche, but she just couldn't stop them. "Don't go to Montana, Jed. Stay here with me. Help me make this place into something again."

"Okay."

"I think we can do it. I mean, I don't really know what makes me think that, but—*What did you say?*"

"I said, okay. I'll stay."

"Really?"

"Unless you want me to rethink."

"No! Don't do that." Suddenly, she noticed— "Hey, you have your coat on. Were you leaving?"

"I was headed down to the stable to check on Lucinda."

"The gray mare?"

He nodded, stepping out and closing the door behind him. "The vet was out today to look at her leg. Her limp has gotten worse, and she can't bend her knee more than about twenty degrees. He gave her a shot of an anti-inflammatory. I just want to check in and see how she's doing."

Joanna extended her hand. "Let's visit Lucinda together."

The simple act of Jed accepting her hand and tucking it into his sent a shot of electricity straight through her.

"Did you mean it?" she finally asked. "You'll stay?"

"I called and turned down the job in Montana this morning. I'm not going anywhere."

Joanna stopped in her tracks and turned to face him. "I can't believe you actually *love me*. Am I dreaming?"

"If you are," he said, placing his gloved hand on her cold cheek, "then so am I. Please, be very quiet so you don't wake me."

"I won't if you won't."

CHAPTER NINE

O h good!" Joanna said from her spot on the floor as Jed came through the door.

She looked so beautiful to him just then with her dark waves falling well past her shoulders, her jean-clad legs folded beneath her, and her small feet covered in thick, gray socks. She'd only been back in Bluegrass Crossing for a couple of weeks, but every day seemed to bring a new discovery about her. About *them*. Just the sight of her lifted his spirits to ridiculous levels.

"I'm glad you're here. I've been going over a few things." Her laptop sat propped open on the coffee table in front of her, and a spiral notebook stood balanced against it. "When is the auction again?"

"The fourteenth."

"And we have four thoroughbreds to put on the block, yes?"

"Yep."

"Okay. Let's figure this out. Either way—whether we keep this place or sell it—we need to get started on repairs and the like. I was thinking—"

Jed crouched next to her and placed his finger over her lips to silence her. "Take a breath," he whispered, "before you hyperventilate."

"There's just so much to think about, Jed, and I—"

"You like to make your lists and plan your next move. I know that. But for just one minute, can I pull you away from all this?"

"No," she blurted. "I'm on to something here, and I don't want to lose my train of thought."

"Even if I have a surprise for you?"

A grin glided over her entire face, and she dropped her pen. "You do? What is it?"

Jed offered her his hand, and when she took it, he guided Joanna to her feet. Placing his hands on both of her shoulders, he looked into her eyes and smiled.

"I'm really sorry your sisters let you down and decided not to come for that family Christmas you wanted so much."

She shrugged, and a pout replaced her smile. "It is what it is. Their loss."

"But my surprise for you is almost as good."

Joanna giggled. "As good as my three sisters?"

He shrugged. "How about just *one* of your sisters?"

Confusion glazed her hazel eyes with an emotional, emerald tint. "What?"

Jed circled her toward the door so she could see who had crept inside, and Joanna froze for several seconds before whirling around, smacking Jed's arm, and flying into those of her sister, Bella.

"I *knew it!*" she cried as they embraced. "We've been praying you'd come!"

Bella snorted. "You *prayed?*"

"I know, right? I have so much to tell you! But we did. We prayed. And here you are."

"After Jed called me three times and guilted me into it, yes. I'm here."

Twirling toward Jed again, she beamed as she flew toward him and nearly strangled him with her arms.

"Thank you, thank you, thank you."

With a gasp, she turned back to her sister. "Oh, Bella! Wait till you see what I have for us. Remember those flannel nightgowns Mom made?"

Bella laughed. "They were awful!"

"Well, I found some just like them for us!"

Her sister's expression drooped. "Oh."

Jed chuckled as he stood back and watched the cyclone that was Jo-Jo, fired up and swirling with hope once again.

Thank you, Lord. I think that look on her face is the best Christmas gift I've ever received.

Her Old Kentucky Home

BY LYNETTE SOWELL

Bella Baby,

I pray the investigators have found you well and happy. I'm sorry I've let so many years get away from us, and that we didn't have the opportunity to spend some time together before my death. You were always my tough little cookie, so strong and determined. I've wondered often over the years about the woman you became, but I know this one thing for sure: you've made your own way. Even as a kid, you did that. I don't really have much more in life than the ranch, and even that belonged more to your mom and you and your sisters than it ever did to me. It still holds my name though, and I've left it to you and the girls to do with whatever you choose. I'll love you always, Bella. Be happy.

Tuck

Trust in the LORD with all your heart and lean not on your own understanding.

—Proverbs 3:5

CHAPTER ONE

Bella Tucker had forgotten the scent of her sister Jo-Jo's favorite perfume, but that all came rushing back as soon as she found herself in a rib-crushing hug.

"You came! You really came!" Beaming, Jo-Jo stepped back, her gaze flicking over Bella's shoulder. "I . . . I almost can't believe it. You're here. At home."

Bella nodded, then gazed at the giant, decked-out Christmas tree in the living room. The tree reminded her of Christmases past—happy days because of her mother. Bella had barely been back to the farm since college, save for grief-filled days after Mom's sudden death during her sophomore year. During that haze she hadn't noticed much about the place she swore she'd never return to. She snapped her focus back to the others.

"Well, this guy over here—" Bella nodded toward Jed, who'd contacted her last week, "—I couldn't tell him no. He was wonderfully persistent."

She wanted to say more about her job, about the whole mess she had left behind in Chicago. But the mess would still be there when she returned after Christmas. Instead, she took a deep breath and willed away the tears that pricked her eyelids. Bella Tucker never cried.

She sensed David's presence at her elbow. The six hours on the road from Chicago had flown past. An easy trip, even if not carefree at the moment.

Jo-Jo's grin widened at the sight of David. "And David. Finally, I get to meet you at last, in the flesh."

Bella shook off the feelings that swirled below the surface of her own smile. "Yes, this is David. David, my youngest sister, Joanna. We call her Jo-Jo." The two shook hands.

"I feel like I know you already, David. You're the other person responsible for making sure my sister came home." Jo-Jo's grin hadn't faded. If anything, she had an extra sparkle in her eye that she cast in Bella's direction. Bella tried not to squirm under her sister's scrutiny.

Instead, she let herself smile. "Yes, and the fact that the bigwigs insisted I use my paid time off between now and the end of the year. You're stuck with me till New Year's. We'll celebrate Christmas Eve with David's parents in Louisville, then we'll make the two-hour drive back here on Christmas Day."

Keeping her tone casual, Bella schooled her jumbled thoughts about being back at the farm. Today was a rare warm day for the second week of December, and the familiar scent of horses drifted on the breeze.

Lord, I'm not prepared for this. Not for the first time did Bella question her decision to come here.

"I'll get your bags," David offered, leaving her side and heading out the door to his car.

"He's not going to stay with us? We have the room." Jo-Jo gave her a quizzical look.

Bella shook her head. "No, since his parents live in Louisville, he's driving there to spend the night. He hasn't seen them in a year or so. He'll be back sometime tomorrow. We'll have plenty of time together here."

"Good." Jo-Jo linked her arm through hers and headed down the hallway. "C'mon, I've got our old room set up for both of us. Won't be quite like old times, but it still looks the same. It's been good to be back. This is going to be the best Christmas ever."

David rolled her suitcase into the house and followed them.

Bella barely heard Jo-Jo's chatter as they headed to their old bedroom—the keeper of all their secrets.

When they were kids, she never could have imagined they'd end up scattered all around the country. *Thanks a lot, Tuck.* She suppressed the recollection of her long-dead dream of her and her three sisters converging with spouses and children on their childhood home as their parents came out to meet them all.

A family Christmas on the farm.

Well, at least she and Jo-Jo would spend Christmas together this year. Her older sisters Sophie and Amy had not been persuaded to come home. Their loss. Last Christmas, she'd been lounging by a hotel pool in Dubai while she sipped something sweet and frozen. She'd taken the year-end assignment on the other side of the world, so a colleague could go home to her own family for Christmas, along with her husband and new baby. This Christmas, because of David and Jo-Jo's persistence and Jed's invitation, she ended up here.

David released her suitcase handle, and she automatically stepped into the circle of his arms.

"Have fun catching up. I'll be back tomorrow," he murmured into her ear.

"Sounds good. I know your parents will be excited to see you again." Bella gave him a swift kiss on the cheek. They hadn't planned any specific activities for their three-week visit to Kentucky other than seeing what their respective families had in mind for Christmas.

After Christmas—after they returned to the routine of their lives in Chicago—she needed to have a serious conversation with David about their relationship. In late January, she was due to spend a week in Germany with one of the European divisions of the company. That is, if she still had a job and if the rumors weren't true.

"I'll see myself out. It was nice meeting you all, and I'll see you again soon." David flashed his winsome, boyish grin at all of them before heading into the hallway. Jed followed him, leaving Jo-Jo and Bella alone at last.

Jo-Jo squealed and flung her arms around Bella once again. "I can't believe it. I'm so happy you're here. And I finally got to meet David."

Bella hugged her sister. "I know. It's a long time coming, isn't it? I'm glad everything worked out just to see the look on your face when you turned around and saw us. I thought Jed would never pry you away from your laptop."

Jo-Jo nodded. "That sneak, Jed, grabbed your phone number from my cell and twisted your arm. You really surprised me. I wish Sophie and Amy would come, too. I still haven't given up on them."

"You're such an optimist. I can't even remember the last time we were all together in one place."

"My high school graduation."

"That's right." Bella picked up her Louis Vuitton suitcase and dropped it on her old bed, trying to forget the sad time before that—their mother's funeral. They had all missed Tuck's memorial service. But his attorney had finally tracked them all down, even though it was too late for his funeral, and delivered a special letter from him to each of them.

"Are you glad you came?" Jo-Jo asked.

"Yes." She smiled at her younger sister and hugged her again. "Very glad."

"I wanted all of us to have one more Christmas here because we might not have this chance again. Jed and I have been talking about the property."

"I admit I haven't kept up with the horse farm's affairs over the years." Bella felt guilty about that. Once she left home, she never looked back. She had no idea her father had returned to the farm after he retired. Not until the letter arrived.

"It's kind of in bad shape, Bella. You could probably tell when you drove up. It's not just the house, but the grounds. Jed and the hands do the best they can with maintenance, but the repairs and upkeep are expensive, and until Tuck's estate is settled, it's tough."

"How's Sarah doing? I was so excited to see you when I got here, I didn't stop to ask about her."

"She's great. In fact, she's running some errands at the moment, but she should be back soon."

Bella smiled. The older woman had been a fixture at the farm forever. Sarah had seemed "old" back when they were kids, but she was probably only in her fifties at the time.

"I can't wait to see her again." She nudged Jo-Jo's arm and smiled with a teasing look. "So, 'fess up. I want to hear more about Jed now that we have some time to talk. Tell me all about this romance with him."

Reluctantly, David drove away from the horse farm, glancing back in his rearview mirror. Part of him wanted to linger, to spend more precious minutes and hours with Bella. She'd barely gotten back from London before she received the news of her father's death, and shortly after that, Jo-Jo's plea to return home for Christmas and help to settle her father's affairs.

Bella and he had been a couple for two years, more or less, and both of them had yet to meet each other's families. Bella's job, and sometimes his, had made their relationship a long-distance one despite the fact they lived in the same apartment building.

She would jet off for a week to ten days, then return to the high-rise where they both lived, two floors apart, then leave again on business. In between trips, they'd make up for lost time with a long date or two.

After almost a two-hour drive through the Kentucky countryside he'd missed while living in the Windy City, David pulled into his parents' driveway in suburban Louisville. He honked. Within seconds, the front door opened, and his mother descended the porch steps.

"Davie!" She let out a squeal he could hear above the car's engine.

He climbed from the front seat and shut the door. "Mom."

Before hugging him, she glanced through the car window at the empty front-passenger seat. "Where's Isabella? Don't tell me she took off on another trip or stayed in Chicago after all?"

He ignored the crackle of judgment in her dark-blue eyes. "I dropped her off at her family's horse farm in Bluegrass Crossing over near Lexington."

"Ah . . . I see." She straightened her spine. "So, she didn't bother to come meet us."

"Mom." Irritated, he hid his reaction and tried to see the situation through her eyes. "You'll meet her soon enough. She hasn't seen her own family in years. I'm staying here tonight, but heading back over there sometime tomorrow."

"That's a two-hour drive."

He shrugged and smiled. "Not so bad compared to Chicago at rush hour." He looked up at the porch. "Where's Dad?"

"Where else? In the workshop, going through his stash of Christmas lights." She shook her head, her platinum curls bouncing. He didn't recall her coloring her hair like that before. "I tell ya, ever since he started replacing the old lights with those new LED strands, he's gone hog wild. You know he'll be askin' you to give him a hand. I think he even bought some computer gizmo that makes the lights flash in time to the music."

"I'll be glad to help deck the place out. You two still have the house lighting party, right?"

"It wouldn't be Christmas without it." Love for him lit up her blue eyes. "I can't believe you're actually home for Christmas. It's been too long. I know I've said so already, but I can't help but repeat myself." Her voice held the faintest scolding tone.

Mom . . . always ready to speak her piece. A lot like Bella. He didn't think it wise to mention that right now.

"You go right ahead, Mom. I don't mind." He popped the trunk and pulled out his carry-on and overnight bag, then joined her at the porch steps. The second stair creaked when he stepped on it like it always had. He needed to help Dad fix that while he was here.

He held the door for his mother, and she entered the house ahead of him, while the aroma of something warm and hearty drifted from the kitchen.

"Supper will be ready soon."

New furniture graced the living room, including a pair of wingback chairs that faced each other in front of the fireplace.

"If it gets cold enough, we'll light a fire before too long. Maybe make some s'mores." She gave him an affectionate look. "You like the new chairs? They're really cozy for your dad and me."

He nodded. "I do. The room looks bigger." His parents had gotten rid of the large sectional that he and his brothers had used to make forts, or employed as a shield when dueling with their light sabers.

That sofa was worn out by the time his younger brother Bryan had gone off to college more than three years ago, leaving his parents empty-nesters at last. If it were him, he would have splurged for new furniture, too.

"Your little brother will be home next weekend after finals," his mother said as if in response to his thoughts. "Time is flying by. I can't believe he's a senior already."

"Me either. Can't wait to see him." David tossed his overnight bag on the piano bench where he and his brothers had suffered through hours of lessons.

Just then his cell dinged in his pocket. Work, probably. He pulled out his phone and glanced at the text. Sure enough. George, his associate broker. The Millers were closing on their building today, a three-unit walk-up, which would be converted into a nice set of condos in the spring. A brilliant return on their investment, he'd insisted, when he showed them the property.

"Are you going to bury your nose in that thing the whole time you're here?" Mom sounded annoyed.

"After today, not much. At year's end, things quiet down long enough for me to leave the business in George's hands."

He typed a response to his associate's question and fired off the message, then muted his phone. "That should do it for now."

He followed his mother into the kitchen and bent to peer through the oven window.

"Chicken cordon bleu, poor-man style," she said. "I haven't made it in ages, with your daddy and I watching our salt and all." His mother peered at the timer on the microwave above the stove. "But I figured you might like a taste of home when you got here."

"Thanks, Mama." He caught himself slipping into a southern accent. If he spoke that way in Chicago, he'd be labeled ignorant. "You didn't have to, but I'm glad you did."

She washed her hands at the sink and wiped her hands on the dish towel that hung from the oven-door handle. "Now go on out and let your daddy know you're here. I still need to make the salad and set the table." As she shooed him away with her hands, he opened the back door and walked to his father's workshop, only a few paces from the house.

David could just make out the tones from an old radio cranked up high that blared with classic Christmas songs, filling the workshop and probably annoying the neighbors. Yet maybe not quite annoying, as the entire neighborhood looked forward to Mr. Christmas's light display. His father had the reputation on the block of being the one with the lightest and brightest display of Christmas lights every season since David could remember. But now that his dad's hearing had started to go, the TV and radio were always turned up too loud for his taste.

"Hey, Dad." He called out loudly enough so he could be heard over the strains of "Rockin' Around the Christmas Tree."

His father looked up from where he stood at a scarred worktable covered with a jumble of Christmas lights. "You made it! Right on time, too. Wait till you see what the yard is going to look like this year. I've got plans all drawn out."

No clap on the back or hug, but David caught the warm twinkle in his father's eye. For some reason, the thought of Bella's confused emotions of grief and anger struck him at that moment. His own throat caught. He didn't want to imagine a world without his father in it. His mother, either. Bella had lost both.

"I'm looking forward to it. I'll be glad to give you a hand while I'm here." He wanted to say, "Not every day," but didn't. He'd figure out the schedule soon enough.

"You think you'll be coming back here someday, permanently?"

Trust Dad to cut straight to what was on his mind. A grin tugged at the corners of David's mouth.

"Actually, I am thinking about it. Very seriously. I've been in touch with Jonathan Daniels. I don't know if you remember him, but we've been talking about me opening an office here in Kentucky and turning things over to George to run in Chicago."

Dad nodded, untangling two strands of lights as he did so. He pulled one to the side and set it onto a pile of lights. "But? I hear a 'but' with that idea."

"But I love Chicago. And then, there's Isabella."

"Ah, yes. Isabella." Dad spoke her name with a shade more tenderness than Mom. "You love her, but I bet she doesn't want to leave the city."

David shrugged. "She's been pretty clear. As long as I've known her, she's vowed never to live in Kentucky again."

CHAPTER TWO

"Sarah is still a fantastic cook, but *oof*, I think I overdid it a little by making up for all those meals of hers I missed." Bella patted her stomach as she sat on the front porch with Jo-Jo after supper. Jed had given them some sisterly space after they ate, but Bella didn't miss the longing look that passed between the two of them as she and Jo-Jo headed outside.

"It's not hard to do. Believe me, I've enjoyed her southern cooking skills for the past couple of weeks, and I'm surprised my jeans still fit." Jo-Jo let out a happy sigh and pulled her cardigan around her shoulders. "*Brr*. It's getting chilly."

"So, about the farm . . ."

"You're cutting right to the chase."

Bella nodded. "It's too much for the four of us to deal with now, or ever."

"The place has grown on me again, Bella. I mean, we grew up here. This is our heritage—our family legacy passed on from Dad. Our great-great-great grandpa homesteaded here. Part of me wants to keep it and somehow make it work."

"You're right. It's our legacy. But realistically, how long can we keep up with it? None of us live in the area. Jed works somewhere else to make ends meet here. The hands aren't paid enough, and I know you probably don't want to let any of them go." Bella gestured toward the stable. "There's the horse auction, you told me about, coming up next week—"

"I think the four of us need to decide together, which is why Amy and Sophie need to be here."

Tuck, what a fine mess you've left us. "I can't argue with that . . . if they'll actually come home for Christmas. If not, I think you and I need to take some time, inspect the house and outbuildings, and determine what needs a little TLC. My vote is to sell it."

"Jed and I have been making a list of what needs to be done already."

"Good. We have a head start." Bella decided to change the subject. "You and Jed seem pretty cozy." She slid her sister a sideways glance. "Have you talked about the future yet?"

A flush crept over Jo-Jo's cheeks, visible in the porch light and gathering dusk. "A little. It happened pretty quickly, but—oh, Bella, I never imagined. Well, maybe years and years ago I did, but it was just a schoolgirl crush back then."

"You two are pretty serious then?"

Jo-Jo nodded. "I can't describe it. It's as if we've known each other forever. If that makes any sense."

Bella wished she could have that certainty. Jo-Jo's eyes had held a glow every time she looked Jed's way during supper. How could true love happen that fast? How could two people be so right for each other so quickly? She knew she loved David, but . . .

She didn't want to burst Jo-Jo's bubble. "I think that's wonderful and sweet. I envy that. I'm happy for you."

"But what about you and David? I can tell you love each other. I know you do."

Bella sighed. "It's complicated. I'm gone so much of the time. I know he loves me, and I do love him—"

"Then what's the problem? Maybe it's time for you two to settle down. Have you thought about looking for another job, one without so much travel?"

"Not really. It would mean a huge pay cut, plus I love to travel."

Jo-Jo reached over and squeezed her hand and gave her a tender smile. "You know, Bell, you never did tell me how you and David met."

"At the apartment gym—at five a.m." She laughed. "Because the weather was so horrible, we had both decided to cancel our outdoor runs and ended up on the treadmills. He had a Wildcats T-shirt on, so we started talking. You know the rest." The memory made her smile.

"I can't wait to get to know him better while you're both here." Jo-Jo snuggled deeper into her cardigan. "How great is it that his parents live over in Louisville? You never mentioned that before."

"No, I guess not. Things have been going a mile a minute for me lately."

"Lately? As in the past few years lately?"

Bella gave her sister a sheepish grin. "You're right. It's been far longer than lately." She thought of the email followed by the conference call, their end-of-year meeting at Sunrise Media Systems.

"Earth to Bella. You zoned out on me for a minute. What's up?"

"Nothing, I hope."

"No way. With that face, it's not nothing. Spill." Jo-Jo reached over and poked Bella in the ribs.

"Ow." Bella grabbed her side, then chuckled.

"See? You can't hurry off Skype when you're right here beside me."

"Very funny." Bella rolled her eyes. "They told us at our last meeting of the year to expect cutbacks in personnel after New Year's. My department, especially."

"Looks like we're two peas in a pod again." Jo-Jo sighed. "It seems like yesterday we were sharing a room, talking about boys and our dreams for the future, and here we are again, doing the same thing."

"You're right; it doesn't seem that long ago." She swallowed hard, unexpectedly emotional. And she never got emotional in her professional life. Coming home had tapped into a place she'd forgotten, memories ignited by the house: The Christmas tree, glowing in the great room when she arrived; the stockings hung from the mantel; the roaring fire, popping and crackling in the fireplace.

Jo-Jo cut into her memories, continuing their conversation. "You should be safe, though, from those personnel cuts, right? You've been in Chicago three years."

Bella shook her head as her gut tightened. "Seniority is no guarantee I'll keep my job. It's all about whether the position is deemed critical. They're offering early retirement incentives for some of the employees who've been there more than eighteen years. The training department seems like it's always the first to go when there are budget cuts. Also, I had to use up the rest of my paid time off by New Year's or I'd lose it.

No cash payouts."

"Well, the second part I'm glad about, so you can be here through Christmas."

"Me, too. It would be great if Sophie and Amy came home, but I'm not holding my breath."

"God has a plan, even if we don't see it—the timing of Dad's passing, Christmas, your job stuff and mine." Jo-Jo sounded like their mom who saw everything through the eyes of faith.

"I've missed you, Jo-Jo. You're always cheerful in spite of everything."

"I don't always feel cheerful. After getting the news about Tuck, I missed Mom even more. I know they weren't together for years, but I can't help but think of them as being together now."

"I hope so."

Jo-Jo rose from her chair. "I want to make some of Mom's special hot chocolate. You want a mug?"

"I'd love some."

"It's too cold to sit out here." Jo-Jo paused in the doorway. "Guess what? You know that carved, cedar box Mom called her Christmas treasure chest? I found it on the top shelf in her closet." Jo-Jo paused in the doorway. "I decided to wait to open it until you got here. Promise me we'll go through it together?"

"I promise. I'd love that." As she watched her younger sister enter the house, she realized she meant those words. The Christmas treasure box, a reminder of the times they used to have.

"Oh, Lord, it's been a while since I've talked to you," she whispered into the gathering dark. "I miss Mom so much. No matter how long she's been gone, I still expected to see her walking into the kitchen tonight. She would know what to do about the farm. I need you so much this Christmas."

Christmas had never been the same since the car accident that took her mother's life. Bella swallowed hard. She couldn't slow down, couldn't let herself think about what she'd lost. Maybe she was more like her father than she realized.

David took an easy morning jog, filling his lungs with cold air, even though his eyes still felt heavy because he stayed up late talking with his parents. But despite the late night, by the time he rolled out of bed, Mom already banged around in the kitchen as she cooked up her customary kids-have-come-home, delectable, country breakfast. Hopefully, he'd burn up a few hundred calories to outweigh her pancakes, sausage, fried eggs, and biscuits with cream gravy.

As he rounded the corner on Vance Avenue, an attractive woman jogged toward him. Whoever she was, she smiled widely at him.

"Hey there, stranger!"

"Catelynn?"

She jogged up to him, and they both stopped, breathing hard. Her cheeks were flushed with the cold and physical exertion. A blue headband that matched her blue running pants and jacket held back her blonde hair. "It's been a while."

"That it has," he said, wondering about the coincidence of running into her.

"I heard you were coming back for Christmas."

In that moment, David knew his mom had orchestrated this "chance" meeting with his childhood sweetheart and former fiancée. Last night, he had mentioned he planned to be up by seven for an early morning run. Inside, he shook his head. Mom always had the best of intentions, but it wouldn't work this time.

"Yes. We got here yesterday afternoon."

"We?"

He caught her swift glance at his ring finger.

"My girlfriend, Isabella, drove down with me from Chicago. She's staying with her family in Bluegrass Crossing. I'm heading back there soon."

"Ah, I see." A furrow crinkled Catelynn's brow. "It's good to see you, though. How have you been?"

"Good. Business has been very good. We're thinking of opening an office near Louisville, maybe Lexington."

"I'm impressed." She gave him a bright smile. "You started that business from the ground up and now look at you."

"You've kept up with my business?"

His former fiancée shrugged as a red blush swept over her cheeks and made her neck glow. "Your mom and I run into each other at church, and she fills me in. I've . . . uh . . . wondered over the past few years how you've been."

Silence hung between them. Had he wondered about her? A couple of times, maybe, but definitely not since Bella came into his life. When Catelynn had called things off between them, the shock had crushed him. He'd healed, but it had taken time. There had been no one but Bella since he and Catelynn parted ways.

"Well, I should finish my run," he said.

"Mind if I join you?"

He hesitated. "No, I don't mind."

They set off along the last part of the two-mile route he used to cover during his high school days and college breaks. Not much had changed about the neighborhood, other than the trees were taller. A few homes had been repainted.

As they jogged closer to his parents' home, old man Webster plucked his newspaper from the mailbox. He waved at the two of them, then trudged up the sidewalk to his house.

David didn't talk to Catelynn during the final leg of his run, and she didn't offer to speak. He imagined Mom would ask her to stay for breakfast, but her ploy wouldn't work.

They continued their run, rounding the corner of his street, and approached his parents' home, then slowed to a walk when they reached the curb. Their breath made puffy clouds in the cold morning air, and David remembered why he preferred to run at the gym in the winter.

Catelynn smiled at him and wiped her brow. She'd always had a great smile, and he found himself smiling back. But he nixed the idea of her staying for breakfast. He needed to hit the road early for the two-hour drive back to the Tucker farm.

Catelynn stopped at the foot of the porch stairs. "It was good seeing you again, David."

"Yeah. Nice seeing you, too." David raised his hand in a half-wave as she jogged away down the street. He couldn't miss the disappointed expression on her face. "They" were a long time ago. She'd been the one to break things off—two months before their wedding.

He took the porch steps two at a time just as his mother opened the door.

"Was that Catelynn I saw running off just now?"

"Yes, it was." He narrowed his eyes a millimeter or so. "Did you have anything to do with that *chance* meeting on my morning run?"

"I have no idea what you mean," she said in a high-pitched voice, then turned on her heel and led the way into the kitchen. "Breakfast is ready, Son, whenever you are. If Catelynn had stayed, I would have invited her in."

"I'm sure," he mumbled.

She rounded on him. "What did you say?"

"I said it smells great." In the space of the fifteen hours of arriving home, his mother had piled on the comfort food. He didn't mind. Much.

Dad, sitting at the table, looked up from his morning paper. "Morning. Sleep good?"

"Sure did." David accepted the cup of coffee his mother extended in his direction. "Mom, you don't have to cook like this while I'm here. I don't mind having cereal for breakfast or grabbing something while I'm out."

"Of course, your dad and I don't eat big breakfasts like this anymore. It's a lot to prepare every day. But I like to cook for my boys. I haven't had that chance in a long time."

"It's me she won't cook for like this," Dad said, shooting Mom a grin.

"Ha. Very funny." Mom tapped him with the poinsettia-print oven mitt she wore on her right hand. "Doctor's orders, Smarty-britches."

David smiled at their teasing and sat at his old place at the table. "When are you planning to hang the lights and get the yard set up?"

"Monday or Tuesday. Should take two days, if everything cooperates," Dad said. "I hope you'll be able to join me. I don't mind the extra pair of hands. It should go faster that way."

"I'll be here. I'll bring Bella with me, too, next time."

"It will be nice to finally meet her." Mom pulled a pan of biscuits from the oven and set them on the counter.

Nice, huh? He almost chuckled at her tone.

"You'll love her. She's smart, beautiful, funny, and friendly. She cares about people and likes to help them."

"Does she love the Lord?" Dad asked.

"Yes, she does. She says she's not where she wants to be spiritually, but she's working on that. As are we all." He set his cup on the table. Mom placed his breakfast in front of him.

"I don't know, Davie." Mom shook her head. "I don't have a good feeling about her. I don't want to see you get hurt. And if you're thinking of moving back here, then what? Will a long-distance relationship work out with this woman?"

Long-distance relationship? They had that already, pretty much. He picked up a piece of crispy bacon and ate it in two bites.

"I don't know." Maybe this move—or possible move—along with Bella's likely reluctance meant it was time for both of them to move on, despite how he felt about her. Part of him could almost see her deciding to move to Kentucky, but like his mother said, then what? If he could convince Bella to move home, would she be miserable? Worse, would she grow to resent him?

He finished off another piece of bacon. He needed to hit the road and get back to Bluegrass Crossing. Hopefully, things would be clearer for him. He could always return the ring he'd bought if Bella was adamant about never returning to Kentucky. But his heart ached at the thought.

CHAPTER THREE

Bella knelt on the floor by the coffee table opposite Jo-Jo, a rectangular, cedar box between them. Hand carved with Christmas images, with the relief stained a darker tone, the box called out reminders of Christmases past.

"You do the honors." Jo-Jo smiled at her and nodded toward the box. Bella lifted the lid, and the scent of cedar filled the room, bringing back memories of when she was a little girl. No one knew where the box had come from originally, but their mother stored Christmas memories inside, along with other treasures.

The scent of old paper met Bella's nose. She caught a whiff of pine and held back a sneeze as she set the box's lid on the coffee table.

A stack of folded programs, special Christmas cards, and some photos were held together with a rubber band.

Jo-Jo frowned at an ancient cookie that crumbled as soon as she touched it. "Eww. I think I was responsible for putting that in there. I wanted to save a bite of Christmas, or something like that."

Bella laughed. "I'm not sure I remember most of these things. But the box seemed a lot bigger when we were kids."

Jo-Jo reached inside for a pressed red rose. "It did. Do you remember Mom bringing it out every Christmas while we decorated the tree? We never knew where she hid it . . . and I looked for it."

"Nosy. I was always hanging ornaments on the tree. None of the rest of you ever cared about the aesthetics."

"You were such a perfectionist." Jo-Jo rolled her eyes. "You even placed the tinsel on one strand at a time."

Bella sucked in a breath. "My snowflake!" She pulled out a tiny ornament made of toothpicks painted white and covered in ancient silver glitter. "I can't believe Mom kept this."

"I remember I broke it." Jo-Jo looked guilty. "But I didn't mean to."

"I know. I sure pitched a fit, though, and then Mom glued it back together." Bella smiled and turned the ornament over to see the painted back. "I was in second grade. I painted the back white, even though Mrs. Parker told us not to. But to me it seemed silly to leave it plain. If someone saw the bare wood on the back, then it wouldn't look like a real snowflake."

Next Jo-Jo pulled out a flat, felt ornament of red and gold, with her name designed with sequins.

"I made this during a Christmas craft night at school. Maybe fourth or fifth grade." Jo-Jo's eyelashes fluttered, and she brushed away a tear at the corner of her eye. "I miss Mom."

Bella felt tears sting the back of her eyes. "Me, too. Maybe we shouldn't have opened the Christmas box."

"No, I think Mom would want us to remember the good times, and maybe if Amy decides to bring Timothy home, we can make an ornament with him."

"That will take a miracle. Keep praying." Bella pulled the dry, cracked rubber band from around another stack of Christmas cards. "I can't think of the last time I mailed out Christmas cards."

"You never have."

Bella laughed. "You're right. I found your birthday card on my desk before I left Chicago. I should have brought it."

"From which year?"

"Uh, I don't really remember."

Smiling sheepishly, Bella pulled out a simple paperback book, no thicker than a quarter of an inch, and covered with photos of cookies.

"Mom's Christmas cookie cookbook." Her throat caught.

"I thought it was lost." Jo-Jo stared at the stained book.

Bella's hand trembled a little as she opened it. Mom had a way of making Christmas special for all of them, and the tradition of cookie making was one of Bella's favorites. That is, back when she still loved the trappings of a traditional Christmas.

She held up the small book and smiled. "I can remember Mom trying to get this to lay flat on the counter when it was new. I would be the one to hold the book open while she read the recipes and sent Sophie and Amy to the pantry for the ingredients."

"At some point all I remember is her using recipe cards. I wonder why?" Jo-Jo said, quirking one eyebrow.

"I think somebody gave her a wood recipe box for Christmas one year, and she copied out her favorite cookie instructions on note cards. This cookbook is falling apart." A couple of pages slipped out on the coffee table. Bella tucked the brittle sheets back in."

"We should make some Christmas cookies while you're here, Bell." Jo-Jo sounded excited. "We can go shopping and pick up everything. The cookie cutters should still be in a drawer somewhere."

Bella couldn't remember the last time she'd baked anything, not even refrigerated cookie dough. "I'd love that. I don't really cook anymore, but doing this together would make the best Christmas . . ."

A tear escaped from her right eye, and she wiped it away.

"Don't cry, Bella." Jo-Jo leaned over and hugged her. "This is a time to be happy. Mom would want us to be happy."

"I know." She smiled through unshed tears, then looked down into the box again at a small bundle of envelopes tied up with string. She pulled the stack from the box and scanned the top envelope.

"Jo-Jo, *look*." Handwritten letters from her father to her mother while he served overseas.

The postmarks were faded—the handwriting as well. "These are postmarked twenty years ago. I would have been eight." Bella handed the stack to Jo-Jo.

"Mom kept these? Why?" Jo-Jo shook her head. "Things were horrible between them when we were little."

"Mom always said Dad was a better writer than a talker. I used to like his letters." *Until they stopped.*

"Should we read them? I feel like we'd be snooping."

Bella took the letters back and studied the first envelope. "This one was never opened."

Jo-Jo tapped the stack of envelopes in Bella's hand. "None of them were."

"I don't know about you, but I need to think about this for a while. I don't know if either of us should read these. What will it change? They're both gone. All has been said and done." Bella put the letters back inside the Christmas box.

When a knock sounded at the front door, Bella sprang to her feet. "I bet that's David!"

Sure enough, when she opened the door, there he stood, wearing the grin that caught her attention the moment they first met.

"Hi." He winked at her, causing her heart to hop a little.

She put her arms around his neck and hugged him. "I missed you."

"It's nice to be missed."

She stepped back to let him enter the great room. "Jo-Jo and I have been skipping down memory lane all morning. If you play your cards right, you just might get the chance to sample some of the Tucker girls' Christmas cookies today."

David glanced from Bella to Jo-Jo, then back again. "Baking? You? Your lavish spending keeps the Italian bakery on the corner in business." He cocked his head at her and grinned. "Are you the real Isabella Tucker or a clone?"

"Hey, we were pretty good back then, weren't we, Jo-Jo? But she's the real baker in the family." Bella shrugged and smirked. "I was pretty good at holding open the cookbook, and I paid attention to whatever Mom did. Anyway, baking is really just chemistry and careful measuring."

"So if your efforts are a success, dare I assume once we get back to Chicago you'll keep it up?"

"I can make no promise of that." She grinned as she picked up the brittle cookbook while Jo-Jo gathered up a few childhood ornaments so they could hang them on the tree.

Jo-Jo placed the lid back on the Christmas box. "I need to take care of a few things around here today. I promised Jed I'd help him with chores before he heads to his other job. Gil is out picking up supplies, and the other two hands are working on a fence. We can make cookies after that."

"We can help, too," Bella said.

Both David and Jo-Jo looked skeptical.

"What? I can shovel." Bella used to dread mucking out the stalls and the smell of manure, although she did like the idea of helping the horses find good homes. Truthfully, she'd realized she missed Jo-Jo more than she could say and wanted to spend as much time as she could with her sister. Not only that, she wanted to find out more about the Jed who'd captured her baby sister's heart. They'd known him when they were kids. But what about Jed, the adult?

Yes, Isabella Tucker could bake if she wanted to, along with clean out horse stalls. Not that she wanted either to be part of her regular routine.

David tromped with the others out to the stable, a foreign place to him. He'd always lived in town, away from the horse culture that ran deep in Kentucky's roots.

"We have several horses stabled here right now," Jed explained to them as he led the way to the barn. "If we divide up the stalls, it won't take long. Grab a pitchfork, pick up any manure or soiled straw you see, and throw it in your wheelbarrow."

Good thing he'd worn his hiking boots. The horses had already been turned out to pasture that morning, but they'd left evidence of their presence behind.

"You can take Lucinda's stall." Jed handed David a pitchfork. "She's got arthritic knees, but she's a great therapy horse."

After twenty minutes of combing through the straw for manure or wet bedding, David felt certain he'd cleaned Lucinda's stall thoroughly. Jed told them not to worry about tossing in fresh straw. He'd do that.

David leaned on his pitchfork and looked over at Isabella in the stall next to him. "This must have been a great place to grow up."

Bella tossed one more pitchfork full of soiled straw into her wheelbarrow and wrinkled her nose. "Except for this chore, it was a great place to grow up. Mom made every season and holiday special for us. Me? I always wanted to feel the rhythm of the city, so I left when it was time to go away to school."

He nodded. "I can understand that. Still, sometimes I miss living here. My parents are getting older and my little brother is almost through with college. Then it's off to a military commission for him and who knows where he'll end up. My oldest brother is an hour away; I'm pretty sure he and his wife and kids will be coming in on Christmas Eve."

David glanced to the other stalls where Jed and Jo-Jo worked, chatting away and sharing the laughter of a couple in love. He had moments like that with Bella, but sometimes she seemed to drift away from him and he didn't know where she'd gone. He used to chalk it up to her being preoccupied with work, or maybe jet lag after a long trip, but lately he suspected something else weighed on her mind.

Bella sneezed. "Can't say I missed this part *at all*." Her dark eyes sparkled at him. Her hair hung in pigtails that skimmed her shoulders, and wisps of hair escaped the bandana tied around her forehead.

"Jed was right," he said. "With four of us pitching in, we're almost done."

"Good." She sneezed again. "I want to show you the rest of the horse farm to see what you think."

"Think?"

She lowered her voice. "Jo-Jo and I have talked about what the four of us should do with the property. You know . . . fixing it up to put on the market."

David left his stall and stopped in the doorway where Bella worked. "What does she think?"

Bella leaned on her pitchfork and wiped the back of her hand on the damp bandana. "She wants to make plans but wait for the others before making a final decision. Stay or go, this place needs a lot of help. We need to work on promoting it, either way."

"It's a good piece of real estate. While part of me thinks selling the family farm would be a shame, considering how long it's been in your family, the business side of me thinks the four of you could make out well financially—with the right buyer. But first, I can tell you from just what I've seen so far, it'll need some fixing up."

"I thought that's what you'd say, and we already know the place needs work. We want whatever suggestions you can think of. I'm prepared to put up some of the funds for whatever work needs to be done. I know Jo-Jo and Amy won't be able to afford it, but that doesn't matter to me. A good sale would help all of us."

"If—and I know it's an if right now—the four of you do decide to go forward with a sale, I hope you'll let me broker it for you. I'll waive my commission, of course." David already knew some of what needed to be done to get the property ready to sell. It would take tens of thousands of dollars. For starters, the house needed a new roof.

Bella frowned. "I didn't think you were licensed to broker real estate in Kentucky."

"Not until a month or so ago. I . . . I've been thinking of branching out and opening an office in the Louisville or Lexington area."

"Louisville or Lexington? But what about Chicago?"

"I would still keep that office open and put George in charge. I'd have to go back and forth between here and there for a while."

"But eventually, you'd make a permanent move to Kentucky, wouldn't you?" It was more of a statement than a question.

"That's the general idea." David groaned inwardly. He'd never planned to discuss this with her in a stable, and it definitely wasn't the way he wanted to break the news to her.

"But . . ."

"But?"

"But what about us?"

David stepped into Bella's stall and took the pitchfork she clutched, leaning it against the wall. "We could still be us." He cupped her chin with his hand.

Bella frowned. "A long-distance relationship is hard to work out. I've been meaning to talk to you about that."

"We pretty much have a long-distance relationship now, don't we?" He studied her face. "You're gone for weeks and weeks every year. But at least we can Skype and talk almost every day while you're away. What would be different if I were living in Kentucky and you in Chicago?"

She frowned at him. "A lot would be different. Your family is here, probably some of your old friends. I'm not a Kentucky girl, David. Not anymore. This horse farm is part of my old life. I'm not a horse person or a homebody. If you move here to Kentucky, I'd feel as if I'd have to move, too. And I don't think that's going to happen."

CHAPTER FOUR

Suddenly, Bella needed air. She tried to scurry from the stall, but David put his hands on her shoulders to stop her. Looking back, she should have known something was up when he insisted on coming home to Kentucky for Christmas, talking about how he looked forward to her meeting his family.

David hadn't said anything since her insistence he'd want her to move to Kentucky. Her shoulders drooped. She didn't deserve someone like him and had been right about her gut feeling to end their relationship no matter how much it pained her. She almost wanted to redeem her frequent-flyer miles and jet away to somewhere warm that didn't remind her of Christmas and the past.

"Why are you running away from me, Bella?" His warm and gentle hands slid down to her elbows. "Where do you want to run?"

"I don't know," was all she could answer.

"That's fair enough." David stepped back and rubbed his forehead. "Look, I'm sorry. This isn't how I wanted to tell you about the Kentucky office. I wanted to do it the right way, at the right time."

"Don't worry about it. I appreciate you being honest about your plans." She tried, unsuccessfully, to stifle the sigh that followed her statement. "In my job, I know exactly what will happen, how, and when. If there's any issue that pops up, I deal with it. If it seems impossible to resolve, I do whatever I need to in order to turn it into a possibility. Then I got the news about Tuck, and now I'm here. Everything reminds me of the family I don't have anymore—"

She raised her hands and let them drop to her sides. She had no idea what to say next.

"You still have your sisters," he said.

"It's not how I wanted things to turn out."

"Bella, we have no guarantees other than what God promises. I would love to have the traditional Christmas like my family has always had, but that could change in an instant. Life can change in an instant. You know that all too well."

She sighed again and nodded. "You're right. This time of year, I really miss Mom though, and now Tuck—my dad—is gone. I miss what could have been."

"I'm sorry." He pulled Bella into his arms, and she laid her head against his chest.

She sniffed back tears, refusing to let them fall. "It's not your fault. I just think about how it was when we were kids and now that's all gone."

"I know your mom did the best she could, raising the four of you while your dad traveled the world on deployments."

Bella nodded. "Tuck loved us. I know he did. He just wasn't very good at showing it . . . or saying it. Until the end. Long ago, I realized the problems between my parents weren't my fault and weren't about me. Their lives were going in different directions. Mom didn't want to spend her life moving every two or three years. Tuck had this never-ending wanderlust and need for excitement that the Marines supplied. I don't want something like that to happen to us. I don't . . . I don't know if I could be happy in Kentucky."

"You know happiness is fleeting. Christ calls us to follow him, and sometimes that road is hard. Not that the road would be too hard—with me." He quirked a smile at her.

"No. I don't think it would. I know happiness is fleeting, but is it wrong to want to be happy?" She glanced up at him, his hazel eyes filled with concern and his expression tender.

"No, of course not," he said. "But my heart tells me this is where I belong. I've prayed about this for months. Things in Chicago are good—with work, with you."

Had she even sought God's will about whether he wanted her to break off her relationship with David? Nothing within her wanted to move back to Kentucky, but she had vacillated between her love for him and her career.

"You never told me you were thinking about leaving Chicago," she murmured against his shirt. "Getting your real-estate license in Kentucky. That's way beyond just *thinking* about making a big change." She stepped back and looked up at him again.

"Like I said, Bella, I'm sorry. I should have prepared you for this. This is a big decision."

"I'll say. Too big to think about right now." A gust of wind swept through the open stable doors. Bella rubbed her arms. Time to buck up and not let this newest development with David sideline her. "On another note, what do you propose we should do about the farm to get it ready to sell?"

She couldn't read David's expression. Did he look resigned or hopeful?

"I need to look up the comps to give you and your sisters an idea of what the current market looks like for properties similar to yours. Then you can make a decision on how much you should spend to whip this place into shape. You don't want to overinvest in improvements."

She nodded. That made perfect sense to her. "In the state it is now, we won't get top dollar. Not that Jed and the hands haven't done a good job taking care of the place."

"I'm glad you understand that in a buyers' market, they have a lot of properties to choose from, and many of them are likely more updated than what you have here."

Bella whirled around when she heard Jo-Jo's voice. "Did you talk to David about our plans to sell?"

"David thinks we should get some comps to see what other properties like ours are selling for."

Jo-Jo frowned. "I do want to start working on the place. There's a lot to do, even if we decide not to sell it. At the least, we need to make some updates and much-needed repairs."

Bella nodded and put her hands on her hips. "We agree on that much. Anyway, with Christmas coming, it's not a good time to start any major renovations, but after New Year's we should make repairs a priority."

After New Year's she'd be gone. She did thank God that Tuck had the foresight to hold onto the property that had been in his family for several generations. The sale would provide a financial legacy for all of them. There was her young nephew, Timothy, to think of, along with any future nieces and nephews that came along in the years ahead. Or her own children? She dashed that idea aside for the moment, her heart still a bit sore from the conversation she'd had with David. If they sold the horse farm, whatever they sold it for would go a long way to investing in the future generation.

When the four of them left the stable, an expensive black SUV—a Cadillac Escalade—was pulling up in the driveway. It stopped behind David's sedan.

An equally good-looking man, wearing a sport coat over a sky-blue Polo shirt and khakis, emerged from the vehicle. He wore costly shades and appeared to appraise the main house.

Bella smelled a rat. What was this guy selling?

Relax, don't be so quick to judge.

She glanced at her sister. They both approached the man where he stood at the driver's door.

"Good morning." Bella stopped at the front fender. "How can we help you?"

"Hey, Dan." Jo-Jo smiled at the guy, who shook hands with Jed, then David. "This is Dan Wentworth. He helps out with the horses sometimes. Dan, this is my sister, Bella, and her boyfriend, David. They're visiting from Chicago."

"Nice to meet you both." He paused for a moment. "I'm here on semi-official business today. I know it's Christmastime, but I wanted to talk to you now. I'd like to be up front. I'd like to buy this place and transform it."

"You're a real-estate agent then?" Bella asked. She could practically see dollar signs dancing in his eyes. But he had an easy smile, a bright-white one. He'd probably never had a cavity in his life.

"I'm a developer. I'd like to turn this place into a housing development, but nothing suburban or cookie-cutter. Five- to ten-acre lots, big enough for families to have a horse or two, maybe a farm. Something sustainable." Dan scanned the yard, the stable, and the pastures beyond. "You've got three-hundred acres of prime real estate here."

Bella nodded slowly. "Well, that's interesting. It would definitely be appealing for families. Whether or not to sell is a decision that's not up to just Jo-Jo and me. Our other two sisters are also on the deed, and they live out of town. We need to consult with them as well. If we decide to go in that direction, we'll let you know."

Wentworth nodded. "I understand completely. I'm always on the lookout for new projects and this one could be ideal for the right buyer. Please, speak with your sisters and let me know if this appeals to you. I can write up an offer. This is a really special place, and I'd like to leave it that way for others who might live on this land someday."

"We'll be in touch with our sisters before Christmas. We'll all discuss it as a family and let you know if that's what we'd like to do," Jo-Jo said.

"Great. I'll be in touch." Wentworth opened the door of his SUV and flashed his grin before he slid into the driver's seat.

They watched as he started the vehicle, then turned it around and left.

"Ladies, I suggest you go forward with the plan to sell this place, if that's what you'd really like to do," David said. "Dan Wentworth might be one of the first to eye this place as an investment, but I can assure you he won't be the last."

"His company is the one that turned the old mansion in town into the Bluegrass Bistro," Jo-Jo said.

Bella nodded. "If someone buys the farm as an investment, they'll tear down everything, so why should we put a lot of time and money into it if that might happen?"

Jo-Jo frowned. "I'm not sure I like the idea of someone coming in and tearing everything apart. 'They paved paradise' and all that. I don't want to sell what Tuck gave us just for top dollar. It would have to be to the right buyer. But I did like Dan's idea."

"I have to agree with you." Bella watched as the SUV turned on to the two-lane road and headed toward town.

⁓

While Bella and Jo-Jo went into town to pick up some groceries for Aunt Sarah, David stayed behind at the farmhouse. Delightful smells drifted from the kitchen, among them the aroma of warm cookies.

He tried to ignore his growling stomach as he pulled out his laptop to do a little research about Wentworth Properties. He had a hard time turning off his work switch; he loved making deals—deals that helped his clients invest wisely in property when they bought, and deals that helped his sellers reap the benefits of their investments.

Wentworth Properties was a viable, thriving company that did exactly what Dan Wentworth said it did. In the past several years, it had developed a number of properties in the greater Lexington area and beyond. Dan had a good résumé on his website, and it went far beyond renovating the antebellum mansion in Bluegrass Crossing.

Then David searched online for local properties up for sale that were similar to the Tucker place. What the ladies had in their favor was that the horse farm already had a working stable with some regular clientele. The right person could step right in and take over. He would recommend they focus on updating areas of the main house and taking care of projects that had been neglected, like putting on a new roof.

"Would you like a snack?" Aunt Sarah stood in the doorway between the living room and kitchen. She held a small plate of cookies in one hand and a glass of milk in the other.

"You bet. I presume those are fresh from the oven?"

"Sure are."

He sat his laptop on the sofa beside him and grinned.

Sarah placed the plate and glass in front of him on the coffee table. "Here ya go."

"Thank you very much. Oatmeal raisin is one of my favorites." He took a bite of a warm, buttery cookie.

"I'm glad you came home with Bella. That one has more of her dad in her than the lot of 'em. Lots of grit and an itch to travel."

"She does a lot of traveling, that's for sure." David dusted crumbs from his fingers.

Sarah shook her head. "Always seemed to be searchin' for something, too—maybe a place to call home."

"You've known her a long time?"

"Since she was a little thing, running around with her sisters all over this place." The older woman sighed. "Seems a shame they might sell it. But that's not my decision to make."

"It's worth a lot of money, especially if they make some repairs and upgrades." He paused. "Since you live here, where will you go if they do sell the farm?"

"I'll make do. I've been here for a long time, but I know this world isn't my home. God will provide somewhere else for me to stay."

David nodded. "That's good to know. What do you think they should do with the horse farm?"

"I really wish they'd keep it in the family. Marlena loved it here. Even after their daddy left, the farm was a happy place for them to grow up. Tuck could've left them all a lot worse off than some absent fathers."

David drained the glass of milk. "Bella never really talked much about her father, just that her parents separated when she was really young and that her dad was a career Marine. I guess they all lost touch with him over the years. I used to encourage her to reconnect with him, but I stopped because whenever I'd mention him, she'd change the subject."

Sarah sat down in the worn leather club chair. "Tuck was a changed man after he came to Christ, and especially so after he got sick. He wanted to make things right with his girls. Well, as right as he could. A man can't make up for a lifetime of missed birthdays, Christmases, and those special firsts. A pity he won't get to walk any of them down the aisle someday." She shook her head. "What about your family? Are y'all close?"

"Yes, we are. I'm the middle of three boys. We keep in touch, but it's been a few years since I made it home for Christmas. I need to spend some time with my folks over in Louisville while I'm here."

"Well, that's a gift." She was silent for a moment as if she didn't know whether to say any more, then she smiled at him. "Whatever happens, David, don't give up on Bella. Because mark my words, I truly believe this is the Christmas that will change everything for every one of the Tucker girls."

CHAPTER FIVE

"Put your laptop away, Bella, and let's get started with the baking." Jo-Jo's voice held a chiding yet warm tone. "Sarah will be gone all day, so now's our chance to bake Christmas cookies. I'm sure the cookie cutters are still in the bottom drawer."

Reluctantly, Bella closed down the file on her desktop. She'd been making notes about upgrades and changes to the kitchen, where her mother and Sarah had made thousands of meals over the years. The appliances could use updating. They could save money by refacing the cabinets and replacing the hardware. She'd also written down: *subway tile backsplash (?)*. At one point, the kitchen had received a facelift, but she wasn't sure what might appeal to a potential buyer.

She opened their mom's treasured Christmas cookie book that lay on the black-marble island. They should probably look for her recipe box, but this was more fun. The book that had been propped open over the years now fell open to Mom's special sugar-cookie recipe. Small hands no longer needed to hold the pages flat.

"I wish we knew if there was any chance Amy and Sophie would change their minds about coming home. We could all make cookies together. Maybe we should wait and see if they do, Jo-Jo. You said yourself you've been praying, and you got me here. I bet Timothy would love to use the cookie cutters like we used to."

Bella knew she was stalling to get out of making cookies. But the excuse sounded feeble even to her.

Jo-Jo turned around and shook her finger at her. "No way. You're not getting out of this, even if you want to. This was Mom's tradition. Plus, Jed and David will eat their share, along with the hands. We'll need a steady supply of Christmas cookies." Jo-Jo tapped the counter with her fingertips. "We can store these, and they'll keep well. And if we run out, we can always make more."

"Yes, ma'am." Bella saluted as she slid off the stool and grabbed the measuring cups from the drawer. "Tell me what to scoop and how much."

As she and Jo-Jo measured and mixed, then rolled out the dough and cut cookies into the shapes of Christmas stars and snowmen, the years melted away. She looked at the doorway into the great room almost expecting Mom to walk around the corner to exclaim over the freshly baked goodness they pulled from the oven.

Bella smiled, knowing that if heaven had windows, Mom was watching two of her daughters laugh and bake cookies in the kitchen of their childhood.

I miss you, Mom.

Aloud, she said, "You're so good at this, Jo-Jo."

Jo-Jo grinned. "I feel the most like myself when I'm in the kitchen. Cooking for people always makes me happy."

"You were always the most eager to learn how to cook and bake. All I could see was the mess we'd make and the heaps of dirty dishes. You've definitely learned how to make all kinds of deliciousness. That lasagna you made last night? I ate some cold leftovers for breakfast this morning."

"That means a lot, coming from you." Jo-Jo smiled widely and wiped her hands off on a dish towel, then slid Bella a teasing sideways glance. "You looking forward to your date night with David?"

"I am. We're doing some Christmas shopping in town this afternoon, then having dinner at Belle Noir. Who knows what else we'll find to do? If Developer Dan is right, I should research what amenities are available in town that would appeal to buyers."

Jo-Jo picked up a still-warm cookie and laughed. "And shopping is *such* good research."

"Someone has to do it." It dawned on Bella she had no idea what kind of gift to buy for Jo-Jo. "So, what do you want for Christmas?"

"I already have everything I want, or need, this Christmas." She took a bite of cookie, giving a happy sigh.

"I'll get you a candle. Or some new socks." Bella grabbed a cookie of her own and bit the leg off a gingerbread man. Not half-bad for dough she'd mixed herself.

"Socks?"

"Everyone wears socks. Do you want wool or cashmere?"

Jo-Jo rolled her eyes much as she had when they were younger. Bella burst out laughing, something she hadn't done in ages.

David felt like a pack mule laden with supplies as he toted half a dozen shopping bags. But he dutifully followed Bella down Main Street toward Belle Noir. He'd heard of Bluegrass Crossing before meeting Bella, but he had never visited until now. He found its charm growing on him—that and the idea of building a life with Bella in Kentucky. A small, square box nestled inside his jacket pocket. He knew it was a risk, especially given their discussion in the stable the other day. But he needed to put his heart and intentions on the line.

Tonight's dinner would be a romantic Christmas surprise for Bella if all went as planned. Tomorrow, they would head to his parents' house where they'd spend the next two days helping Dad get his light display up and running.

Bella paused in front of him on the street. She tucked a receipt into her wallet and turned toward him. "Oh, here. Let me take a few of those. I'm sorry. I didn't bring you along just to carry my things." She grinned at him.

"I don't mind." He handed her two of the bags, one filled with an assortment of toys meant to appeal to a young boy, the other containing a cashmere sweater (on clearance) in a pretty shade of blue for Jo-Jo.

Something in her face softened. Right there on the street, she gave him a quick peck on the cheek. "Thank you. For being you. I can't imagine anyone else with me here right now, and I wouldn't want to." She paused, as if she were gathering her thoughts to say more.

"I'm glad." He used his free hand to brush wayward strands of dark hair away from her face. "Because there's nowhere else I'd rather be."

An icy gust of wind swept down the street. A cold front was blowing in, reminding them that winter had descended upon Kentucky.

Bella shivered. "We should get these to the car and head into the restaurant."

"Sounds like a great idea." Unbeknownst to Bella, he'd arranged for a special dessert for the two of them to share—a molten-chocolate cake. He'd also ordered a dozen red roses that would be waiting for her at their table.

They headed for the downtown parking lot where he'd parked the car around the corner from Main Street. David popped the trunk, then loaded their shopping bags inside. Hand in hand, they walked toward Belle Noir.

"You know, this is a lot like our dates in Chicago," Bella observed. "Dinner out on the town. It's a bit quieter though. Bluegrass Crossing has a lot more to offer than I remember."

"When was the last time you lived here?" David squeezed her gloved hand.

"After I graduated from high school. I came home during summer breaks the first two years of college, but then my junior and senior years I had internships."

They rounded the street corner and as they did so, a fresh gust of wind made them scurry to the restaurant. "Well, it has some nice-looking storefronts." David held the door open for her. "Another plug for you to market the farm. Minutes from downtown, with quaint and charming shops and restaurants."

As their server led them to their table, he didn't miss the surprise on Bella's face when she saw the roses on their table. He helped her with her coat.

"Roses." She leaned to sniff the blooms. "Beautiful." She glanced at the other tables. "Oh. These are from you? Thank you, David. They smell so sweet, and they're gorgeous."

He smiled. "I'm glad you like them." They settled onto their chairs and ordered their drinks and appetizers from the waiter. His folded, wool topcoat on the chair beside him still held his biggest surprise of all. That would come after the server brought their dessert.

During the meal, he kept their conversation light and full of laughter while he dug into his steak, and she cleared her plate of the grilled trout with lemon butter sauce and capers. They shared more stories of their respective childhood escapades, him growing up in an all-brothers household, her growing up with sisters only. He laid his chin on his hand and smiled at her, the light from the candles reflected in her expressive eyes.

After finishing her last bite of fish, Bella laid down her fork. "What?"

"You look especially beautiful tonight."

"Thank you. And thank you for making tonight special for me. I've enjoyed spending time with Jo-Jo, but I wanted some time alone with you while we're here. It's like I'm seeing Bluegrass Crossing for the first time right along with you."

The server cleared away their dinner plates and returned with a tray that held the small, molten-chocolate cake and two steaming cups of coffee.

"Another surprise." Bella reached for one of the two spoons on the plate, garnished with a drizzle of chocolate sauce and adorned with a raspberry. She took a nibble of the cake and the runny chocolate goodness that escaped from the center of the cake. She closed her eyes. "Amazing."

As they both ate from the same plate, David tried to gauge when to produce the ring. If he were closing the deal on a commercial property, he'd know exactly when to time it. But judging the right moment to ask the woman he loved the most important question he'd ever ask? He had no clue.

"You're quiet." She wiped her mouth with the snowy-white napkin from her lap.

He reached for her hand. "Bella."

"Yes?"

Without stumbling to the carpet like he did when he had a particularly disturbing dream of this proposal the other night, David made it onto one knee in the restaurant. The oxygen left the room, or maybe his lungs were not cooperating. Without looking around, he knew the other diners were focusing on Bella and him.

"Isabella Tucker, I love you. I can't imagine my life without you, wherever that might be, and I know I want to spend the rest of my life with you. Will you spend the rest of your life with me? Will you marry me?"

The words came out smoother than he hoped, although he fumbled a bit with the black-velvet box when he removed it from his coat pocket. He opened it to reveal the diamond, the one he'd caught her looking at wistfully in a Chicago jewelry store window last summer.

Bella sat unmoving, her mouth open.

Chapter Six

It was *the* ring, the brilliant-cut solitaire she'd seen at Waverly & Sons back in Chicago. Bella sucked in a breath and choked, gasping for air. She grabbed her goblet of water and sipped.

David had proposed. He'd really proposed. After a beautiful dinner, and the roses and the utterly decadent dessert. He'd orchestrated everything this evening. She should have guessed, should have known something was up.

But David needed an answer. He looked at her, expectantly. "Are you okay, Babe?"

She nodded and coughed. Sputtered.

Will you marry me?

She couldn't imagine her life without him either. She didn't want to. But since coming home to Bluegrass Crossing, she'd thought a lot about what life without him would be like. If he came back to Kentucky and she stayed in Chicago . . . the idea made her hurt inside.

Would their love be enough? So far their long-distance relationship in Chicago had survived in spite of her misgivings. They'd found friendship and love in her big city. But would it survive if they moved to Kentucky?

"I . . . I need to think about it. I do love you, David."

He pulled the ring from the box. "Please, wear this while you think about it. I know tonight was a surprise—"

"Yes, and what a lovely surprise it was."

"I know you're not a fan of surprises."

"This was definitely worth being surprised for." Bella let him slip the solitaire on the third finger of her left hand. The diamond winked at her in the candlelight. She turned to face him where he still knelt and kissed him.

She could give presentations before hundreds in auditoriums or crowded boardrooms filled with corporate suits, but the applause now coming from fellow dinner patrons made her face warm as if she'd just finished a jog.

"Are you ready to go?" he asked. She nodded.

David paid the check and they left. During the whole drive home, she played with the solitaire on her usually bare ring finger. Some of Bella's friends from her college days had married, convinced they were in love, only to divorce a few years later. Even college sweethearts. She'd skittered away from love and romance herself until David. Until now. She glanced at him, and he took his eyes off the road a brief moment to look at her.

"When I said, think about it," he said, "I didn't mean you have to give me an answer by tomorrow. Or Christmas. Or even New Year's."

"I know." Bella didn't want to keep him waiting—not for long.

"Okay. I wanted to make sure you knew that. Take your time. I'll be here. I'm not going anywhere. But I would consider it an honor if you would say yes. No pressure though."

"Thanks for giving me time to process this." She decided she would call one of her colleagues to see if he'd heard anything more about the company restructuring the Chicago office.

Turning off the two-lane road, David pulled into the long, familiar driveway to the horse farm. Lights still glowed in the house. It wasn't that late really, so everyone must still be up. When Jo-Jo saw the ring, she'd freak out and want to know all the details about their wedding plans.

Plans? She didn't have any at the moment, but the ring on her finger told her she needed to make some decisions. Typically, she knew exactly what she wanted and how to reach her goals. Lately, a few curveballs had struck home in every aspect of her life and career. Then tonight, David had proposed unexpectedly. She should have known it would happen someday. He'd shown her how committed he was to making their relationship work. But how committed was she?

David smiled at her as they held hands, walking up the stone porch steps. Then she stopped and looked back, remembering.

"The shopping bags. We left them in the trunk."

"I'll get them. You go on inside." He descended the steps as she opened the front door.

"Hey, we're home." Christmas music—a carol played on a mandolin—met Bella's ears as she entered the toasty great room. "It's freezing out there."

Jo-Jo looked up from where she sat on the worn leather sofa, looking at something on Bella's iPad that she'd loaned to her. Her little sister couldn't afford her own, so Bella had decided it would make a great Christmas present for her along with the sweater. Louisville should have an Apple store.

"Did you have a good time?" Jo-Jo asked.

"The best."

"Next time, if you go for breakfast or lunch, you should try the Bluegrass Bistro. It's really good. Jed and I have been twice." Jo-Jo held up the iPad and turned it to face Bella. "I've been looking at roofing materials tonight—isn't that exciting? Here, take a peek."

When she reached for it, Jo-Jo grabbed Bella's hand and gasped. *"What's that on your finger?"*

"David proposed tonight at dinner."

Jo-Jo shrieked and tossed the iPad on the sofa beside her before enveloping Bella in a hug.

"Bell! I'm so happy for both of you."

"Well, I . . . I haven't exactly said yes yet."

"What's wrong with you?" Jo-Jo stepped back and shook her head, her dark hair bouncing past her shoulders. "You've been dating for years, and now you're hem-hawing around?"

"He had roses ready at our table before we arrived and arranged for a special dessert. It was all such a big . . . surprise." Bella fumbled for the words. *"Where's Jed?"*

"At home, working on plans for the horse auction. Stop trying to change the subject." Jo-Jo's eyes widened as David carried the shopping bags into the house. "Oh my. You did do some shopping."

Bella nodded, relieved David had interrupted their conversation. "The shops downtown had some good sales. I wanted to make sure there's something under the tree, especially gifts for Timothy, just in case by some miracle Amy and Sophie decide to come. We can always send them by UPS if they don't. I think we guessed well, choosing things a seven-year-old might like. Don't you think so, David?" She knew she was talking too fast.

David glanced between her and Jo-Jo, a questioning look on his face. He finally nodded. "I think we did. It's been a long time since I was seven. Uh . . . I'll let you two talk and take the bags to your room."

"Thanks." Bella loved this man's thoughtfulness.

Jo-Jo hopped back around the coffee table to the leather sofa. "Don't tell me you've already decided no!"

Bella's heart quaked inside her. He'd proposed. It had really happened. And all her "hem-hawing," as Jo-Jo put it, now put her in a bad spot. What if she told him no after all she'd put him through? She would end up hurting the man she loved. But did she love him enough to marry him?

"No, it's not that." Bella darted a look down the hallway, then lowered her voice to a whisper. "I'm scared, Jo-Jo. I don't want to end up like Mom and Dad. David doesn't deserve that. Out of all of us, I think I'm the most like Tuck."

Jo-Jo hugged her again. "Stop it. You need to stop those thoughts right now."

"I don't know how."

"I do," Jo-Jo said. "You aren't our father. Take the letters Tuck wrote to Mom when you leave for Louisville tomorrow and read them. Find out what really happened to their marriage. While you're gone, I'll be praying for you to make the right decision."

An icy wind bit into David as he and his father propped the ladder on the side of the house. Inside, snug as bugs in the proverbial rug, Bella and his mother were having coffee while looking at a myriad of family photos. David didn't know whether he should go inside to run interference or let his history unfold for Bella picture by picture.

"Okie-dokie." His father eyed the roof. "I wanted to start with the roof first. But this wind makes getting up there, and probably staying up there, a mite tricky. Maybe this year I'll just outline the roof instead of zigzagging strands of lights on top."

David almost sagged against the ladder in relief. He wasn't super keen on heights anyway and didn't mind this change of plans one bit. "Maybe tomorrow the wind will die down, and I can go up there for you." He hoped.

Dad nodded, scratching the stubble on his chin. "Then again, when it snows, the lights would be covered up anyway. We'll just decorate the rosebushes with the extra lights."

"Did you ask Mom about covering her roses with lights?" His mother fussed over those bushes like children.

"Aw, it won't matter. Poor things'll be too cold to notice anyway."

David tried to ignore his numb fingers while helping Dad with the same decorating ritual he and his brothers had groaned about when they were kids. After all, how many more Christmas seasons would he have the chance to do this with his father? With the passing of Bella's dad, even though they were estranged, it was a reminder of David's own borrowed time with his parents.

They took turns scaling the ladder while one of them held the strand of lights on the ground.

"Alrighty." Dad climbed down from the ladder, the last string of lights now edging the roof. "Next, we'll trim the windows and around the doors."

For the next several hours, until the sun slid behind the barren maples to the west, David worked beside his dad, attaching strands of lights to the house. Tomorrow would be devoted to setting up the standing displays of reindeer, a sleigh, and candy canes.

Lights glowed in the living room windows. How had the afternoon gone for Bella and his mother? He hoped Bella didn't regret coming with him.

CHAPTER SEVEN

Mrs. Moore didn't like her. The woman smiled and welcomed Bella into her home, but Bella's gut told her the older woman was putting a good face on things for the sake of her son.

They sat around the dining room table, now cleared of the supper dishes. Bella had offered to help load the dishwasher, but David's mother declined. Instead, water ran, dishes clanked, and the coffeepot gurgled as it brewed another pot of coffee.

After David's mother served them fresh coffee and cheesecake, David and his father dominated the conversation, discussing the Kentucky winter so far, whether the kids would get snow for Christmas, along with the real-estate market in the area. Silently, Bella ate her slice of cheesecake and wondered how she could break through the polite, but cool, exterior of David's mother.

"So, how did you like all those family photos? Did Mom put you to sleep after a while?" David took a sip of coffee.

"No, she didn't put me to sleep at all. I loved seeing the pictures. You all look like you had a lot of fun growing up."

"We did. With all the stitches, broken bones, and bumps that come with a bunch of boys," David joked.

"That's true enough." His father polished off his cheesecake. "I can't remember how many trips we made to the emergency room."

"I can." Mrs. Moore dabbed her mouth with a napkin. "Nineteen stitches, one broken nose, two broken wrists, a few sprained ankles, and one concussion. Oh, and one broken leg."

Bella laughed out loud. "Wow. Were y'all accident prone or just ornery?"

"Both." David slid his arm around her. "What's with that *y'all* I just heard?"

"I'm off the clock and on vacation." She smiled up at him. "It was a momentary lapse."

"You can take the girl out of Kentucky, but you can't take Kentucky out of the girl." David's Dad raised his coffee cup to Bella in a salute.

Bella shrugged. "Maybe so."

"Tell us about your family, Bella," Mrs. Moore said. "Davie said you own a horse farm."

"We do. My father passed away not too long ago, and my sisters and I inherited it. It's a working farm for retired racehorses. Some are eventually sold as riding horses, and some are kept for therapy purposes or teaching children to ride here. We're still deciding whether to sell the property since none of us live in the area."

"That's sad," David's mother said. "It's a shame you can't keep it in the family."

"At least one of us would need to make a big life change to move back here. Then there's the cost of upkeep on the horses and maintenance on the house, stable, fencing, bunkhouse, and outbuildings." Surely the woman could understand that reasoning. Plus, Bella resented the need to justify her family's decision to a virtual stranger.

"Well, we do what we can for family," Mrs. Moore said, smiling tightly. "Your father left that farm to you. What do you think he would say of your decision?"

"Now, Barbara, it's really none of our business," David's father interjected.

"Mom . . ." David shook his head in warning.

David's mother waved their words away. Bella felt her stomach tighten as she put on her corporate face, anger building inside her, but she held tight control over her emotions.

Mrs. Moore turned to her son. "I think if the tables were turned, I'd appreciate someone else giving you something to consider. Isabella, you're wearing David's engagement ring. Since you have both committed to spending the rest of your lives together, surely I can tell you what I think?"

"If we had a close relationship, of course. But you don't really know me, do you, or where I've come from or my family dynamics? I barely knew my father, and my mother passed away when I was nineteen and away at college. I have no ties to that property. In fact, none of us have lived there in years. As your husband pointed out, it really is none of your business."

"Well, I never! Catelynn would never speak to me in such a manner."

"Who's Catelynn?" Bella asked, trying to remain calm.

"She and David were engaged. In fact, she stopped by the other day after David arrived."

Something snapped inside her. Bella stood, her face hot with anger and her nerves frayed. If she had driven herself, she'd put David's ring on the table in front of the nosy woman, walk out, and drive back to Bluegrass Crossing alone.

Christmas music played softly in the background. She hadn't noticed the music before. "Silent Night." Right. She could use a silent night. How dare the woman!

Bella touched the ring David had given her. It shouldn't matter to her that David had been engaged before. In a matter of a few days, since being here in Kentucky, she found that her inclination to step back from their relationship had turned into an inclination to move forward. This revelation, though, brought her to a standstill.

David stood, his expression pleading for her understanding. "Bella, that was almost six years ago."

Bella nodded curtly. "It doesn't really matter to me whether you were engaged before." The words were out before she really thought about them. Did it matter?

"Let's go for a walk," David said, taking her hand.

She tugged her hand away. "It's freezing out."

"I'll take you somewhere warm, where we can talk."

David's mother stood and looked at her son. "Now, honey, I wasn't trying to cause any trouble. You just need to think things through."

"I have, Mom."

Bella maintained control, but she could tell David was almost as angry as she was. "I love Isabella Tucker and I know she loves me." He took

Bella's hand and squeezed it. "She's been through a lot, and we've been through a lot together. Love is work, but both of us are hard workers."

Without another word, she and David hurried through the kitchen and out the back door, leaving their coats behind. They made the short trek to his father's workshop. Within a few minutes, David had the portable heater up and running.

"There. Better?" He settled onto a stool at his father's workbench and patted the stool next to him.

"Better, thank you." She lifted her hands. "You don't have to explain about Catelynn to me. Like I said, it's all right."

"I want to, okay?"

She hesitated before nodding yes.

"Catelynn and I grew up together and graduated in the same high school class and headed off to the same college. After we graduated from college, it was sort of expected we'd end up together. I proposed; she said yes. We made wedding plans. Then right before she mailed out the invitations, she called everything off."

"Ouch. That must have hurt." Her anger lowered to a simmer.

"It did, very much so. But then I went to Chicago and eventually met you. Catelynn and I had been split for three years before you stepped into my life. You were like a breath of fresh air in my world."

Bella focused on the workbench beside her, staring at a group of Christmas bulbs scattered on the top. She lined them up, one by one, sorted by color.

He lifted her chin and turned her face to look at him. "You've been safe for me, Bella, with our schedules and your traveling. I realize that. There's been nobody else for me, and I know there's been nobody else for you since we've been together, even with all the hours we put in at work." He reached for her hand. "I don't want to just feel safe anymore. I'm grateful Catelynn called off the wedding. That's why I spread my wings, got out of my comfort zone, and moved to Chicago. I would have never met you otherwise. For that, I'm grateful to her."

Bella squeezed his hand. "Thank you for telling me. I'm not upset or angry you never told me until now. I'm glad you did, but your mother—"

"I know, I know. She crossed the line. I'll talk to her."

Bella searched his eyes and finally nodded. She cupped his face in her hand, and he kissed her palm. ·

Two forces of nature had collided tonight. Bella worked with COOs and other upper-level management for companies around the world. And she proved tonight she could hold her own against one persnickety mother, namely his.

His mother had never acted this way before. Then again, she'd known Catelynn throughout their school years so there was never that getting-to-know-you period.

Once they returned to the house, they bypassed David's parents, who had retreated to the family room to watch TV. David and Bella mounted the stairs and said good night outside his kid brother's bedroom door.

"Everything will be fine," David said, rubbing her arms. "Tomorrow's a big day for Mom. She always makes a ton of food. Wait till you see how the whole neighborhood shows up to celebrate Dad's light display. It's a tradition in this area to officially kick off the Christmas season."

She looked up at him, her brow furrowed in the dim hallway light. "What about your mother? Does she even want me here now?"

"Of course, she does. Mom's probably stressed out by all the changes in my life, compounded by preparing all the food for tomorrow. She'll want your help cooking or at least being her gofer. Just keep your cool. I've never seen her act this way before."

Bella stuck out her chin. "I'm game. I can always run to the store if things get tense. But I'm not sure how I can convince her I'm not evil."

He kissed her cheek. "She's being protective of her little boy, I guess. Things will be better in the morning."

"We can only hope." She laid her head on his shoulder for a moment. "Good night, *Davie*. I'll see you in the morning."

"Sweet dreams, Beautiful."

After Bella closed her door, David headed down the hall toward his own room, then changed his mind and descended the stairs, the banister adorned with pine garland and white lights—Mom's special touch. His parents didn't bother with a tree anymore since he and his brothers had left home. Instead, Dad put all his efforts into the light display, and Mom decorated the inside of the house to make it festive for all the guests who would stop by between now and Christmas.

When he got back downstairs, his mother was washing out the coffeepot and setting it up for the morning. She looked up when he entered the kitchen.

"You heading to bed soon?" she asked.

"Soon." He paused. "About tonight."

Her shoulders drooped. "I'm sorry. I know I was out of line, but I love you, Son. I don't care how old you get; I still don't want to see you hurt. Who's to say Isabella won't run out on you like Catelynn did?"

"There are no guarantees in life, Mom, but I don't believe she will." He crossed his arms and leaned back against the counter. "If you're so concerned about how Catelynn treated me when she called off our wedding, why are you hinting around about her now, filling her in on what I'm doing?"

She said nothing for a moment but instead pulled the dishwasher detergent from under the sink and poured some into the dispenser. "Catelynn has changed. She's matured and grown up. She's solid and dependable. I know she still loves you and regrets how she treated you."

"I'm happy for her. I pray she meets someone special someday." He settled onto the stool at the breakfast bar. "But that someone isn't me."

His mother shook her head. "Be careful with Isabella. I'm sorry she has had a hard time of it, especially losing both of her parents. You mentioned her job's in jeopardy, too, but will she even want to move back to Kentucky?"

"Honestly? I don't know, but it's going to be okay. Regardless of what happens with her job, regardless of what happens between us, I'll be fine."

She cast him a doubtful look before turning on the dishwasher.

CHAPTER EIGHT

Bella bunked in David's younger brother's room, the walls still covered with school-spirit banners and trophies from high school and college. Sports memorabilia, including a signed baseball, rested on the top of a bookshelf.

She felt tired and cranky. She didn't want to confront David's mother about her rudeness, because Barbara Moore might be right. What if Bella wasn't good enough her son? Not that she was inferior, but David deserved someone ready to settle down and start a family. Bella loved her career and the travel. Could she be satisfied in a traditional marriage role, being home for good instead of on the road most of the time? No wonder Mrs. Moore had misgivings about her.

With a sigh, Bella sank onto the twin bed. She should have stayed at the farm and let David come here alone to spend time with his parents. The ill-fitting diamond slid sideways on her finger. But he had been thoughtful enough to notice her enthusiasm when she saw it in the jeweler's window.

Her phone lay on the nightstand where she'd left it after dropping her overnight bag on the bed. She rolled onto her side and picked up her phone. A text from Jo-Jo, asking how things were going with the parents. Another text from a colleague, Jeremy, the director of program development at work.

Call me. It doesn't matter how late. Your position is being phased out, but I caught wind of something else I think you'll be ideal for.

Something else? But that first part of the text—her position being phased out? She stared at the felt pennant pinned to the ceiling above the bed. The news didn't surprise her, but it still hit her hard. She'd held out hope the restructure wouldn't affect her job. But there it was, displayed on her phone.

Maybe she should think about moving to the farm for a while after New Year's, but how would she, or even could she, survive there? She needed to think rationally. It wasn't as if Kentucky was a third-world country. But she was used to keeping her suitcase ready and collecting new stamps on her passport. A new hotel, another culture to visit. God had made a big world, and she loved getting to see much of it.

She called Jeremy's number. He answered on the second ring.

"Good, I'm glad you took my message seriously and called right away."

"Of course. Tell me what you've heard."

"The London group can't stop talking about the great job you did a few weeks ago. Their head of program development resigned. Family issues. We talked about the restructuring here and your current position. Send me an updated résumé so I can refresh their memory about you, and the job's as good as yours."

Bella sat up. "With the London group? As in me working in London full time?"

"Well, you wouldn't live in Paris."

She laughed at that. "I suppose not. Salary package?"

"Whatever you're making now, plus ten percent more. Stock options, vehicle allowance, *housing stipend*. And you wouldn't have to travel as much."

"London is expensive." She hesitated. "I'll need to consider it carefully."

"I thought that's what you'd say. Don't consider it carefully for too long though, Tucker. New Year's is coming, and you'll be out of a job unless you apply for the transfer."

"Thanks for letting me know, Jeremy. It's an amazing opportunity."

"You're welcome. Happy holidays. See you after the first of the year."

After they ended their call, Bella stared at her cell. London—half a world away. During her most recent trip there, she'd reveled in the British countryside, the Brits' manner of speaking, and especially the dry humor of her colleagues abroad. But move there? Not as much travel.

That might be a negative.

Then she studied the engagement ring on her finger. What should she do?

The idea of moving an ocean away from her family tugged at her heart. With Jo-Jo and Jed likely heading to the altar, that would mean babies in the future. She loved talking to her nephew Timothy via Skype, and she could still do that, but she'd missed so much of his childhood already. Yet Amy and Tim lived in New Orleans, even farther away from Chicago than Bluegrass Crossing.

Then there was David—his sweet warmth and strength. She couldn't hug him, or spend quality time with him on an Internet connection. How often would they even see each other? But what else could she do if she walked away from this job of a lifetime?

What else could Tuck have done if he'd separated from the Marines that he loved so much and stayed home to raise his family? Would he have been happy or miserable? She laid back and stared at the ceiling again. The memory of an old argument between her parents returned unbidden.

"I'm tired of this, Tuck," her mother had shouted. "I can't do it anymore. If you leave this time, that's it for us. I want a husband I see more than once a year."

"There's another choice, and you know it," he yelled back. "You and the girls can follow me to Germany."

"I told you I won't drag our daughters halfway around the world while you play soldier."

"Then stay here without me." His angry voice had scared Bella. "I'm a Marine and always will be. When you figure out what's more important to you—this horse farm or me—let me know."

After Bella heard her dad slam out the front door, Jo-Jo crawled into her bed, and they cried themselves to sleep. The next morning, her father had said good-bye, and she never saw him again.

Now she wished she had brought the letters Jo-Jo had pushed into her hands before she and David headed to Louisville. But she'd set them on the hallway table in the entryway and walked out without them. Part of her didn't want to know what Tuck had written. Had her dad apologized? Begged her mother to move to Germany?

"Dear Lord," Bella whispered, "help me know what to do. From the time I was a kid, I knew I wanted to travel. What I do helps make people's jobs easier. I've always loved solving business problems. How can I do that in Kentucky? It wouldn't be the same. If I say no to the London offer, I'll need to find another job. And please, help me to decide whether I should say yes or no to David."

The entire block showed up for the annual "Lights-On Celebration" given by the Moores. David felt almost the same sense of anticipation he had when he was a little boy, waiting for his father's yearly light display. They expected at least fifty neighbors from this block and beyond to stop by and see the lights.

This year there was an addition of tens of thousands of LED lights programmed to play in conjunction to the rhythm of the music. Tonight, visitors would enjoy trays of appetizers, snacks, and cookies thanks to Bella and his mother. When Mom developed a migraine midafternoon, Bella took over the rest of the food preparation.

"I can't promise everything I fixed is as good as your mother's," Bella said as she stood by David's side.

He stamped his feet in the cold and hugged her with one arm. "I'm sure it's all tasty."

"Ha. But thank you. I couldn't bear to see your celebration be anything less than spectacular. I know how it is when a plan goes sideways and there seems to be nothing you can do." Bella's breath made cloudy puffs in the frigid air.

When she slipped her arms around his waist, leaning against him, he kissed the top of her head.

"You're amazing, you know that? I know Mom hasn't been easy to deal with."

"She loves you and doesn't want to see you hurt again. I get that. I'd probably be the same way." Bella smiled at him. He flashed her a wry grin. "I don't think this will be the last time you two don't see eye-to-eye. You're sort of like her."

"Thank you . . . I think?" She hugged him tighter.

He meant every word. After the disaster last evening, the atmosphere between his mother and Bella had warmed slightly at breakfast, although they really didn't say much to each other at the table. He hoped the rest of the morning had gone smoother.

How best to introduce inquisitive neighbors to Bella? He did it simply as, "This is Isabella." The rest sorted itself out and no one asked any questions if they noticed her ring.

He wanted her to be his bride, wholeheartedly. He reaffirmed within himself that he wouldn't ask her again, but would let her give him her answer, whether that be yes or no, in due time. After his morning prayer times, he felt convinced God would have him remind Bella of his love for her, and God's as well. They were both unconditional. Well, he hoped his was unconditional. He did his best.

Would he still love Isabella Tucker if she declined his proposal? Tonight he gazed down into her sparkling eyes and knew he would. Her refusal would wound him deeply as would her decision not to follow him to Kentucky. But with God's help, he would survive. He hugged her tighter.

They stood off to the side of the yard where they could see the faces of the crowd, lit by the street light on the corner. The rest of the yard remained dark.

"All right, folks, it's time," David's father called out above the chatter of the group gathered by the front curb. "The display is bigger and better than ever. Let's count down from three. Three—two—one!"

Dad flipped the switch, and the yard came to life with colorful lights—the roof, windows, and doors; the trees and bushes clustered in the front yard; Santa and reindeer on the lawn; and lighted archways lining the front walk. They'd put in a good eight hours yesterday and nearly ten today.

Bella gasped. "Oh, it's beautiful. I had no idea it would look like this. You did a great job."

His dad trotted indoors and soon the first strains of the Trans-Siberian Orchestra blared from a small speaker. When the lights began to flash in time to the music, the neighbors applauded.

David had to applaud, too. Dad had pulled it off again. "We did it. It actually worked." He smiled down at her.

Bella nodded. "I never doubted it would." She glanced toward the front door. "There's your mom. I'll help her with the snack trays." With that, she headed into the house.

During Bella's days in Kentucky, her laugh had come more easily, her smile more frequently. David prayed she'd see this place was doing her plenty of good, that slowing down didn't mean stopping her life, and that her wardrobe needed a closet rather than a suitcase.

He'd loved his days in Chicago. The city had a pulse and an appeal unique to it. But home? There was no other place like it. He tried to get around the cliché, but he couldn't. Nothing could compare to seeing his father's pride at his yard display, nor his mother passing out lovingly prepared snacks to her neighbors. Nor Bella, finding her place among them and rediscovering her place with her own family.

Lord, please, somehow let this work. If Bella needs convincing to marry me though, I don't want her to stay if one day she'd resent her decision.

As the evening progressed, he introduced her to the newer neighbors on the block. Old man Webster brought queso dip for the party with his Chihuahua prancing beside him on a red-and-green leash. He approached David and Isabella, his left hand holding a Caprese bite and his right hand holding the leash and a cup of steaming cider.

"Good to see you again, young man." Webster's voice held the same gravelly tone it always had. "I'd shake your hand, but both of mine are full right now."

"Good to see you, too, Mr. Webster." He turned to Bella. "I'd like to introduce you to Isabella Tucker. She's visiting her family over in Bluegrass Crossing."

"A pleasure to meet you, ma'am." Webster inclined his head in a courtly gesture.

"Nice to meet you." Bella flashed her wide smile at him.

"You here for long? Are you spoken for? If not, I'd like to take you out for supper one night." The old man's eyes twinkled.

"I am spoken for, Mr. Webster, but thank you for the invitation."

"You're most welcome." Webster shook his head. "I had to ask, you know. David, my boy, don't let this one get away."

With that, he trudged off toward David's mother, who held a tray of chicken wings.

David didn't respond to Webster's comment. Instead, he faced Bella. "Thank you for helping Mom. She's completely in her Christmas element right now."

She nodded. "This is a lovely tradition for your neighborhood." Her voice sounded wistful.

David wanted to tell her she was already revisiting her family's traditions and maybe was on the way to making some new ones, but he didn't.

CHAPTER NINE

So, how did it go with David's family?" Jo-Jo flopped onto her pillow and stared across the bedroom at Bella. "I know what happened the first night—horrific—but how was everything else after that?"

"Better, a lot better." Bella bit her bottom lip.

"But?"

"But I heard from the office. The company is phasing out my job for sure."

"Oh, no." Jo-Jo sat up. "I'm sorry, Bell. What will you do?"

"Here's the deal—there's a position for me in London if I want it. Better pay, less travel."

"Less travel? But you'd be thousands of miles away."

"I know." Bella frowned. "It's a great opportunity though."

"Did you tell David?"

She shook her head. "No. He was busy all day yesterday, setting up the lights, and I helped his mother. Then, there was the party . . ." It sounded like a flimsy excuse, which it was.

"You didn't tell him on the ride home today?"

"No. I still don't know what to do."

"Have you prayed about it?"

"Yes, but I don't feel like there's a clear answer." Bella sighed, drawing her knees up to her chin. "I love what I do. Like I said, this is a great opportunity. Lots of Americans live and work overseas. I'm still young. I'm not married, and I don't have any children."

"But you have a ring on your finger and a decision to make."

Bella lifted her hand and looked at the diamond. "He's so good to me."

"And here comes another *but.*" Jo-Jo swung her legs over the side of the bed.

"You know me too well." Bella stood and paced the yellow-and-white room. "*But* I don't know if I can stay here, because here is where I'll end up if David moves back to Kentucky. My place will be with him. I'm afraid, Jo-Jo. I'm afraid our love won't be enough. I saw Mom's journals. She loved Tuck, but it wasn't enough to keep them together. What if David's love, as amazing as it is, won't be enough for me? I'm afraid I'll end up like Dad, dying alone with a pile of regrets because of decisions I made. He always said I was his Tough Cookie—made from the same dough he was."

Jo-Jo rolled her eyes. "That was a metaphor, silly. You're you. Sure, you were bitten with the travel bug like him. But you've seen the consequences of our father's decisions and have learned from them. Anyway, even if he and Mom had stayed together, we'd be right where we are right now: deciding what to do with an old horse farm in serious need of help."

"Maybe we all would have stayed closer to home if Tuck had stayed here, and things wouldn't have fallen apart like they did. . . . Our family wouldn't have fallen apart." She paused at the window that looked out on the stable.

"All those maybes don't change things now." Jo-Jo joined her. "We might have spread far and wide from the farm, but you and I are here together now. Tuck would approve. Speaking of which, did you take the time to read those letters yet?"

"No. I forgot and left them here." She'd found the stack of letters on her bed when she returned home. "Evidently, Sarah put them on my bed."

"I think you should read them. Tonight." Jo-Jo faced her. "I'm praying for clarity for you, Bell."

Jo-Jo hugged her and left. Jed was due home any moment from his job at the other horse farm, and no doubt her sister wanted to catch up with him after the day's work.

Bella looked over her shoulder at the letters on her bed. She crossed the room and picked up the stack, tapping them against her other hand.

Maybe she'd read a few. What could it hurt?

The first letter had an APO postmark from an October when her father was serving in Kuwait. She opened the envelope and tried to ignore the salutation to her mother. She did look curiously at a coin with Arabic writing on both sides. She skimmed the letter. It was full of news and how much he missed them all. He asked her to send some beef jerky and his favorite brand of bath soap and more razors since their small Post Exchange ran out of those items quickly.

He told her how much he loved her and that he couldn't wait to see her again and hold her in his arms. Thankfully, the romantic part of the letter didn't contain anything more than his proclamations of love and longing.

Then, his letter's focus switched to messages for each of the girls.

Bella had never known that. He'd sent them each a message specifically for them? But then Mom had never opened these letters. Evidently, she had given up on him long before they separated.

Her message from her father was that he hoped she was working hard in school, and that he couldn't wait to get a letter from her also. He said he included a coin for her that he picked up while patrolling through one of the local bazaars.

The letter overall made her smile. The next couple of letters were postmarked the fall of the same year—two in November. Then came a letter postmarked in December.

She skipped to the part intended for her, still feeling a bit shy about reading what wasn't meant for her eyes, words that no one else had seen since her father wrote them before tucking the pages into an envelope.

My sweet Isabella,

As I look at the big sky here in this desert, I can't help but wonder about the Magi who probably passed through this very place on their way to see the baby Jesus. I'm not much of a praying man or real religious, but I know there is a God who will show us the way, like He showed the wise men where to find the newborn king.

After I finish this deployment, I'll take you fishing. Can't wait to give you a great big hug, my Tough Cookie, and wish I could hug you this Christmas.

Bella wiped her eyes with the back of her hand.

I know there is a God who will show us the way.

Even back then, her father who admitted his own shortcomings spiritually, knew God would lead them. Maybe it came too late for her parents' marriage. Her mother wouldn't give up her life here to follow the man she loved. It made her sad.

She set the letter atop the stack. Maybe this letter had remained unread until now for a reason. Bella looked at the postmark. She would've been five or six when the letter had been mailed. What child of that age would have understood Tuck's words?

As she thought over Tuck's words to her, she realized what she had known all along: London paled in comparison to a future with David. The plum job in England wasn't going to bring her the joy she knew was here in Kentucky. Everything she needed was here. Jo-Jo's words came back to her. Ruminating about the could-haves, should-haves, and would-haves wasn't productive. It would change nothing.

Lord, forgive me for doubting David's love. He has loved me without condition. He showed me he was willing to love me, even at the prospect of losing me. She touched the ring. *Whether I stay or go, he loves me. Thank you for the gift of this man in my life. Thank you that I realized this in time before throwing away something beautiful.*

She went to the vanity table and sat, quickly brushing her hair and touching up her makeup. She and David Moore needed to have a very important conversation.

David filled the horses' water troughs in the stable since Jed had other chores to finish. He had pitched in so the poor guy could spend a few extra moments with Jo-Jo this evening.

"Hey there," Bella said.

David looked up and smiled at the sight of Bella, her hair falling around her shoulders in soft waves.

"Hey yourself." He turned off the water supply. "What brings you out here?"

"I was looking for you." She reached out her hand. "Walk me back to the porch?"

"Sure. This was my last one anyway."

The late afternoon twilight lent little warmth to the remains of the day as they held hands. Night would soon fall, and temperatures would drop. They climbed the porch steps where Bella stopped and turned to face him.

"I wanted to let you know, I received news that my job is definitely eliminated, but there is another position for me—in London." She fell silent.

"And?" He couldn't breathe.

"I also wanted to let you know, I'm not taking it."

Relief washed over him, followed by concern. "I'm sorry, sweetheart. I know you worked hard to get where you are, and I know you loved that job."

Bella shrugged. "It's okay. I'll receive a hefty severance package. After the New Year's holiday, I'll go back to Chicago with you . . . like we planned."

"Good." He smoothed away a strand of hair that blew across her face.

She blinked, then licked her lips. "But I wanted to give you an answer to a question you asked the other night. I didn't want you to wait any longer because that's not fair. I'm sorry I've made you wait this long."

He nodded and waited some more. Looking at her serious face, his breath hitched.

"So, what I'm trying to say is, my answer to your question is yes."

"Yes, to what?" Hopeful, but unsure, he put his arms around her.

Bella tipped her head back to look him in the eyes. "Yes, I want to marry you. I want to spend the rest of my life with you, no matter where we are. If it's Kentucky, or Chicago, or even Europe someday."

Thrilled, he pulled her to him. "You really know how to give a guy a heart attack. I thought—"

"Don't think." Stepping back, she stood on her tiptoes and kissed him. "Merry Christmas, David."

"Merry Christmas, Bella."

"Let's go tell Jo-Jo. I want her to be the first to know." She tugged at his hand, grinning as she opened the front door. But he resisted. "What's wrong?"

David closed the door. "Nothing. Let's savor the moment instead." He pulled his future wife back into his arms for a long embrace full of promise. The temperature outside didn't seem so chilly after all.

David pulled back, gazing down into her eyes. "Welcome home, Isabella Tucker."

"Home for me will be wherever you are." With that, she tugged on his hand and led him inside.

I'll Be
Home for Christmas

BY BARBARA J. SCOTT

My Sweet Sophie,

I'm writing to you one last time, hoping my attorney can track down your most recent address. You'll always be my little cowgirl. I remember that light in your eyes as clearly as if it were yesterday when I carried you on my shoulders out to the stable. You sure loved taking care of those horses, didn't you? I never saw a little girl more suited to riding tall in a saddle than you.

By the time you read this, I suspect this old Marine will be long gone. The horse farm belongs to you and your sisters now. I can only hope my death will bring the four of you back together—back to the home you once loved so much. I'm sorry I wasn't around much when you were growing up, but I want you to know, I love you, and I always will.

Tuck

Children are a heritage from the LORD, offspring a reward from him. Like arrows in the hands of a warrior are children born in one's youth. Blessed is the man whose quiver is full of them.

—Psalm 127:3–5

Chapter One

Sophie Tucker loosened her white-knuckled grip on the steering wheel of her 1999 white Ranger pickup as she gradually slowed to pull into the ice- and snow-covered driveway. Home . . . *finally*. She heaved a sigh of relief.

What should have been a three-and-a-half-hour drive from Nashville to Bluegrass Crossing outside of Lexington, Kentucky, had turned into six hours, and she'd spent another half hour creeping along the rural road to the horse farm where she'd grown up. As she gently turned the steering wheel to the right, the truck's rear-end fishtailed. Panicked, she turned into the skid to stop her slide into a deep ditch. Instead of gaining control, her truck spun around, one wheel hitting the gravel shoulder. She gunned the engine, but that only made things worse.

Her anxiety level hit the stratosphere when she realized what she feared most was happening, almost as if in slow motion. Her Ranger slid sideways down the six-foot embankment, and she thought it might roll over. She screamed, "Jesus!" over and over again until she came to rest at a 45-degree angle, the downhill side of her truck buried in snow.

Breathing hard, her heart throbbing in her throat, Sophie shut off the engine and dropped her head on the steering wheel. When someone rapped hard on her side window, she whipped her head around, trying to see through the frost. Someone yanked on her door handle. She turned the key back on and rolled down her window, looking up into the bluest eyes she'd seen in a long time. Not since high school anyway.

Ice crystals pelted her face. "Matthew Weatherly, you scared the life out of me."

"Right back at ya, Soph. I had just walked out of the stable when I saw you skidding into the ditch."

"What are you doing here?"

Smiling in relief, he poked his head inside, his warm breath caressing her cheek. "Looks like I'm rescuing you, Peanut. We need to get you out of there before your pickup decides to roll. Unlock your door."

Sophie's heart slowed now that she was safe, and she felt the return of those melted-chocolate feelings she once had for her first real crush. Not that he'd ever known how she felt about him back when they goofed around in their church's youth group and rode horses together. He was a senior when she was a lowly sophomore. He had all the girlfriends he wanted, and she didn't qualify. Then he'd graduated and joined the military—*traitor*—just like his hero Tuck. Her father's nickname stuck in her throat.

She broke his friendly stare and reached for her truck keys. "I don't need rescuing. I push around thousand-pound thoroughbreds for a living, remember?"

"How could I forget, Dr. Sophia Tucker, equine veterinarian extraordinaire?" he drawled. "Your daddy was really proud of you."

Sophie bit her tongue, aware of the cold steel door that slammed closed in her heart. What she wanted to say was, *Oh, you mean the father who abandoned my mother and his four daughters and ran off to play war games? Like I care what he thought.*

Before taking out her keys, she raised the window and unlocked the doors.

"I'm not sure we can get your door open," Matt yelled from outside. "Maybe it would be safer if you crawled out the window."

"Let's try the door first."

With Matt's help, she managed to crack it open, and with him pulling on the handle, they finally opened it far enough for her to squeeze out.

She pulled her duffle bag with her, but before she could swing it out, Matt took it out of her hands. The pickup door slammed shut. Then he helped steady her as she stepped into the deep snow to climb up the embankment. The full force of the wind hit her, making it hard to stand upright.

"Let's get inside before we freeze to death," he said. "A blizzard's moving in. We're supposed to get sustained winds of thirty-five to forty miles an hour and a foot or more of snow."

Her brows furrowed in worry as she shouted over the whistling wind. "Did all my sisters make it home okay? I didn't let anyone know I was coming."

"No one's heard whether Amy is coming, but Jo-Jo and Bella are stuck in Lexington."

When Sophie's leather-soled cowboy boot made contact with the road, she slipped and fell against Matt, all six foot three of him. She felt small, even at five foot ten. With his free hand, he quickly grabbed her arm and kept her from face-planting in the snow.

"Watch your step. There's a solid sheet of ice under this white stuff."

"Thanks for the warning." She glanced toward the house, but could barely see it through the driving snow. "Why on earth would they drive over there with weather coming in?"

"This storm was supposed to head north of us. Now they're saying it could be a record-breaker. Besides, you know Jo-Jo. She got it into her head to go Christmas shopping at the mall. Bella and her boyfriend, David, piled in with her."

Sophie gripped Matt's muscled arm, and together they plowed up the driveway, holding on to each other. They tucked their heads close to block the blinding snow mixed with ice crystals.

"Now they're stuck," she said.

"Yeah," Matt bellowed. "Dave checked into a hotel, and your sisters are staying with an old friend of Aunt Sarah's—Mrs. Shaffer."

"Nice lady. Are Jed and the hands here?"

"No. They delivered some of the horses to auction near Louisville and got caught in this. They're bunking down over there."

"At least they're all safe." Burying her face against his sleeve, Sophie put all her effort into making it to the porch. As they drew closer, she noticed the old farmhouse fully outlined in large, colorful bulbs of red, green, and white—just like when she was a kid. Had Jo-Jo done that? Her sister had definitely inherited the Christmas gene passed down from their mother, Marlena.

Taking care not to slip on the icy stone steps, Sophie opened the door, scraping her boots on the poinsettia welcome mat before crossing the threshold onto the gleaming, gray French oak floors.

"Sophie, there's a blizzard out here." He gently pushed her inside, out of the wind, snow still caking his boots, and quickly shut the door behind them as he dropped her duffle bag on the floor.

"Now look what you've done to your Aunt Sarah's clean floors," she scolded him.

"Don't get all bent out of shape, Peanut. If you'd stomped your boots much longer, we woulda had a snowdrift a foot high in here."

Sophie swung a punch at his arm. Grinning, he playfully blocked her, both of them falling back into their childhood roles. Matt had practically grown up on the farm with his younger cousin, Jed, taking care of the horses while his uncle managed the property. His Aunt Sarah helped with the house, enabling Sophie's mama to focus her attention on the business side of things. Sophie and Matt were always roughhousing, competing to see who could climb the highest tree or race the fastest horse across the pasture.

Sarah strolled out of the kitchen, a big grin on her face. "All right, you two. No fighting in the house. You're both adults now."

Sophie looked at one of her favorite people in the whole world and giggled. "Tell *him* that."

"Look at the stranded kitten I rescued, Aunt Sarah," Matt said. "She drove her truck into the ditch."

"I did not! It *slid* into the ditch."

"It's a wonder you made it drivin' all the way up from Nashville in this storm." Sarah's smile lit up her seventy-something face. "Come here and give me a hug. I've missed you."

"I've missed you, too." Sophie stepped into her warm embrace and gazed at the vision of lights over the older woman's shoulder. "You put up a Christmas tree."

Every handmade ornament dangling from the fragrant branches took her back to her childhood days when, each year, she and her three sisters helped decorate the biggest Virginia pine Tuck could find on the property.

"Jo-Jo talked Jed into it," Matt said.

"It's beautiful." The tree almost touched the fifteen-foot, beamed ceiling of the great room.

Sarah smiled and put her arm around Sophie's waist. "It's about time, too. It's been far too long since Christmas kissed this old place. Jo-Jo dragged the boxes of ornaments and strings of lights out of the attic."

"Mama loved Christmas and went all out, but I don't remember the last time we had a tree like that one. Once Tuck left, we took to putting up those little puny ones from the Monty family's lot." Sophie's eyes continued to roam from branch to branch, from memory to memory.

"I remember," Sarah said matter-of-factly and bustled toward the kitchen. "The Christmas before your daddy left home."

The thought of her father left a hollow feeling in Sophie's stomach, one she'd rather ignore. "Is that fresh coffee I smell?" She shrugged out of her coat.

"You know it is, and I stocked all your favorite creamers, too, just in case you girls decided to come after all. They've got a new one out just for Christmastime—chocolate peppermint."

"What, no hug for me?" Matt draped his arm around his aunt's shoulders and stooped to kiss her on the cheek.

"You've only been gone an hour," Sarah said, smoothing the front of his blue-checked flannel shirt and then giving his flat tummy a pat. "Are the horses all tucked in for the night? It's gonna be a cold one."

"Yes, ma'am. Stalls mucked out, fresh straw on the floor, feed and water, and blankets. Thermostat set on forty-five."

"You're a good boy, Charlie Brown." Sarah patted his red cheeks. "I wish Jedediah and the rest of them hadn't taken off early this morning. Thanks for drivin' over and fillin' in."

"No problem. Oh, and before I hiked down to the stable, I stacked a bunch of firewood on the porch and brought in a couple of armloads to keep the fireplace goin' until this storm passes."

"No tellin' how long that'll be. In March of '15, we lost electricity for a week. I had to cook on a skillet in the fireplace. Cold as blue blazes, too."

Sophie and Matt followed Sarah into the kitchen, pulled out bar stools from the island, and plopped down side-by-side as if Sophie hadn't been gone for years. How many hundreds of times had Sarah set out a plate of warm chocolate chip cookies for all the kids and poured them glasses of milk? Almost every afternoon after school.

Guilt niggled in her gut. She should have kept in better touch with Sarah after she left home. When she was in college, she'd made it a habit to drive over from Lexington every week or two to visit Bella and Jo-Jo . . . until they left; later she found out Tuck was retiring and returning to the farm. She'd found the job in Nashville and made herself scarce, and then she told herself she was way too busy to call.

When her mother died in a car accident, Sarah had been there for Sophie and her sisters. Grieving the loss of her mother had been one of the hardest things she'd ever gone through.

Shaking off the dark thoughts, Sophie sighed when the woman who had become a second mother to her set a blue mug of dark-roast coffee in front of her and fetched the bottle of chocolate peppermint creamer from the fridge. Even at seventy-something, Miss Sarah was still a beauty with snow-white hair and porcelain skin that looked like a proper southern lady's, one with the good sense to avoid the sun.

"Where's mine?" Matt asked.

Sophie took a sip of hot coffee made just the way she liked it and looked over at him. "Well, aren't we spoiled. How hard is it to drop a K-cup into the machine? I'd tell him to make his own, Sarah."

"I'm sure you would." Matt put his arm around her and pulled her to him, kissing the crown of her auburn hair. "I'm glad you're home, Peanut. We've really missed you. Haven't we, Aunt Sarah?"

"Yessiree."

"Jo-Jo will be over the moon that you decided to come home for Christmas after all," Matt continued. "Besides, it's been pretty dull around these parts since I moved home. With you gone, I didn't have anyone to save from falling out of trees or from drowning in the river when the canoe tips over."

"You left town first. And you're one to talk. If I remember right, you had your share of accidents, like that broken arm you got from trying to jump a horse over the back fence. A horse that had never been *trained* to jump a fence, by the way. You were trying to impress what's-her-name."

He laughed. "Missy Taylor. Happy Gal dug in her heels, and I went flying over her head."

"Ah, so you do remember."

Scrubbing his five o'clock shadow with the back of his hand, Matt winked at her and sipped from the matching blue mug of coffee Aunt Sarah set down in front of him. "Not one of my finer moments."

Laughing, his aunt playfully slapped his hand when he reached for the cookies and moved the plate to the black-marble counter. "Not till after supper. You'll spoil your appetite."

"This from the woman who always taught us, 'Life is hard. Eat dessert first.'"

"Don't go quotin' me to me, whippersnapper."

"And did you mention supper? Am I invited? I'd love to, but I'd better get on home before I'm stuck here."

"You *are* stuck here," Sophie said. "No way your Aunt Sarah's letting you drive home in a blizzard."

"That's right. If you think you're leaving in this kind of weather, you've got another think comin,'" Sarah said as if there were no room for argument. "I'm not stayin' up all night, worrying about you sliding into some ditch like Sophie did. You can sleep in Tuck's room tonight. There's fresh sheets on the bed and a couple of heavy quilts folded on top."

"You don't have to worry about me wrecking my truck," he said. "I'm a whale of a better driver than *Miss Sophie Pants*. She failed her first two driving tests."

Sophie frowned and folded her arms. "I did not. I only flunked once, and that's because my truck was too long for those stupid orange cones they set up for the parallel parking test."

"All right, ladies, I'll stay. Somebody needs to take care of the womenfolk and a stable full of horses."

Sophie smiled at his aunt. "We'll let him think that to massage his inflated ego."

Matt burst out laughing. "You've always gotta have the last word, don't you, Peanut?"

Sophie's heart hadn't fluttered like this since Matt gave her a peck on the cheek before he walked out of her life on his way to Naval Station

Great Lakes. She had loved him with her whole heart, and still he left her—*abandoned* her—just like Tuck had left her mom. But unlike Tuck, Matt had come home after his tour as a medic with the Marines, hung up his uniform, and gone back to school to become an RN.

"Do you have any animals at home that need taking care of?" she asked in concern.

"Nope."

"Not even a dog?"

He shook his head. "It's hard to take care of critters on my crazy schedule."

Sarah bent down to open the oven door and check her pot roast. Sophie looked over at Matt and found him staring at her with those gorgeous blue eyes, surrounded by the kind of long, dark lashes any woman would kill for. With a soft smile, he reached over and tucked a lock of hair behind her ear. Sophie's heartbeat sped up, stealing away her breath.

"I'm really glad you're home, Peanut."

Matt had abandoned her once as a friend, but those deep feelings for him still lingered. Only stronger, if that was even possible. Until this moment, she had resigned herself to live life as a single woman. The men she had dated in the past never so much as caused a blip on her EKG. Yet one touch from Matt, and she felt like a love-struck teenager again.

CHAPTER TWO

Early the next morning while it was still dark outside, Matt tossed back the covers and hopped out of bed, fully awake. His inner alarm clock always went off at 5:00 a.m., no matter what time he went to sleep. Before throwing on the clothes he'd worn the day before, he dropped and did fifty push-ups, then fifty sit-ups.

After he made coffee by the dim light shining from the vent hood over the stove, he ventured onto an ice-covered porch. Pulling up his coat collar, his Stetson low over his eyes, he stepped out into freezing rain. Miserable weather, but the stable *guests* couldn't take care of themselves.

It took an hour or so to muck out the stalls, spread fresh straw, and feed and water the horses. When he returned to the house, his cheeks chapped red by the cold, he walked into a bright kitchen that smelled like fried bacon. Aunt Sarah looked up and broke an egg into her bowl.

Smiling, he tugged off his gloves, stuffed them in the pockets of his frozen jacket that he hung on a peg by the door, and then washed his hands at the farm sink.

"Sophie up?" He dried his hands with a paper towel before mounting one of the wooden stools at the kitchen island.

Aunt Sarah turned and studied him for a moment before she turned back around. "Not yet."

"Lazybones."

"I suspect she's pretty tired after that treacherous drive yesterday." She whisked a bowlful of eggs with a little cream, added salt, and poured them into a sizzling hot skillet coated with butter.

"I imagine." He sat on his hands to warm them up. "The snow has turned to freezing rain again. Everything's coated with a thick layer of ice. We've already got tree limbs down."

"Welcome to Kentucky."

He rubbed his still-cold hands together and blew on his fingers.

Sarah glanced over her shoulder. "Why don't you go stand by the fireplace and warm up your backside?"

"I'm okay. Nothing a little hot coffee won't cure."

"You know where it is."

"It's a pain to make it one cup at a time," he grumbled, glaring at the Keurig on the counter. "I'm not about to waste my money on those K-cups."

"I know, but it was convenient for Tuck. For a big, tough guy, he sure liked those fancy flavored coffees. Besides, I'd feel guilty getting rid of that machine since it still works. When it breaks, I'll go out and buy a Mr. Coffee."

Matt stood and grabbed a mug out of one of the gleaming white, glass-front cupboards, set it under the Keurig spout, and popped in a K-cup before pressing the blinking, blue button. When he thought his Aunt Sarah was otherwise occupied, he stole a couple of pieces of hot, crispy bacon off the paper towel-covered plate. She smacked his hand.

"Ouch."

"Mind your manners." She stopped and looked up at him with a serious expression. "Now that she's home, you gonna tell that girl how you feel about her?"

He felt warmth surge up his neck to flush his face red. "What?"

Aunt Sarah planted her hands on her jeans-clad hips. "You know what I'm talkin' about. Nobody's ever been good enough for you but Sophie, and she's obviously not found anybody better than you. It's time you two settled down together."

Matt schooled his expression to remain passive. He stared into his black coffee, not wanting to look his aunt in the eye and lie to her, and then took a sip before he answered. "We're just friends, always have been. We haven't even talked to each other in years, let alone thought about each other."

"Then why are you still single?"

Matt took another sip of coffee, avoiding her eyes. "Just haven't found the right woman to marry yet."

"Uh-huh." His aunt set a plate of fluffy scrambled eggs and crisp bacon at his place, and he sat down to dig in. "Keep tellin' yourself that, Mattie boy, and you'll wind up like poor Tuck, dying alone."

Not wanting to admit her words nicked his heart, he ignored what she'd said and grinned at her. "You bake any of your famous buttermilk biscuits this morning?"

"You know I did."

Aunt Sarah opened the oven door and used a thick dish towel to pull out a pan of tall, golden-brown biscuits. She picked up a couple of them with her bare hands and tossed them on his plate. Then she set the antique, cut-glass butter dish in front of him.

"Now I suppose you'll be wantin' some of my apple butter."

He grinned like a kid and ran his hand through his sandy-blond hair that crackled with static electricity. "Yes, ma'am."

She pointed a gnarled finger at him and opened the fridge with her free hand. "You think about what I said. You're not gettin' any younger, you know."

"You got that right. They'll be cartin' me off to the old folks' home before you know it," he teased, slathering his first biscuit with butter. He looked down at his plate and forked eggs into his mouth, hoping she'd change the subject.

He didn't want to think about how he felt when Sophie skidded back into his life yesterday—still tall, long-legged, with a mop of wavy, dark-auburn hair, those steely-blue eyes, and not a lick of makeup. Even when they were in high school, she never needed it. He swallowed a chuckle, wondering if that scrunchie-thingie she used to pull back her hair into an off-center ponytail was the same one she used in middle school. It looked the same anyway.

Nobody could ever accuse Sophie of being a clothes horse. The only time she ever wore anything but faded blue jeans was at Easter services. Mainly because that's when her mama made her wear a dress. And it was at one Easter service that he'd first noticed she didn't look like a boy anymore. She was thirteen—he was fifteen—but she looked eighteen in that swirly, spring-green dress with yellow flowers.

That was when he'd started dating lots of girls instead of hanging out at the creek with her all the time, skipping rocks and fishing. If he hadn't joined the military when he did, he might've asked her out, but then he thought about what Tuck might have done to him for kissin' his little cowgirl. Nope. Better to leave town and not look back. He thought he'd get over her, but at night in the desert, he'd pull out a picture of her and think about what might have been.

Even back then, Sophie knew she wanted to be an equine vet. He wanted to be a doctor, but he couldn't afford college, so joining the Marines as a medic after his stint in the Navy to get his medical training was as close as he would ever get to that dream. The Marines were so picky about their medics, they only took the best corpsmen the Navy had to offer and then turned them into Marines. Not everybody made the cut. They wanted to know you could get down in the mud with them during a live firefight and bandage a guy shot in the gut.

Sophie looked like he'd betrayed her that day when he told her he was leaving for Great Lakes right after graduation. That put him in the same class as her father—military—and she didn't hold Tuck in high regard. As far as he knew, she'd never talked to the man again after he left her mama to "play soldier" as she called it and started calling him Tuck instead of Daddy.

Matt shoveled egg into his mouth. A shame, really. After Tuck came to the Lord, he wanted to make amends with his girls, but they hadn't made it easy to find them. The only address Aunt Sarah had for Sophie was a P.O. Box in Franklin, Tennessee, where all those rich country stars lived. They'd tried to contact them all before Tuck passed. Jo-Jo never answered her phone or email, Bella seemed to be on one perpetual business trip, and the oldest girl, Amy, was so bitter he doubted she'd so much as give a hoot that Tuck had died of cancer. Alone.

There was so much they deserved to know about Lt. Col. Robert "Tuck" Tucker—his bravery, his loyalty to his country, and especially his desire to keep America safe for his girls after 9/11. He had a chest covered in medals, including the Silver Star, but in the end, Tuck had told him he would trade them all for the chance to tell his girls he loved them one more time. Sad. Matt hoped he had brought Tuck some comfort in his last days. He swallowed past the lump in his throat. He still missed the Marine who died too soon from lung cancer. He suspected he always would.

"Morning, sleepyhead," Aunt Sarah said, interrupting his thoughts.

Matt looked up at Sophie, who scuffed into the kitchen, yawning, wearing green-flannel PJs and an old, red-checked flannel bathrobe. She hadn't even washed her face yet, but it looked soft and flushed, pink with sleep. Her mussed auburn hair fell in waves at her shoulders.

The feelings for her he'd suppressed all those years couldn't be denied any longer. But if she knew what he was thinking about doing with his future, she'd never forgive him if he carried through on his plans. He sighed. Maybe they weren't meant to be together after all. Maybe God knew she needed someone better—someone not scarred by what he'd seen on the battlefield. At least she had forgiven him for joining the service now that he was an RN.

Matt took another bite of his biscuit and enjoyed the view of Sophie.

"Coffee," she said, groaning, with her eyes half shut. She shuffled over to the coffeemaker, grabbed a mug out of the cabinet, set it under the spout, and popped in a dark, French-roast K-cup. He didn't know why she even bothered to drink coffee. She always dumped half a cup of flavored creamer into every serving. Leaning against the refrigerator with her eyes closed, taking her first sip, he swore she could have done that drill blindfolded.

"Sit down before you fall down, Peanut." He grinned at her and patted the seat beside him. She slid onto the stool and all but gulped her first cup of coffee. "How do you manage to get up in the middle of the night and take care of a sick horse?"

"Practice." She yawned. "Like a fireman, I lay out my clothes every night and get my coffee ready to go. All I have to do is turn on the switch and dress while it percolates, pour it into a thermos, and drink it all down before I get to where I'm going. Takes me fifteen minutes, max. Five in an emergency." She leaned on her elbow and looked up at him with those eyes that appeared ice blue in the morning light. "Did you know the latest research shows that drinking at least four cups of coffee a day staves off Alzheimer's? Plus, the caffeine jump-starts my brain."

"That's four cups a day . . . not an hour," he said.

Sophie drained her cup and sang, *"You say potāto, I say potăto, you say tomāto, I say tomăto . . ."*

Matt burst out laughing. Sophie made him happy. She always had. Whenever they were together, all seemed right with the world. Without her all those years, he realized now that his world had been slightly off kilter.

"What do you want for breakfast, sugar?" Sarah interrupted, smiling. "Scrambled eggs, bacon? Or I can whip up some pancakes right quick if that sounds good to you."

Sophie groaned and shook her head. "Nothing, thank you. I can't eat eggs in the morning. They make me sick. I'll have a protein bar later."

"No wonder you're so skinny, girl." Sarah frowned. "You used to eat a hearty breakfast every morning before school. At least have one of my biscuits."

Matt waggled his eyebrows at Sophie, dabbing at the butter running down his chin with a paper napkin. "She makes the best biscuits in all of Kentucky."

"You think I don't know that?" Sophie snatched the rest of his biscuit and popped it in her mouth.

"Hey!"

Grinning, she chewed, her cheeks bulging like a squirrel with a nut, and then turned her coffee mug upside down and shook it over his plate.

"Thanks a heap."

"You're welcome." Sophie batted her eyelashes at him. Oh, if she only knew what that did to him. "If you're *really* glad I'm home, maybe you'll fetch me another cup of coffee. Please?"

"Manipulator."

Grinning wickedly, she teased, "I'm a horse whisperer, you know."

"Yeah, but I ain't no horse." He grumbled, took her mug, and doctored another cup of coffee, setting it in front of her. "You gonna laze around all morning, or get dressed and go check on those horses? We've got a mare down with the flu."

"The flu?" No kidding around now. "Why didn't you say so? Why wasn't she vaccinated?"

"She was a rescue, and before Jed could inoculate her, she presented symptoms. Probably picked it up at the racetrack where we got her. She's on the mend though."

"How long has she had it? Is she staying hydrated?"

"A week to ten days. And yes, Jed's done everything he can. You know how much he loves those animals."

"And the others?"

"They're fine. Just in case, he kept her isolated, even though they've all had their shots."

Sophie ran her fingers through the silky, reddish-brown strands before taming it with the hair do-dad she pulled from the pocket of her robe.

"Give me five minutes, and I'll meet you back here." She turned and scuffed out of the kitchen.

"Yes, ma'am," he said, saluting with two fingers, a smirk on his face.

Matt looked over at Aunt Sarah and pushed away his empty plate, folding his arms on the kitchen island. "Is it me, or is she getting bossy in her old age? I wonder if she'd be that worried about me if I got the flu."

"Depends," she said, her expression deadpan.

"On what?" He pulled his boot up to retie the damp laces.

"On whether you could infect her beloved thoroughbreds."

"People can't give the flu to horses—"

His aunt burst out laughing as she ran water into her iron skillet before wiping it out quickly and setting it to dry on the back of the stove.

"Ha, ha." Matt would have thrown a dish towel at her head, but she *was* his elder.

"Sometimes you're just too easy," Aunt Sarah said. "You better hustle. She'll be here and halfway to the stable before you pull your gloves on. That girl doesn't let any grass grow under her feet."

Chapter Three

Just as Sophie stuffed her arm into her blue down jacket, the lights flickered and went dark, plunging her old bedroom into murky shadows. The weak light from the windows barely penetrated the gloom.

Great. Just great.

She poked her head out of the door. "You guys have any lights out there?"

A flashlight blinded her, and she reached out to shove it away.

"No, they just went out in *your room*."

"Wiseacre," she said to Matt.

"I'll turn on the water in the bathroom and kitchen sinks so the pipes won't freeze."

"Why can't we just fire up the generator?" Sophie zipped her stained work jacket and pulled on her worn, leather gloves before picking up the black bag that contained everything she needed as a vet. Matt had made another trip out to her truck for it yesterday afternoon before it turned dark.

"Can't."

"Why not?"

She looked up at him as he suddenly stood much too close. Her breath hitched. Brushing past his firmly muscled frame, she put some distance between them as she strode down the hall.

"Conked out last winter." His voice came unexpectedly behind her right ear. "Nobody had the money to replace it."

His nearness never used to bother her this much. Of course, he was a teenager the last time she saw him. She had to admit he'd grown into quite a man—a broad-shouldered, blue-eyed man who oozed . . .

maleness. All those old feelings bubbled up inside her and exploded like the Fourth of July fireworks show on the riverfront in Nashville.

"Maybe your place still has power," she said. "You can always head home now. I can take care of the horses."

"I'm sure you can, Peanut, but I'm stuck. We're all stuck. There's a thick coating of ice on the roads and every tree and fencepost in-between."

He followed her into the great room. At least they had more light filtering in from the windows.

"So we're all just supposed to freeze until someone digs us out?"

Matt leaned back against the doorway, folded his arms across his chest, and gave her that lopsided grin she remembered so well. "Pretty much. The Sophie I remember would have thought this was a grand adventure."

"The Sophie you remember grew up."

"Yes, she did," he said softly, his gaze locking with hers.

"Well, there's nothing to be done about it. I need to examine all the horses to make sure they're healthy."

"They are . . . except for Sophie. She's the one with the flu—"

"What?"

Aunt Sarah sat down in Tuck's worn, brown-leather club chair. "That red-haired horse kind of adopted him. I named her Sophie, being that you two were best buds and all when you were kids."

Sophie looked back and forth between Matt and his aunt, trying to discern the unspoken message they exchanged.

"There was also the fact that he was the only one who could get close to her when she was sick," Sarah said. "Never seen anything like it. Totally bonded."

Sophie tipped her head with a quizzical look on her face. "So you named her Sophie because . . ."

Aunt Sarah giggled—*actually giggled.* "Because you and Matt were thick as thieves when you were growin' up." Picking up her knitting, she concentrated on the stitches of the nearly finished cable-knit sweater. "If you weren't racing those thoroughbreds on the track or pushing each other into the creek, you were grossing each other out drinkin'

Coca-Colas and having belching contests."

"I never!" Sophie felt her face flame.

"Short memory," the older woman said.

Sophie stepped to the front door and tried to turn the knob. It was frozen shut. She couldn't even exit with dignity. With her chin held high, she brushed past Matt and escaped into the kitchen. "I'll be in the stable for a while."

Matt shoved away from the door. "I'll come with you. It's pretty slippery out there."

She almost ran to the back door and threw her words over her shoulder. "You're not my nursemaid, Weatherly. I can take care of myself."

Famous last words. With that, she closed the door with a solid *thunk!* and promptly slipped on the top step and fell hard on her fanny. At least *he* hadn't seen her make a fool of herself.

She'd been in love with him when they were kids—whatever love was at that age—but now she could hardly be in the same room with him without her heart speeding up. She thought it best to avoid the risk of being alone with him at all.

After firing up the wood pellet stove in the stable, Sophie pushed thoughts of Matt out of her mind and took her sweet time examining each of the horses now in her care, starting with the auburn, flu-afflicted mare.

"Hello, sweet girl," she said, reaching into the stall to stroke the velvety nose. "You must be Sophie, huh? Me, too. Pleased to meet you." No fever. She swung the door open, moving slowly, and caressed the mare's neck. "Let's listen to your lungs, okay?"

Sophie gently placed her hands to close off the mare's nostrils until the horse tossed her head and fought to inhale, then she listened to her throat and trachea. She repeated the procedure, moving the stethoscope down the thoroughbred's sides to listen to her lungs. Since horses were nasal breathers, it was hard to hear their vitals when they were at rest.

Finally, she stroked the mare's neck and smiled. "All done. You've kicked that flu in the backside, girl."

Only three stalls stood empty and waiting for more rescues. Still, she completed her cursory exams in a short amount of time. She didn't have the equipment for pre-purchase tests. X-rays were expensive for a $5,000 horse, but once she set up her clinic, she'd give them a more thorough going-over.

Without electricity to keep the stable above forty-five degrees, Sophie employed every blanket she could find and made sure each stall had a nice, thick layer of straw to insulate the floor. Hopefully, the temperature wouldn't drop much below freezing, or she'd be down here all night stoking the stove.

Once she left the stable, she hunted around to find a branch to use as a walking stick. A nice fat one had fallen in just the right spot atop the ice to reach it. Grabbing the limb, she slid along the ice-covered snow, using the piece of wood to anchor herself step by step. She had almost reached the front porch when Matt rounded the corner of the house, his blue eyes stark against the white, snowy background.

"Hey, Peanut! You took so long I thought you were spending the night down there."

"I . . . uh . . . the horses—" Sophie had never been at a loss for words around Matt, but she seemed to be dumbstruck at the moment.

"I figured you gave each one a complete examination." Matt, on the other hand, didn't seem to be at a loss for words at all. Pushing back his hat, he seemed to move in slow motion as Sophie watched him stoop to pick up an armful of wood to carry into the house. "You should see Aunt Sarah. She's as excited as a kid going off to camp. She's already made you guys a bed on the pull-out sofa in front of the fire and had me drag out one of the twin mattresses so I can sleep on the floor tonight. I think she piled on every blanket and quilt in the house."

Shaking her head to clear it, Sophie reached back for their easy, bantering relationship. "Are we having hot dogs on sticks and s'mores, too?"

"I wouldn't be surprised." He grinned, and she melted into a puddle of warm goo inside.

Matt jiggled the front doorknob to knock the ice loose, and it opened like magic in front of him. Her hero. "After you, milady."

"Talk about Sarah. You're acting like a big, goofy kid."

He grinned. "Thanks. I think."

"You two can stay up all night laughing and snorting—"

"I do not snort," Sophie said. Then she ruined her denial with a giggle, and her head tipped back, resulting in another snort.

Aunt Sarah sighed and turned over, pulling a pillow over her head.

Matt snickered. It wasn't that what Sophie said was so funny, but they had been reduced to nine-year-olds, trying to best each other with who could produce the silliest laugh they'd ever heard.

Sophie stiff-armed her hand in front of Matt and clutched her chest, her breath huffing in and out. "Stop! I can't breathe. I'm going to pass out."

"Okay, if you admit that you snort like an overloaded donkey when you laugh out loud."

"All right. I give."

Matt chuckled and took a gulp of his Coke, fascinated with watching Sophie's eyes twinkle in the firelight. When she laughed, her whole face lit up, and she became . . . *irresistible*. He wanted to reach over and stroke the curve of her soft cheek and finally take that leap to steal the kiss he should have stolen when they were in high school.

Instead, he pretended to grow solemn. "I've needed to ask you a really serious question since you came home."

Sophie immediately sobered. "What?"

He sighed, then looked up with a twinkle in his eyes. "Are you still as ticklish as you were when you were a kid?"

Sophie held up a stern finger. "Don't even think about it, Weatherly. No tickling. In fact, if I ever marry, I intend to include a clause in the pre-nup agreement that says there will be no tickling *ever* for the duration of the marriage."

He opened his mouth to speak, but she interrupted him. "And absolutely no whistling in the morning before my first two cups of coffee. Maybe three."

"Hey," he said, spreading his arms wide. "It's your pre-nup. Throw in the whole enchilada. Not that anyone would ever marry you under those conditions."

"Then I'll stay single," she said, shrugging her flannel-robed shoulders.

They stared at each other, and then the moment was spoiled when a loud snore sounded from under his aunt's pillow. They both burst out with huge belly laughs, then tried hard to suppress them so as not to wake his aunt.

"How's that working for ya?" Matt finally asked. He leaned back against the club chair, his hands clasped behind his head.

"How's what working?" Sophie's eyebrows knitted into a V.

"Being single."

Sophie reached into her bag of cheese puffs and crunched on a couple more. The girl had decimated the bag, turning her fingers bright orange and spreading a clown smile across her adorable face.

"I don't know." She licked her index finger. "How's it working for *you?*"

He plucked a couple of tissues from the box on the side table nearby and handed them to her, pointing at her mouth.

She scrubbed her face. "Better?"

"Better."

"You didn't answer my question," she said.

"I know, but I asked you first. Any guys waiting in the wings, wanting to put a ring on that?"

Sophie pulled up her knees and wrapped her arms around them. "No."

"Has there ever been—"

"No, no, and no."

He grinned at her as she licked the corner of her mouth. "I didn't ask you anything."

"But you were getting ready to. No, I've never had a steady boyfriend. No, I've never been engaged, and no, I don't have a husband stashed in the back of my truck."

She grinned and dusted off her fingers. "Now you get to answer. How's single life working out for you?"

He was silent for a moment, wondering whether to answer truthfully, or maintain the light mood. He opted for the truth. If not now, then when?

"Not well." Matt's gaze locked with hers. "By this age, I thought I'd be married and have a couple of kids. It gets lonely sometimes."

Sophie nodded as if she understood all too well. At least he hadn't scared her off. "Yeah. I mean, I love my work. I thought it would be enough, but—"

"But there's a hole in your heart shaped like someone special, and Mr. Right hasn't ridden into your life yet."

She sighed. "You know what I worry about the most, Matt?"

"What, Peanut?"

"That he rode into my life, and I waved as he rode right back out again. I mean, how do you know when you've found that special person you're supposed to spend your life with?" She plucked at a carpet thread. "It shouldn't be this hard."

He tapped her hand with one of his size thirteen, stocking-clad feet. "No, it shouldn't. Maybe it's just the timing that's been off. Maybe your Prince Charming had to save the kingdom before he got back to the business of finding the girl who fit the glass slipper."

"Or maybe he's a clueless knucklehead," she said dryly.

He chuckled. "That's another option."

How could he tell her she was his girl, that she was the one he'd been looking for all of his life? He couldn't. If he was the right man for her, then she had to know it in her own heart first.

"My Miss Right is probably out on a date with the clueless knucklehead," he said.

She giggled. "I've got an idea."

He took a sip of warm Coke before stoking the fire with the poker. "What's that?"

"Let's dump those losers and marry each other."

He wondered if he looked as shocked as she did by what just came out of her mouth. A Freudian slip, or something she'd thought about before? She softly gasped and clapped her hand over her mouth.

"Hmm, a possible third option. Maybe this is worth exploring. We've known each other forever, so we're not hiding any deep, dark secrets.

We've always been great friends, so we wouldn't have all that drama—" He tapped her hand with his toe again. She absentmindedly massaged his foot, setting off waves of electricity through his entire body.

"And we're a brick-load smarter than those jerks we've been waiting around for," she said.

"Right," he muttered. Sophie continued to massage his foot, and he half closed his eyes like a cat ready to purr. "We may be on to something."

Abruptly, Sophie stood up and yawned, ruining the moment when she hopped under the covers next to his aunt. "I don't know about you, cowboy, but I'm exhausted. Set your alarm for three, and I'll get up to check on the horses."

"Sounds like a plan," he said, setting his cell phone for a wake-up call. "I hope I've got enough juice left in this thing."

Matt launched himself onto the twin mattress and dove under the mountain of quilts. Silence, except for the popping fire, filled the room until he heard the one person's voice he definitely didn't want to hear. He could only groan inwardly when Aunt Sarah whispered, "Chicken," and rolled to her other side.

Chapter Four

Bundled in a purple T-shirt, a red-flannel shirt, and her blue down jacket, Sophie felt almost too warm in the stable with the wood pellet stove cranking out the BTUs. Just as she unzipped the jacket and threw it over the empty stall wall, Matt sauntered in, causing the skin at the nape of her neck to tingle. With his presence, the horses moved restlessly in their stalls, shuffling their hooves, and filling the barn with the fresh scent of dust, straw, and manure.

Quickly, she grabbed a curry brush and started grooming Sophie's auburn coat, her conversation with Matt last night still fresh in her mind.

"You should warn a girl before you sneak up on her," she said, purposely avoiding those gorgeous blue eyes.

Hunching over the stove, he held his gloved hands toward its warmth. "No sneaking here. You're the one who's jittery."

Sophie left that remark on the stable floor without comment, avoiding the landmines lying in wait down that road.

"Have you thought about whether you want to sell the farm?" Matt asked. "Jo-Jo seems pretty set on keeping it in the family. I guess she and Jed have some pretty lofty ideas about where to go from here, but I think everyone else thinks taking the offer is the best way to go."

She stood up straight, the curry brush gripped in her hand and hanging at her side. "What offer? Nobody said anything to me about an offer to sell the place."

Matt shoved his hands into his pockets and rocked back on his boot heels. "Oh, maybe I wasn't supposed to say anything."

She strode over to him, forgetting her attraction for the moment. "Spill."

"Your sisters probably wanted to talk to you first. A land developer is interested in building some of those five-acre horse estates. You know, the ones parents buy for their twelve-year-old daughters so they can have their own horses."

"Over my dead body. This land has been in the Tucker family for generations," she said, pointing the curry brush at Matt. "I plan on buying out my sisters to start my own equine practice. I can't compete with some big developer."

He lifted his hands in surrender. "Hey, I'm on your side. I didn't know whether you even planned on staying in town with the way you felt about your dad."

"You bet I'm staying," Sophie said, angry that something might stand in the way of her dream. "This land was homesteaded by my three times great-grandfather. It's always been a horse farm. Besides, they can't sell it without my permission. When Tuck died, he left it to all four of us."

"I know," Matt said, pulling off his gloves and coat. Then he ran his hands up and down her arms as if that would calm her. "I don't think your sisters are disputing that fact."

She pulled away from him and started to pace, throwing the brush at the work bench. She'd never be able to afford this property if her sisters wanted to make a big profit. She thought legacy meant more to them than—

Sophie's conscience took a big bite out of her thoughts. Of course, she'd never *actually shared* her secret dream with any of them. She thought that's all it was—a dream.

Suddenly, all those Sunday school lessons on forgiveness came rushing back . . . that she should forgive because God forgave *her* when Jesus died for *her* sins. She didn't know what she'd expected of the future, but it hadn't been for Tuck to die so young.

Unbidden, a sob burst out of her throat and tears streamed down her face, clogging up her nose. Matt pulled her into his arms, and she hesitated as she suddenly caught a whiff of her dad's pipe tobacco hiding in the fabric of his insulated shirt-jac. Sophie remembered that her mom had bought it for her dad from L.L. Bean one Christmas. That's when she realized Matt must have borrowed some of her dad's stuff to wear since he didn't have a change of clothes with him.

"Everything will work out just fine, Peanut. Your sisters are reasonable."

She was crying so hard, she couldn't talk, but he held her anyway. She snuggled against his chest and thought of all the fun times she'd had with her dad before he and Mama separated. Sophie always blamed him for the break-up, but now that she was an adult, she realized there were always two sides to every story. Still sobbing, she choked and coughed.

"Baby, you're gonna make yourself sick," he said, rubbing comforting circles on her back. When she could barely breathe anymore, Matt pulled an old-fashioned white hankie out of his pocket. Her dad always carried one, too. He was probably wearing a pair of Tuck's pants, the realization making her cry even harder.

Leaning against her longtime friend, she let herself blubber out all her guilt and loss and pain until her tears finally slowed and she took a deep, shuddering breath, blowing her nose on the hankie. Matt still cradled her in his arms.

"I . . . I never forgave him, Matt. He died, and I never even got to say good-bye." Tears trickled down her cheeks. She felt as though she had a huge, empty hole in her heart that threatened to pull her inside out, straight down into it. "That day he left, I screamed, '*I hate you!*' over and over and over. He died thinking I hated him. But I didn't. I felt like it was my fault he left. I know that sounds stupid."

Matt kissed the top of her head and rocked her in his arms. "No, that doesn't sound stupid at all. I think that's how most kids feel when their parents split up. I was mad at my dad for years after he died in that plane crash. If he'd just listened to Mom about the weather . . . if he'd stayed in Dallas till the next morning . . . he wouldn't have died. I think that's why I idolized Tuck and wanted to be a Marine. He became my hero—sort of a substitute dad."

Sophie closed her eyes and leaned into Matt's comforting embrace. It felt so nice—*so right*—to let him hold her in his arms. When had she started thinking of Matt Weatherly as her Prince Charming? Maybe he had always played that role, and she never realized the depths of how she felt about him.

She sniffed and pressed the wet handkerchief against her nose. "Then when you left, I not only lost my dad to the military, but my good friend, too. I was so mad at you."

He laughed softly. "I know. You never answered any of my letters."

"Honestly . . . I burned every one without reading them. I have no idea what you wrote." She looked up at him, knowing she probably looked a mess.

A chuckle rumbled deep in his chest. "Probably stupid stuff anyway. I wasn't the English major in the family, you know."

"Neither was I," she said with a tiny smile. She snuggled in his arms again. "But I should have read them and written you back—told you how I felt."

"You felt abandoned. Again."

She nodded and felt the nubby texture of her daddy's shirt against her cheek . . . smelled the sweet distant scent of his cherry pipe tobacco . . . remembered her dad teaching her to ride when she was only four.

"You were his favorite, you know," Matt said, pulling her down beside him on a hay bale. He kept his arm around her, and she tucked her head into the hollow that seemed made just for her.

"No, I wasn't. I was always sassing him."

"You were a handful. I'll give you that. You wanted to spread your wings and fly, but he held you close to keep you safe. Good thing he did or you might never have gone to vet school."

"Why not?" She looked up at him, and he cupped her face in his hands.

"Because I probably would've asked you to marry me when you turned eighteen, and we would've had six kids by now."

Sophie's heart lurched, and her eyes grew round at his confession. "You never looked twice at me. You were always off on a date with some popular girl."

"Because I suspected your daddy would've tanned my hide if I'd so much as looked at you. He might have loved me like a son, but you were the daughter who inherited his family's love for horses. He always said thoroughbred blood ran through your veins."

Sophie looked up into his eyes and felt that same yearning as she did when she was fifteen years old. She wanted Matt to kiss her, just like she'd fantasized about so many times. The moment seemed right . . . natural . . . ordained. Their eyes locked, and they both leaned forward slowly . . . just as her recovering patient Sophie nosed in and licked Matt's ear.

They both burst into laughter.

"Too mushy, Soph?" She popped up and patted the horse's neck, then looked into Matt's smiling face. "Evidently, your girl's jealous of me."

"Apparently so." His voice turned husky. Matt stood and traced the curve of her cheek with his forefinger. "We'll continue this discussion another time."

She wanted to continue it *now*, but she guessed the mood had been broken. After all those years of waiting, her first kiss with Matt needed to be special, with the time to savor every sweet moment . . . like the first bite of Sarah's pecan pie topped with real whipped cream.

Did she dare dream about a future with Matt, or was it just the Christmas season and the weather's forced isolation from the real world that drew them close together again?

Matt stretched out his legs toward the blazing fire in the hearth, content to snuggle beside Sophie and not talk. Aunt Sarah, their faithful chaperone, huddled closer to the fire in Tuck's leather chair.

"I'm bored," Sophie said out of nowhere, nibbling her lower lip. "I wish I knew how to make cookies over an open flame."

Matt looked down at her for a long moment, trying to hold back his laughter, but finally let loose with a big belly laugh.

She smiled and elbowed him in the side. "What? Don't you think they made cookies back in the olden days? I bet we could figure out how."

Matt looked over at his aunt, and she just shook her head as though Sophie had taken leave of her senses.

"I'm sure they did, Peanut, but you're liable to burn down the place if you try. Cooking was never your strong suit as I recall."

Her lips puffed out at him in a pretty pout. "I can cook."

"Sophie Rose Tucker, don't you know lying is a sin?" he said. "The only time I remember you ever baking cookies was when you almost blew up the kitchen."

Aunt Sarah picked up her knitting. She pulled on a thin pair of cotton gloves with the fingertips cut off before her metal needles started to click.

Sophie smirked. "Mama got a new kitchen out of it, didn't she?"

"That she did, Peanut. That she did."

Matt remembered the disaster Sophie had left in her wake. It was a wonder she hadn't killed herself. Everyone deemed it a miracle that the match somehow failed to light the gas until she'd stepped out of the way.

"Blew that old oven door right through the window," Aunt Sarah said, snickering. "If your daddy had been home, you probably wouldn't have been able to sit down for a week."

"I never got spanked," Sophie said.

"Not sayin' you ever did, but you sure scared the living daylights out of everybody that day."

No one said anything for a moment, drifting back down into comfortable silence. Suddenly, Sophie pulled on Matt's shirtsleeve.

"While we're on the subject of food, how come you call me Peanut?"

She had to be kidding, right? He'd called her Peanut since she was eight. "You know how come."

"No, I don't." She scooched away from him to lean against the arm of the worn leather sofa and stretch out her legs.

"No way." He lifted one brow. "That day is etched forever in *my* memory."

"Not mine."

"You really don't remember?"

"Not a thing," Sophie said. She looked over at Sarah. "What's he talking about?"

"Matthew, you tell her," the older woman said, looking up at him from her knitting. "He's the one who got you in trouble that day, Sophie Pants. Course, you were both about even by the time you grew up. Never seen two kids who could get into so much orneriness together."

"Even at school we were voted Mr. and Miss Mischievous for the school yearbook," he said, grinning at Sophie.

She pushed against him with her foot. "You're off topic. Tell me why you call me Peanut."

"As I recall it . . ." he started.

Aunt Sarah looked over her reading glasses at him. "Remember, I'm here to fill in any parts you leave out."

"Yes, ma'am," he said. "Well, one afternoon when you were about eight, we were sitting on the back porch in the sun, dropping peanuts into our Coke cans."

"Why?"

"I don't know. I think we saw your sister Amy do it one time. Something about the combination. Anyway—"

"So that's why you call me Peanut?"

"Not exactly," Aunt Sarah said, the corners of her mouth lifting in a small grin. "Go on, Matthew."

"So you dared me to stick a peanut in my ear," he continued.

Sophie giggled. "And you were dumb enough to do it?"

"Yeah, and I almost couldn't get it out. Your fingers were smaller though, and you were finally able to dig it out before we had to call your mom or Aunt Sarah."

"So that's why you call me Peanut."

"No. . . . Then I dared you to stick a peanut up your nose."

She put her hands to her cheeks. "And I did it?"

"Yes, you did," Aunt Sarah said. "Your daddy almost had a conniption. He and your mama rushed you to the hospital and had to pay some doctor to stick an instrument up your nose to retrieve it. If it'd gone too far up your sinuses, they woulda had to operate."

Sophie's eyes widened. "I don't remember any of this.

"Too traumatic, I guess," he said, and then popped a Frito into his mouth.

"Don't eat all those, Matthew," Aunt Sarah said. "They're for the chili pie."

He glanced at the cast-iron pot, bubbling at the center of the fire. He dusted the Fritos off his fingers and handed the almost-full bag to his aunt. He turned to face Sophie straight on, loving every minute of this. He couldn't believe she didn't remember.

"As I recall, you made the doctor save the peanut in a little urine sample cup and kept it in your room until your mama finally threw it away."

"Gross!" Sophie said, making a face.

"I can tell you this much," Sarah added, "Matthew made himself pretty scarce for a few days until your daddy settled down."

"And that, my dear Sophia, is why I call you Peanut." He grinned.

"Don't call me that!"

"I told you, I've always called you Peanut."

"No. *Sophia.* You know how much I hate that name."

"Blame that one on your mama and your Italian great-grandma, Sophia Rose. I can still hear your mother calling out your name." He pitched his voice into his falsetto range. "Sophia Rose, you better get yourself back to this house before I come looking for you. I told you to clean up your room before you went out to play."

Sophie stuck her fingers in her ears. "La, la, la, la, la. Let me know when you're done insulting me."

"I swear, you two remind me of a couple of grown-up kids. And argue worse than an old married couple," Aunt Sarah said in her soft, southern voice.

If only . . .

CHAPTER FIVE

Matt folded his arms and turned back toward the fire, staring mindlessly at the bubbling chili pot, the sound of its clanking lid creating a musical rhythm. Eventually, Sophie scooted back over to his side and laid her head on his shoulder.

"So, are you looking for a job?" she asked.

Oh, boy, this was one conversation he had hoped to avoid. He didn't want to lie to her, but he wasn't quite sure whether *omission* measured up to an out-and-out lie.

"I thought I'd wait until after the first of the year to make a decision," he said finally.

"Does that mean you have more than one offer?"

He paused before answering her. "Sort of."

"What's that supposed to mean? Either you do or you don't."

Matt sat up straight and put his arm around Sophie, pulling her against him. "I *thought* I'd made a decision . . . until you came home. Jo-Jo said you were staying in Nashville for Christmas."

"What have I got to do with it?"

Aunt Sarah laid down her knitting without looking at either one of them. "I think I'll go crawl up under a bunch of quilts and take a nap in my room."

"Won't it be too cold for you away from the fire?" Sophie asked.

Aunt Sarah waved back over her shoulder as she left. "I'll be fine. I just need a little catnap. You two have a lot to talk about, and you don't need my two cents thrown in."

With that, she disappeared down the hall toward the bedrooms, and Matt glanced at Sophie's quizzical expression.

"What's going on?" she asked, straightening. "And don't you lie to me, Matthew Weatherly."

"I'd never lie to you, Peanut," he said in a soft voice. "It's just I never thought we'd reconnect. It's like time has stood still since I saw you last."

She smiled, her cheeks pink in the glow of the fire. He caressed her face with the back of his hand. "Your ponytail is crooked."

Sophie inched away from him. "Okay, I know when you're stalling."

He sighed. "I haven't signed the papers yet—"

"What papers?"

"When I thought you weren't coming home, I talked to a Marine recruiter about the benefits of re-enlisting now that I'm an RN."

She shot to her feet, her hands fisted at her sides. "You can't be serious!"

Now he'd done it. Why couldn't he have waited to find out how she felt about him before he opened his big mouth?

"I was . . . till I laid eyes on you when I rescued you from that ditch. The signing bonus is generous, and with my degree now I'm eligible for officer training school."

"The Marines? You'd actually re-enlist *in the military?* After all this family's been through? I thought you loved it here. I thought—" She turned away from him, crossed her arms, and stared into the fire.

"You thought what?" Matt stood and put his arms around her, pulling her to his chest. She was wound tighter than a spring.

"Nothing," she said flatly.

He turned her around, but she wouldn't look at him. "I know this is fast, Soph, but I need to make a decision about my future. Now that Mom and Dad and Tuck are all gone, there's nothing to hold me here, especially if you all decide to sell this place and you go back to your life in Nashville."

"I told you I won't agree to sell." She clenched her teeth.

Matt bent down to look into her eyes. "I need to know how you feel about me, Peanut, because . . ." He took a deep breath and stepped off the cliff. "I'm still in love with you after all these years, as crazy as that sounds. But if you're going to walk out of my life again, I need to move on."

"How am I supposed to know?" She looked up at him with fear in her eyes. "I just got here."

"Do you love me, Soph? Do you think you *could* love me? Because if you do, I'll rip up those papers right now."

When she stepped away from him and put her hands into her back jeans pockets, his heart fell.

"I don't know," she said. "I don't know if what I'm feeling is love or if I still have a teenage crush on you."

He pulled her to him, and she slid her arms around his waist, leaning her head against his heart.

"You're the only one who knows the answer to that," he said softly. "All I know is that I love you. I've always loved you, and I think I always will. But you have to feel the same way if I'm going to base life decisions on us having a future together."

"I know," she mumbled into his shirt. "But I'm afraid, Matt." Sophie tilted her head back and searched his face. "I'm afraid you'll end up leaving like my dad did."

"I won't."

"But how do I know? I don't know why Tuck left. What if you get restless or angry or decide you've made a mistake and just walk away? I'm not sure I can take that chance."

"Life is full of unknowns. We can either stand on the beach or get our feet wet. Maybe you need to spend some time praying about this. Nothing I say will convince you if you don't believe in us. Love takes a lot of faith, Peanut."

She stepped back from him again and pulled the scrunchie out of her hair, letting the auburn waves tumble to the top slope of her shoulders. He wanted to run his hands through its silky strands, but he resisted.

"Yeah, I guess it does," she said. "But I'm not sure I have that kind of faith. Mama did, and look how things turned out for her. Besides, I haven't been to church in a long time."

He sighed and leaned his hand on the mantle, studying all the names on the stockings Jo-Jo had hung there. Even when she didn't know whether her sisters would come home for Christmas, Jo-Jo had still hung a stocking for each of them, convinced that God would answer her prayers.

Matt turned and looked into Sophie's steely-blue eyes that changed color with her mood. He gave her a loving smile. "I have enough faith for both of us. I'll pray the Lord will give you the assurance you need, but you also have to seek him out for yourself. That's a relationship you've got to repair on your own. I do know this. Until the ice melts off the roads, and I pull out of your driveway, I'll be here for you. I'll stay through Christmas."

She looked at the colorfully wrapped presents under the giant Virginia pine and nodded her head. "I think I'll head down to the stable and throw some more pellets into the stove. I need to . . . be alone for a while." With a gulp, she added, "I never expected this when I came home, Matt."

"Neither did I," he said and caressed her cheek. He planted a quick, soft kiss on her cheek, but not the one he wanted to share with her. That would come later.

I hope.

Sophie sat on a scarred, wooden stool and rubbed oil into the dry leather of a halter. Most of the equipment was in good shape, but the ranch hands hadn't gotten around to taking care of everything. Matt had told her Jed had taken a job at one of the local horse farms to help pay the taxes until the estate could be settled. Not many men would have done that, but Jed was a Weatherly, too.

Matt Weatherly had never failed her until he left when he was eighteen. She was in love with the boy who had dropped a garter snake around her neck to scare her, but also the one who sat beside her in companionable silence while they fished for sun perch. What kind of man had he become? His experiences of the world were far broader than hers. He had seen things she would never see. He had served in a war zone.

Since she was a kid, she had breathed, slept, and lived for horses. She studied everything there was to know about a horse. She knew every bone, muscle, tendon, organ, and all the diseases that could affect them. She knew how to communicate with horses and how to doctor them back to health. Her life focus had narrowed to a horse-shaped pinpoint.

At some juncture—probably after her dad walked away—Sophie had learned to depend on no one but herself, especially not God. He never answered her prayers about bringing her dad home, so why should she trust him now?

Sophie dipped her rag into the can of oil and rubbed it liberally on the left lead and wondered . . . had God abandoned her or had she abandoned God? A prickle in her heart answered her question. She had given up on him. When she was still in college, she occasionally attended church on campus, but after a while she couldn't get up on Sunday morning after a hard week of studying. And that was that. No more church.

Once she finished oiling the tack, she hung it to dry and washed her hands with Lava soap in ice-cold water, hoping they'd get power back soon. The sun shone brightly today, and the ice on the coated trees had started to melt. The large thermometer on the porch had registered thirty-three degrees when she left the house.

What was Matt doing? She thought he might follow her down to the stable and convince her to take a chance on a relationship with him. He loved her. Why had he never told her?

After throwing more pellets into the wood stove, she plopped down on the same hay bale and leaned back against her namesake's stall. Sophie whinnied and blew the hair on the top of her head. Smiling, she reached up and stroked the mare's soft nose.

"What would you do, Soph? Would you take a chance on Matt?" The horse nickered. "I'm sure you would, being best buds and all."

After a few silent moments, she clamped her eyes shut and tried to remember how to pray.

Lord? Are you still there? This is Sophie Tucker. I know it's been a long time since we last talked, but I wanted to tell you . . . I'm sorry I blamed everything that happened with my daddy on you. You didn't make him leave. I know that now. Mama didn't blame you, so I don't know why I did. I was just a kid, I guess.

She sighed and lifted her face. *I suppose you know what Matt told me—*

that he loves me and all. He wants to know if I feel the same way. I don't know what to tell him. Maybe if you and I were on speaking terms again, you'd let me know what I should do.

A Scripture rose in her mind even though she couldn't remember where it was from in the Bible: *I will never leave thee, nor forsake thee.* Peace flooded into her heart. She closed her eyes, and let her namesake nuzzle her cheek. It made her smile.

She remembered the story about Jesus sitting and talking with a group of little children who surrounded him. The disciples basically said He was wasting his time—that there were more important people to talk to. But instead of agreeing with his disciples, he scolded them.

In some ways, she still felt like that little girl her father had deserted. She had been stumbling through life ever since, but evidently, Tuck had come to the Lord and received forgiveness. She needed to forgive him . . . and ask God to forgive her for blaming Him.

Please, Lord, hear my prayer. I forgive my daddy for leaving Mama and me and my sisters. I don't understand why he left, but I know I need to forgive him for it. I choose to forgive him. I'm glad he made peace with you before his passing.

Please forgive me for blaming you, too. It wasn't your fault. Even though we're your children, you give us the freedom to make our own choices. Sometimes we make bad ones. I want to make good choices from now on. I want to be like one of those little children and lay my head in your lap and my burdens at your feet.

A tear squeezed from the corner of her eye as she pictured herself as a little girl resting at Jesus' feet.

Please tell me what I should do. Is it your will that I love Matt with my whole heart and trust him? Everything in me wants to. I know it will take a leap of faith. Please help me to step out into the unknown and trust you to catch me. I love you, Lord. I really, really do. Amen.

Sophie wiped the tears from her eyes with both hands. She sniffed and wished Matt were there to lend her a hankie. She didn't know what she had decided about the future, but she knew she loved Matt. She had loved him her whole life, and she wanted to believe he would be there if she decided to take that leap of faith.

Sighing, she slipped her arms back into her work jacket and zipped it before putting on her gloves. The stove had enough pellets to burn a few more hours, the horses were warm and toasty, and she needed to spend some time with Matt.

When Matt heard the back door close, he quickly returned the small photo album he'd put together for Tuck and set it on the side table beside the bed. When the old Marine knew he was dying of lung cancer, he'd asked Matt to go through all the family picture albums for the best ones of his wife, daughters, and the rest of the family. Matt's favorite was a picture of Sophie and him, hanging upside down from a tree limb about twenty feet off the ground. Tuck had taken it. If Sophie's mother had seen them, she might've grounded her daughter for a month.

He buttoned a second red-flannel shirt on top of the one he already wore from Tuck's wardrobe. The pants were a little long, but at least he hadn't needed to wear the same clothes since he'd been stuck here. Not that he was complaining about their forced confinement. It had given him the chance he needed to finally share his feelings with Sophie. He hoped he hadn't made a big mistake and spooked her.

When he walked into the great room, Sophie was pulling a knitted hat off her head. Static electricity turned her hair into a horse's tail, and he couldn't help but laugh.

"What's so funny?" She leaned one hand against the mantle and tugged off her boots.

"Nothing," he said, grinning.

"That's the first peep I've heard out of him since you've been down at the stable," Aunt Sarah said, wrapping some yarn around a needle. Her hands stilled. "He's been moping around here like he lost his best friend."

"I have not," he said, shoving his hands into his pants pockets. "I just didn't feel like talking."

"That'd be a first," his aunt said.

Sophie grinned at him. "She's got a point. You're definitely an extrovert."

"The way he can tell a story, he shoulda gone into sales."

Matt flopped down at one end of the leather sofa and crossed a leg over his knee. "It's a good skill for a nurse. Haven't you ever heard laughter is the best medicine?"

"He's got a point, Sarah," Sophie said, sitting on the other end of the sofa, still wearing her stained down jacket.

Matt sniffed deeply. "Hey, what's that perfume you're wearing? Eau de horse manure?"

"Ha, ha," she shot back. "It's a good thing we both smell like horses or we wouldn't be able to stand each other. I'd kill for a hot shower about now."

"You and me both," he said. "I haven't felt this grubby since . . . well, maybe ever."

"You poor little thing," Aunt Sarah said, looking at Matt with a twinkle in her eyes. "It's a good thing you were born in this century—"

"I wasn't," he sassed. "You need a calendar?"

"You know what I meant, Mr. Smarty Pants. In the old days, they never took baths during the winter. Thought they'd come down with the *ague*."

Sophie, who wore pink- and orange-striped socks, pulled one leg under her, looking for all the world like the teenage girl he once knew so well. "What on earth is the *ague*? Sounds like something that could kill you."

Matt lifted his finger in the air. "Actually, I know the answer to this one. I had to take a medical history class once. You'd be amazed at all the diseases we've eradicated."

"You're not auditioning for *Jeopardy*, you know," Sophie said, raising an eyebrow.

Matt uncrossed his leg and turned toward the woman he loved. "A lot of people think ague was the modern-day flu or pneumonia, but actually, it was probably malaria. Sweating, chills, violent shivering."

"Oh, how delightful," Sophie said. "Thank heaven for the discovery of antibiotics."

"And bathtubs with showers," Sarah said dryly.

Suddenly, the Christmas tree lights came back on, Bing Crosby sang *I'll Be Home for Christmas* on the stereo next to Tuck's old chair, and the lamp beside Sophie cast a soft, flattering glow on her pink-tinged cheeks. Best of all, the furnace kicked on with a *thud*.

"Hallelujah!" Aunt Sarah said, setting her knitting aside and grabbing the bag of Fritos. "Anybody else want some hot tea?"

"No thanks," he and Sophie said at the same time, their eyes locking.

"I'll be in the kitchen then," she said, walking briskly out of the room. "I've been craving chocolate all day. Now I can bake a pan of fudge brownies. Maybe I've got some Reese's Pieces in the pantry, too."

As Sarah banged around in the cupboard, Matt scooted closer to Sophie and put his arms around her, easing her toward him, enjoying the warm feel of her next to him. She tucked her head into the hollow of his shoulder and sighed. He had been afraid she might run like a jackrabbit. Instead, she snuggled closer to him as if it was the most natural thing in the world. He had wanted to kiss her since he was fifteen; but now he was a man, and he realized Sophie was the love of his life. It made a difference. If he kissed her the way he wanted to now, he wasn't sure he could stop.

Barely able to breathe, his heart thudding in his chest, he finally coaxed himself away and cupped her face with his hands. "You don't know how long I've waited to kiss you, Peanut—"

Her eyes twinkled. "Probably as long as I've wanted you to." She leaned toward him, but he stood up and reached out with his hand.

"—but I think we should wait a little longer before I do something to get me in trouble. Maybe we should take a walk."

CHAPTER SIX

L et's not. I'd rather sit here with you."

Sophie pulled Matt back down on the sofa and laid her head in the hollow of his shoulder again. He made her feel safe and . . . treasured . . . loved. He started to say something, but she put her fingers to his lips. "Shh . . ."

"Does this mean—"

"This means I love you, Matt," she said with a touch of sadness in her voice. "I always have, and I always will." She cuddled closer, not wanting the moment to end. But . . . Matt wanted an answer, and she didn't have one yet.

"Does that mean we—"

To shut him up, she put her hand over his mouth and then traced the line of his jaw with her finger.

Matt moved back and searched her face, pure love in his eyes, a smile on his face.

It kind of scared her. She stood abruptly and put her hands into her back pockets, creating some distance between them.

"What?" He stood and took her by the shoulders, his eyes fastened on hers. "Does this mean you want me to stay, Soph?"

Looking down, she kicked at the nubby area rug with the toe of her boot. "Yes."

He whooped, picked her up off the floor, and swung her in a circle. Then he gave her a big smacking kiss on her cheek and pulled back with a wide grin on his face, only to let it fade when he saw her serious expression. "What's the matter?"

"I love you, and I don't want you to leave."

"I hear a *but* coming." Slowly, he let his arms drop and stepped back, his expression guarded. "If you're going to break my heart, just do it. I'm a big believer in ripping off the Band-Aid fast."

"I just need more time," she said, trying not to sound desperate or whiny. "I did what you asked. Jesus and I are talking to each other again."

Matt's face softened. "I don't think He ever stopped talking to you."

She shrugged her flannel-clad shoulders. "I suppose I was the one who stopped talking to Him . . . and to you . . . and to Tuck."

"You're still having a hard time referring to him as your dad." He sat in Tuck's old leather chair and tugged her down onto the arm.

"You playing Santa Claus now?" she joked, but he didn't let her off the hook.

"Have you forgiven your dad for leaving you?"

She nibbled her lower lip. "Yes, I think so. I don't hate him anymore. I'm trying to see him through adult eyes."

"Forgiveness is a choice, Peanut, not a feeling. Feelings change, but if you've forgiven him, the feelings will follow eventually."

"It's still hard for me to trust anyone, even though I prayed about it. I've been on my own, making my own decisions, for a long time."

"So have I," Matt said, stroking her arm, "but people change, especially when they lay down their will at the foot of the cross. Let Jesus change your heart."

Sophie looked back at him. "I prayed about us, but I don't have an answer yet. Can we go back to just being good friends—at least until after Christmas?"

"I think we're way beyond *good friends*," he said.

She smiled and stroked his cheek, and he reached over to trace her bottom lip with his thumb.

A tingle of electricity shot through her. One thing she couldn't deny was their attraction, but could she really trust him not to leave her? She needed more time to figure that out—to pray about their relationship and where it was going. When she was a kid, Sophie was fearless. But once Tuck and Matt exited her life, she had started to question every step she took.

Sophie ran her fingers through Matt's sandy-blond hair. "Your hair's sticking up."

"You should see yours," he said, chuckling.

She smacked him on his bicep. "You're supposed to tell me how beautiful I am."

"Okay, you're beautiful. You're changing the subject again."

"Instead of talking," she said, standing and offering her hand, "let's go join Sarah, and we can make Christmas treats together. We always made Christmas cookies with Mama."

Matt groaned and held his stomach. "Jo-Jo and Bella made enough Christmas cookies to supply Santa and all the elves for the next twelve months."

"I didn't find any."

"I guess Jed, Dave, and the hands ate them all."

"I could always make you a kale salad. Yum, nice and healthy."

He slapped the other arm of Tuck's chair. "Christmas cookies it is. Kale tastes like a pot scrubber."

A couple of days later, a warm wind blew in from the south, and the ice melted off the trees and the blacktop road.

"By tomorrow, we can hook a chain to your pickup and pull it out of the ditch," Matt said as he leaned his arms on the kitchen island, watching Sophie mix up more cookie dough. He was afraid to ask what kind these were. The first several batches had been inedible or burned to a crisp. "I can probably make it home today if I'm careful."

"It froze again last night," she said, avoiding his gaze. "Lots of black ice. You probably should stay another night to be on the safe side."

"So you want me to stay, huh?" He grinned at her, but she concentrated on dropping spoonfuls of dough on the cookie sheet. She didn't answer, and his heart sank a little lower.

Maybe he was wasting his time. Sophie had avoided the topic of a future together whenever he tried to bring it up the past couple of days. So he had given her space, but maybe he'd given her too much of it.

"You wanna lick the bowl?" She looked up at him and popped a fingerful of dough into her mouth.

"Nah, I don't think so. What kind are these?"

"Chocolate chip. Sarah stocked up at Sam's Club before the holidays. The recipe is on the bag, so I didn't think I could mess it up. We're about out of everything else though. I should probably call Jo-Jo and ask her to stop by the store on the way home."

"Have you even told her you made it home?"

"Not yet."

"How come?" Why wouldn't she have called to let her little sister know she was home, especially since Jo-Jo had wanted all of her sisters there for Christmas?

"I don't know," she said, shrugging. She grabbed the old red bowl he remembered from childhood and set it in the sink, then popped the cookie sheet in the oven. "I didn't want to disappoint her in case I decided to turn around and head back to Nashville. Then the storm blew in, and you know the rest. My cell died."

He looked down at the island and twirled the salt shaker. "You could have called her after you charged it up—let her know you were here."

"I guess."

"You planning on running out on all of us before she gets home?" His question was pointed, but he meant it to be.

Her head snapped up, and her eyes flashed with anger. "What's that supposed to mean?"

"It means I'm not sure what you want out of life, Sophie. You say you want to start a vet clinic here . . . you tell me you love me . . . but you won't talk to me about any of it. I want a future with you, but I have a tough decision to make, and all you want to do is kid around and avoid the subject."

"That's not fair!"

"Isn't it?" he pressed. "I'm not a teenager anymore."

"That's for sure," she muttered. "You were more fun then."

Without a word, Matt stood, grabbed his coat and hat off the hook by the back door, and opened it. He didn't even look back.

"Where are you going?" she asked, her voice wavering.

He looked over his shoulder. "Home. Tell Aunt Sarah I'll see her later."

With that, he closed the door and walked through the slush toward his pickup truck.

———

When Sophie opened the back door and stepped out, avoiding the icy patches in the shade, she watched Matt drive toward the main road. He made a right turn and drove out of her life—*for good?* Her heart beat in her throat, and it felt as though a horse had fallen on her chest. Then . . . she got mad, stepped back inside, and slammed the door.

"What in tarnation is going on in here?" Sarah said, walking in from the laundry room, folding a dark-blue towel.

Sophie grabbed a dish towel and viciously wiped flour and bits of dough from the kitchen island, most of it landing on the wood floors. "Matt left and went home. He said to tell you he'd see you later."

"Just like that? Why'd he slam the door?"

"I slammed it." Sophie clamped her jaw tight and continued to scrub the island, pushing more of the mess to the floor.

"So what did you fight about?"

"Nothing."

"He wants to marry you, and you wouldn't give him an answer." Sarah dropped the towel on a stool, planted her hands on her hips, and shook her head.

Sophie looked up, her jaw dropping open. "How did you know?"

"Because he told me. Both of you are stubborn as mules—headstrong—not wanting to give an inch."

"I don't like feeling pressured." Sophie grabbed the broom from behind the door and made a worse mess on the floor, scattering flour everywhere. "I need time to think."

"Pressured? You've loved that man since you were kids. If you take any more time to think about how you feel, you'll be an old lady like me. You either know, or you don't know."

Sophie didn't have an answer. She grabbed the dust pan and swept most of the crumbs into it before dumping them into the white plastic trash can.

"Did you hear what I said, Miss Sophie Pants?"

"Yes, ma'am."

Sarah slid onto the other wooden stool and patted the black-marble counter. "Do you love him?"

Sophie looked into Sarah's sympathetic eyes and nodded.

"Then what's the problem, girl?"

Sophie leaned against the island and dropped her head into her hands, her auburn ponytail falling to one shoulder. "I don't know. All I keep thinking about is Tuck leaving Mama. They supposedly loved each other, and look how they ended up."

Sarah reached over and pulled Sophie's hands away from her face. "Come here, Sophie Pants." She picked up the bath towel and patted the stool beside her. Sophie sighed, rounded the island, and slumped down on the seat. "Just because your mama and daddy had problems doesn't mean you and Matt will. There's more to their story than you know. Your daddy always felt like a failure, trying to live up to his father's expectations. Your granddaddy was a hard man. This horse farm produced Derby winners in the past, and he expected the same from Tuck."

"I don't remember much about him."

"He died younger than he should have—heart attack. It's no wonder, the way he let his temper fly."

"But that doesn't explain why Tuck left *us*. Why did he leave Mama all alone to run this place?"

"Honey, this horse farm has been in your family for generations, but your daddy didn't want to spend his days racing thoroughbreds. It meant everything to your grandpa, but Tuck just didn't have the heart for it. From the time he was a boy, he wanted to be an officer in the Marine Corps, but your granddaddy wasn't about to pay for his college tuition if he pursued it. Since your daddy had to pay for college on his own, he stayed in Kentucky and went to Western in Bowling Green. They've had a military leadership program there since the first World War. That's where he met your mama and married her as soon as he graduated."

"Mama married him even though he wanted to run off and join the Marines?"

"Yes, she did, with her eyes wide open. She just didn't fully realize what she was signing up for. Your daddy always felt that leadership in the Marines was what he was meant to do, the one thing he was really good at. The Marines . . . now that was where he excelled.

"The big problem between your mama and daddy was that the Marines eventually came first—over her and you girls. It wasn't until he was close to retirement that he realized the men he trained and led always moved on or out. They had wives and kids. They had lives besides the military. By the time he realized his only sense of stability and security came from his family and the legacy of this horse farm, it was too late. Your mama was gone, and you girls had gone off in your own directions. That's when Matt invited him to church."

"Daddy never went to church with us."

"I know. His faith came late in life. After a few sermons, he realized the Marines had become his god and that's when the Lord got ahold of his heart. He became a different man than the one you knew, Sophie."

Tears burned at the back of Sophie's eyes. "He was?"

"Mm-hm. Totally different. He had the light of Christ in his eyes, and he spent many an hour sitting in that old chair of his, reading the Scriptures. He told Matt he regretted so many things, but he especially regretted leaving Marlena and you girls to fend for yourselves while he went out to slay the dragons."

Sophie played with the crumbs still on the island, rolling them into a ball of dough in her fingers.

Sarah placed her hand over Sophie's with a sigh. "Near the end," she went on, "he wanted to tell you how much he loved you and how sorry he was for leaving you. His only comfort was the thought that he would spend eternity with you girls and your mama. He talked a lot about that once he got sick. Matt was right by his side when he slipped away, you know. Tuck told him he saw the Lord holding out his hand. His face glowed when he passed."

Silent tears ran down Sophie's face, and Sarah pulled her into a hug. "Matt isn't your daddy, sugar. My nephew loves the Lord with all his heart and soul, but he loves you, too, and he would give up the world for you. He'd be happy as a clam to settle down on this farm with you."

Sophie swiped at her tears with both hands and grabbed a paper napkin from the holder to blow her nose. "I've really messed things up, haven't I?"

"Pretty much," Sarah said matter-of-factly. "If I were you, I'd give him a call and ask him to come back."

"You think he would?"

"You'll never know unless you do it. There comes a time in life when you have to choose one side of the fence or the other. You can't just straddle it all your life. Are you gonna live the life God has planned for you or be paralyzed by fear the rest of your days?" Suddenly, Sarah sniffed and looked over at the oven. "Something's burning."

"Oh, no! Not again."

Sophie jumped off the stool and raced to open the oven door. A cloud of dark smoke billowed out, choking both of them. The smoke alarm went off with deafening shrieks.

"Throw 'em to the birds," Sarah yelled.

While Sophie opened the back door and tossed the whole cookie sheet into the melting snow, Sarah retrieved a clean dish towel from the drawer and waved it in front of the smoke detector until the alarm shut off.

"All I hope is you can make enough money as a vet to hire a cook," Sarah said, coughing. "Otherwise, you and Matthew will surely starve to death."

CHAPTER SEVEN

After washing the dough off her fingers and eating the rest of the chocolate chips in an attempt to fill the aching hole inside her, Sophie closed her bedroom door and plopped down on the pale-yellow duvet.

Yellow. Bella's favorite color. And since neither Amy nor Sophie had cared much about how they decorated their room, Bella had taken it on and given it her own frou-frou style.

She stared at her cell phone, building up her courage, and finally dialed Matt's number. It went to voice mail after several rings. She hung up without leaving a message, uncertain about what to say anyway.

She redialed his number and again it went to voice mail. "This is Matt. I'm not available to take your call right now, but if you'll leave your number and a brief message, I'll get back to you as soon as I can." Sophie waited impatiently for the beep.

"Hi Matt, this is Sophie. Give me a call, will ya?" Then she hit the button to end the call.

Since she rarely checked her own voice mail, she decided to text him with the same message, then sat there for fifteen minutes, staring at her phone, willing him to text her back.

Nothing.

Her heart sank. Maybe he didn't want to talk to her. Maybe she'd blown her last chance with him. Defeated, she laid back on her pillow, clutching her cell to her chest.

When it rang, she startled, but the caller ID showed it was Jo-Jo. Even though she'd been at the house for almost a week, she still hadn't called her youngest sister to let her know she was home. At first, she didn't know whether she'd stay . . . until Matt poked his head in her truck window and smiled. She had been afraid to see Matt again—afraid he would break her heart. And now . . . she had broken his.

"Hey, sis, what's up?" she answered.

"What's up with you?" Jo-Jo asked. "Have you given any more thought to coming home for Christmas? Bella's here. We got caught in that blizzard that came through, and we've been stuck in Lexington at Mrs. Shaffer's house. The roads are almost clear though, except for a few patches of black ice. Just in case, we're waiting until morning to head back to the farm."

"I'm here," she said.

"What? Here *where*?"

"At the farm."

"You are?!" Jo-Jo squealed. "You really came home for Christmas? How long have you been there? Why didn't you call me?"

Sophie sat up and leaned against her white headboard. "I drove up in that same snowstorm. My truck's still in the ditch."

She heard a little gasp on the other end of the line. "Are you all right?"

"I'm fine," she reassured her little sister. "My cell went dead though. We didn't have power out here for a few days."

"Are you and Sarah okay? Did you stay warm enough? Jed called me and said Matt was stuck there, but he didn't say anything about you."

"Yes, we're all good."

Jo-Jo's voice took on a teasing tone. "You and Matt were trapped in the same house?"

Sophie rolled her eyes. "His Aunt Sarah was here, too."

"Did he kiss you?" she pressed. "Do you have anything juicy to tell me?"

"No . . . and besides it's none of your beeswax if he did. What time will you be home tomorrow?"

"Sometime around noon. We'll wait till the roads are clear and dry. Do you need anything? Can we stop at the store for you? You must be running low on everything."

"That would be great. We *are* out of pretty much everything. Oh, make sure to pick up more flour, sugar, and butter to make Mom's Christmas cookies."

"I'm so glad you decided to come home, Soph." Sophie experienced a pang of guilt for not calling her sister sooner. "Now if we can just persuade Amy to drive up from New Orleans, it will be a real Tucker Christmas."

Sophie sighed. "I wouldn't count on Amy, Sis. I don't want you to get your hopes up."

"I prayed you'd come, and now here you are. God can do anything!"

"I hope so," Sophie said, wishing it were so. "See ya tomorrow."

They said good-bye, and Sophie disconnected the call. While talking to Jo-Jo, she had received a text from Matt: *Sorry I missed you. I called a towing service to pull your pickup out of the ditch. Can you meet me about 11:30 tomorrow at the Bluegrass Bistro? Let's talk.*

Relief untied the knot in her stomach. He wanted to see her. She had so much to apologize for. She started to call him but had second thoughts.

What if he wanted to tell her he had signed his re-enlistment papers? She didn't want that kind of news over the phone. Plus, what she had to express needed to be said face-to-face. She just hoped he would listen. If not, she'd probably spend the rest of her life alone. What a thought. Life without Matt.

But it had to be a good sign that he wanted to talk, right? She remembered seeing Bella's Louis Vuitton suitcase propped against the dresser in her sister's bedroom. Makeup wouldn't be a problem. Bella always packed the expensive kind. Sophie hadn't styled her hair with a blow dryer and brush in so many years, she hoped she still knew how. Matt seemed to like her hair down.

She texted Matt back that she would meet him there. Then she glanced at the time on her cell phone and jumped to her feet. Time to go check on the horses. It had been easier with Matt here. But she was on her own now until Jed and the hands got back.

Walking down to the stable, slipping on the ice and snow that still covered the ground, she thought a lot about wanting to set up her vet practice here. But how could she ask her sisters to sell her the property for a rock-bottom price? Matt said the offer from Dan Wentworth was a really good one—more than fair.

She stuffed her gloved hands into her stained jacket. But what if Matt left town? She'd have no reason to stay. Maybe selling the property, no matter how much it pained her, would hurt less than living here without Matt.

Matt rinsed and dried off his one white plate before placing it in the cabinet next to his one cup and one glass. Before Sophie came home, he hadn't thought about how simply he lived. The small, one-bedroom house he had rented on the rural road had been converted from a garage. When his mother died and after he had sold her house, he didn't need a lot of elbow room anyway. Most of his inheritance had been used to pay off his school loans, so he was at least debt-free. Not a lot of people could say that.

He moved to the tiny living room and placed another log on the fire, staring at the flickering flames and wondering which turn his life would take: a future with Sophie or a career in the Marines. He knew which road he wanted to walk—but he wasn't sure Sophie could commit to him. He'd never fully realized how much Tuck's leaving had affected her.

Matt toed off his boots and kicked back in the oversized, brown-leather lounge chair he had splurged on. He crossed his hands behind his head and looked around the sparsely furnished room. Living by himself, he didn't need much: a modest flat-screen TV, his lounge chair, and a side table to hold a glass and a couple of fishing magazines.

When Tuck had taken sick—lung cancer—his hero had decided not to go the chemo route. Tuck was stage four, and the man didn't want to spend his last days on a therapy that would make him sick. Matt couldn't blame him. Not really. So before Tuck died, he'd spent most nights at the farm taking care of him, and this house was just a place to wash his clothes and eat takeout food.

As they usually did, his thoughts drifted back to Sophie. He practiced what he'd say to her, but he had no idea how she would react. Would she walk out on him, or listen to what he had to say? He was driving himself crazy with all the possible outcomes.

Matt reached over and picked up the remote, turning on the TV and flipping through the channels. He settled on Animal Planet and closed his eyes, letting the narrator's voice lull him to sleep.

Sophie woke up before daybreak. Not that she'd gotten much sleep the night before. Her mind had been like a freight train with no brakes, barreling down a mountain, shimmying this way and that. When it was obvious she couldn't sleep any longer, she got up, threw on her stable clothes, and made a cup of coffee while trying not to wake Sarah. They had stayed up late talking about all those things she had never known as a kid. So many secrets. So much going on with the adults in her life.

After mucking out the stalls, feeding and watering and brushing the horses, she stepped out of the stable and watched the sun rise. Its baby blues and pinks and golds streaked over the horizon, reminding her that no matter what happened between her and Matt, their relationship remained in God's hands.

When she opened the back door after returning from the stable, the smell of blueberry muffins beckoned. She hugged Sarah and gave her a kiss on the cheek.

"You're up early," the older woman said.

Sophie shrugged. "I woke up and couldn't go back to sleep."

Sarah wiped her hands on the apron tied around her waist. She was still dressed in her rose-pink robe. "Thinking about Matt?"

She pulled off her boots without answering and hung her coat on a peg by the door. "I need to wash my jacket today. Even I can't stand the smell of it anymore."

"Matt and I had a long phone conversation after you went to bed. My call woke him up."

Sophie padded over to the oven and turned on the light. The muffins were perfectly brown on top. After washing her hands, she grabbed a dish towel, took out the muffin pan, and set it on top of the stove. She almost burned her fingers when she grabbed one and dropped it on a plate.

"You're ignoring me, Sophie Pants," Sarah said.

Leaning on the kitchen island, she blew on the muffin and peeled off part of the steaming top—the best part. "No, I'm not."

"Coulda fooled me."

"Okay, so what did you talk about?"

The corners of Sarah's mouth turned upward. "Oh, so now you're curious."

"Maybe." A blueberry burned her tongue, and she rushed to the sink for a drink of water.

"I told him the same thing I'm gonna tell you." Sarah plucked the rest of the muffins out of the pan and piled them on a plate. "Get over yourself."

"What?"

"For a couple of risk-takers, you two have turned into cowards at too young an age." Sarah stood with one hand on her hip. "Both of you used to be fearless. Now you're dancing around each other, making up all kinds of excuses about why you can't take a chance on being together. And none of them hold water."

Sophie sat on a stool and slowly ate a bite of muffin, but she could hardly swallow past the lump in her throat. "He just walked out."

"He asked you to lunch, didn't he?"

"Yeah, probably to tell me he's leaving town. I'm not sure I'm going to the lunch. None of Bella or Jo-Jo's clothes fit me. All I've got with me are raggedy old jeans and T-shirts."

"Now if that isn't the most pathetic excuse I've ever heard." Sarah sounded disgusted with her.

"In high school, he only dated cheerleaders and homecoming queens. Look at me. Half the time, I've got manure on my boots and dirt under my fingernails." Sophie sighed and rested her chin in her hand.

"Last night, you were all set to have lunch with him. Don't chicken out now." Sarah walked around the island and took her crumb-covered hand. "Come with me."

CHAPTER EIGHT

The petite woman was stronger than she looked. Sarah dragged Sophie down the hallway to her mother's bedroom—her parents' bedroom. Opening the closet door, Matt's aunt pushed back the hangers with Tuck's clothes to reveal her mother's wardrobe.

"You saved Mama's clothes?"

"None of you girls wanted to go through her things when she passed. Then Tuck came home, and he sure didn't have the heart to let go of anything. There's a sweater outfit she used to wear to church somewhere in here." Sarah's voice sounded muffled as she made her way deeper into the closet. "Here it is." She poked her head out, beaming, and held up the soft blue sweater, trimmed with seed pearls. "It matches your eyes. I know the skirt will be too short, but you can try on a pair of her jeans. She always had to wear high heels, especially with her dressy jeans, because they were too long on her. You got a pair of flats with you?"

Sophie shook her head. "No."

"Well, we've got shoe polish under the bathroom sink. You can shine up those cowboy boots of yours. You'll be right in style."

"This sweater's awfully wrinkled," Sophie said, holding it up and sniffing it. The faint scent of her mother's perfume still clung to the fabric.

"Put it on a padded hanger on the curtain rod while you take a hot shower. Those wrinkles will come right out. Now go."

"You sure are bossy this morning," Sophie grumbled, feeling the nerves jumping in her stomach. Yesterday, she'd been eager to see Matt again. But in the light of day, she wasn't so sure.

"Somebody's got to take the reins. You two act like nervous, green-broke horses."

Sophie knew she was right. She loved Matt. He loved her. So what was her problem?

Straightening her shoulders, Sophie rifled through her mother's clothes until she found a newish pair of jeans that looked long enough for her. She could always tuck them inside her boots to hide the bottoms if they were too short.

"Good girl," Sarah said. "Now go make yourself pretty. I'm sure Bella's got a whole makeup collection tucked away in her suitcase. Not too much though. Matt likes you just the way you are. But a girl needs to look her best at the Bluegrass Bistro."

"It's that fancy?"

"Well, it's not Burger King."

While Sophie cleaned and polished her boots, Sarah called out to tell her the tow truck driver had pulled her pickup out of the ditch and moved it up toward the front steps of the house.

"Thanks, Sarah," she shouted back.

By the time she emerged from the shower, she was running a little behind. She used makeup sparingly—a light foundation, a little blush, eyeliner—not too dark—and some lipstick that flowed on like warm butter. Sarah helped tame her hair.

After they finished, Sophie examined herself in the mirror. How long had it been since she'd worn makeup? Not since her last date a couple of years ago with another vet. Bella's shampoo and conditioner must have cost a fortune. They had left her hair full and shiny, and Sarah had styled it into soft waves with the blow dryer and a large, round brush they found in Bella's things. She almost didn't recognize herself.

"You don't think it's too much for a lunch . . . thing?" She wasn't about to call it a date. She and Matt had never been on a date. This was just two friends getting together over coffee.

"Trust me," Sarah said. "It's not too much. You look like a prom queen. Now scoot before you're late."

Sophie furrowed her brow. "My truck's all muddy. Maybe I should hose it off first."

"Believe me, Sophie Pants, Matt's not gonna be looking at your truck." Sarah gave her a hug. "Now go and have fun." She nudged her toward the front door.

Sophie blew out a lungful of air. "I'm not sure when I'll be back. Anything you need at the store?"

"Forget the store! Now go before he thinks you stood him up."

"Yes, ma'am."

Sophie slipped into her good jacket, grabbed her old leather handbag, and pulled out her keys. After she opened the door of the Ford Ranger, she looked back at Sarah. She felt excited and scared all at the same time. "Pray for me."

"I've never stopped, sweetie."

Sophie closed the mud-splattered door, started the engine, and headed down the driveway, praying she wouldn't make an idiot of herself.

Sophie parked in front of the three-story, red-brick building with tall, white columns and a porch that spanned the length of the historical house. Like a lot of old mansions, the home in downtown Bluegrass Crossing had been rezoned for business and restored to its former glory. Although the large sign in the front yard read WENTWORTH PROPERTIES, a smaller, tasteful sign next to the front door designated it as the location of the BLUEGRASS BISTRO.

She opened the heavy wooden door with the etched-glass window. When she turned the silver knob and entered the foyer, she noticed another sign, marking the entryway into the bistro, which was obviously the former dining room of the mansion. She paused under the tall arch of polished, quarter-sawn oak, scanning the room for Matt. Since he was one of only a few customers, he was easy to spot when he stood and gave her a subtle smile. She suspected, however, that even if the room had been crowded with customers, his broad shoulders clad in a dark-brown wool blazer would have made him easy to spot. She wondered if he was as nervous as she was after their argument.

Clutching the strap of her black leather purse, she wove between the cute little bistro tables, the aroma of freshly brewed coffee permeating the air, and gave a cursory glance at the walls lined with photos of past

Kentucky Derby winners and colorful local artwork for sale. When she reached the table, Matt was still standing there, looking down at her. Finally, he pulled out the wooden café chair across from him.

"Hi," he finally said after returning to his seat, staring at her as though she were a prize thoroughbred. "You look . . . really nice."

"Thanks." He had never complimented her on how she looked. Nervously, she smoothed out a nonexistent wrinkle from the front of the soft, blue, cashmere sweater.

"Really, *really* nice."

Clearing her throat, she clasped her cold hands together on the cloth-covered tabletop and gave him a jittery smile, feeling a pink flush rise in her cheeks. "You don't look so bad yourself. I've never seen you in a blazer."

"Yeah, it's kind of new." His words sounded a bit stiff.

Could it get any more awkward between them? Had their fight totally destroyed their friendship? Unbidden, a memory of him flashed through her mind, and she couldn't help but giggle.

"What's so funny?"

"I take that back," she said, teasing him. "I remember the jacket you wore with that matching, baby-blue, ruffled shirt for your senior prom."

Matt groaned, which seemed to break the block of ice that had separated them. "Don't remind me. I suppose by the time your senior prom rolled around, baby-blue tuxes were out of style."

"Actually," she said, playing with the cut-glass salt shaker, "I didn't go to the prom. I was in the hospital having my appendix out."

A look of sympathy crossed his face. "Bummer."

"Tell me about it. I'd already bought my dress. I think my date was relieved he didn't have to go. He wasn't much of a dancer."

He chuckled and rubbed the back of his neck. "Neither was I."

Their gazes locked, and Matt suddenly reached over and covered her cold hand with his large, warm one. "I talked to Aunt Sarah last night."

Sophie nodded. "She told me."

He grimaced. "Did she tell you she gave me an earful?" He caressed the back of her hand with his thumb, sending tingles up her arm.

"She didn't let me off easy either."

"I'm sorry I walked out on you, Peanut. That wasn't fair."

Sophie shrugged, and her pulse beat a little faster. "I didn't exactly make it easy on you. I'm sorry I was such a brat."

"I should have been more understanding, not pressured you so much. It's just that I've already wasted so much time. I should have come looking for you years ago."

Matt took her other hand, and her stomach fluttered when he continued to caress her skin. She wanted to reach across the table and smooth his brow—trace every line on his sun-kissed face. Every fiber in her wanted to lean forward and feel his warm lips on hers.

"It's not your fault, Matt. You couldn't have found me anyway. I was too busy hiding from Tuck . . . from everybody, really. I thought if I moved on and made a new life for myself—cut all ties with my past—the pain of you both leaving would go away."

"Did it?"

"No, of course not. I needed to face my feelings instead of stuffing them down. When I talked to your Aunt Sarah last night, she told me a lot of things about Daddy I didn't know—about how he was raised. He made a terrible mistake when he left us, but it was unfair of me to judge you by the same yardstick I used to judge him." She squeezed his hands and gave him a soft smile. "I'm glad you were with him at the last. At least he had someone who loved him."

"I'm glad he found the Lord before he passed on. That gives me some comfort."

Sophie nodded in agreement.

"But I didn't ask you here to talk about Tuck," Matt said, staring intently into her eyes, his expression serious. His words stabbed her heart with fear. Had he re-enlisted already?

When he let go of her hands and stood, she wondered if he might walk out on her. Her mouth felt dry with dread. Instead, he dropped to one knee just as another couple entered the dining room—and he took her left hand in his.

Her eyes widened. "Matt!"

Unexpectedly, he grinned and winked at her. "You deserve the full deal." He reached into his pocket and pulled out a gold engagement ring with a single diamond. "Sophie Tucker, will you marry me?"

"For real?" she squeaked.

"For real. Forever and ever, till death do us part."

She couldn't think. Or breathe, for that matter. All Sophie could do was . . . nod.

"Is that a yes?" he asked, looking hopeful.

Taking that leap of faith, believing God had brought them back together at just the right time, she silenced the voices of doubt, inhaled sharply, and said, "Yes!"

Matt tried to slip the ring on her finger, but it was too small. "This was my mama's engagement ring. I can buy you another one that you like better." His brow knit into a V.

"No." Sophie took the ring from him and slid it onto the pinkie of her left hand. "It's beautiful. We can have a jeweler resize it later."

While they had focused on each other, the lunch crowd had thickened. Choruses of congratulations and applause rang out from the patrons and bistro employees.

"Now could you get up?" Sophie whispered, embarrassed at the fuss they had caused.

Matt pushed up off his knee and sat back down, not letting go of her hand. "I love you, Sophia Rose."

Trying to hide her smile, she growled in her throat. "You know I hate that name."

He laughed. "You better get used to it. The pastor will use your full, given name at our wedding."

Despite their audience, they leaned forward and gave each other a quick kiss. Sophie sighed. She hoped the touch of his lips would always make her heart leap and send warm honey through her veins, like it did just then. How would it feel when he finally kissed her . . . *really* kissed her?

The waitress interrupted. "I hate to break into your romantic moment, but can I get you anything? Coffee, tea, water—"

At the same time, they both replied, "Sweet tea, please."

"Sweet tea it is. Have you made a decision about what you'd like?"

"Oh yeah," Sophie said, giggling. "I think I'll have a big slice of pecan pie with lots and lots of real whipped cream."

"She's kidding," he said, looking up at the server.

Sophie sat up straighter. "No, I'm not."

"You don't want a sandwich? Soup and salad? They make a fantastic baked potato soup."

Sophie didn't even look at the menu in front of her. She leaned over and squeezed his hand. "Don't you remember what your Aunt Sarah always said?"

Matt looked puzzled and then a light went off in his eyes. "Life is hard. Eat dessert first."

"Exactly," she said, smiling, love for him thrumming through her entire being—spirit, body, and soul. "I think it's about time we ate dessert first."

"Pecan pie, it is," Matt said, grinning at the waitress. "And don't be stingy with the whipped cream on top."

Please Come Home for Christmas

by LENORA WORTH

Dear Amy,

I'm sure it will be a surprise to you if the investigator locates you and delivers this letter into your hands. You're my oldest daughter, and I haven't so much as looked into your eyes or heard your voice in years.

I want you to know that when I called you after coming back from overseas, I didn't blame you for hanging up on me. You were old enough to understand how dramatically I failed the family when your mom and I split, and wise enough to know you didn't want any part of me afterward.

I'm so sorry, honey. I wish we could have talked just one more time before the cancer took me. I feel sure you grew into a woman who's strong and kind, and I only want to make sure you know that, with all my faults and weaknesses, I've loved you with my whole heart for my entire life.

I've left the horse farm to you and your sisters. Do with it as you see fit. Just know this: I've made my peace with the God your mom pointed toward every day of her life, and I want to believe I've made my peace with you as well. Sweet daughter, I'll love you always.

Tuck

If you forgive anyone's sins, their sins are forgiven; if you do not forgive them, they are not forgiven.

—John 20:23

CHAPTER ONE

"Order up!"

Amy Tucker Brosseau folded the wrinkled piece of paper and put it back in the pocket of the old sweater she usually wore while working the early morning shift at the Garden District Dish Café. She'd read the letter from her now-deceased daddy several times over in the last few weeks, but the shock of seeing his words there on the stark white paper always left her feeling cold and empty.

"Hey, I need more coffee."

Grabbing the French toast and bacon from the pass-through window, Amy hurried by the man holding up his coffee cup. "Be right back, Mr. Purdue."

Amy set the order down on the old oak table that shined with an aged patina. "Okay, anything else for you folks?"

The newlyweds didn't even bother answering. Instead, they both started cutting into the shared plate of thick brioche French toast while gazing into each other's eyes with a sweetness that rivaled the powdered sugar on the golden bread. Amy envied their happiness . . . and their honeymoon.

New Orleans was beautiful during the Christmas season.

And the Garden Dish, as the locals liked to call the café, was always busy from Thanksgiving through New Year's Day.

Amy's feet hurt just thinking about the next couple of weeks of holiday frenzy. But she needed this job since Timothy had a long list ready for Santa. Amy's focus had to be on her seven-year-old son, no matter how many times her sister Jo-Jo called to convince her that she was needed at the rundown, failing Kentucky horse farm their wayward daddy, Tuck, had left them after he died from cancer.

All three of her younger sisters were back in Bluegrass Crossing now. Joanna, Bella, and Sophie had all returned after they'd received letters from Tuck following his death. Over the last month, they'd come home one by one to decide what to do with the once-thriving horse farm. At first, they'd all agreed to sell it and be done. But in a twist that could only happen in the Tucker family, each of her sisters had found true love right there in good old Kentucky. Now they were all leaning toward keeping the ranch and making it grand again with the help of the men in their lives. She was the last holdout. No man, no urge to go back, and no energy to save the Tucker ranch.

Amy knew she should feel something for the daddy she called Tuck, but each time she thought of the ranch back in Kentucky, she also thought of her mama. And then she got angry all over again. She missed Mama with all her heart. But she couldn't conjure up any sympathetic emotions for her father. Except maybe a side of regret to go with that simmering anger.

Robert J. Tucker had lived and breathed the Marine Corps and had served way beyond the call of duty while his wife and four girls tried to keep up the horse farm that had been in the Tucker family for generations. Even now, the ranch hobbled along as a rehab center for retired racehorses, a place where an aging star could be retrained to become a family horse or be trained as a therapy horse. People brought their children there to learn how to ride or to experience being around those truly magnificent animals.

But Amy left all of that behind after her mother died. She headed to Nashville with her high school sweetheart, Tim. After they were married, she worked part-time and took a couple of college courses before they moved to New Orleans. Tim was electrocuted two years back in a freak accident down at one of the shipyards. Now her daddy was gone, too. The Marine Corps father who'd been absent from their lives for the most part had left his four grown daughters strapped with a money pit.

You won't have to work three different jobs if you pack up and go home to live on the farm.

Home to Kentucky.

Home to the ranch, a place she'd left with the solid plan of never going back. Ever.

You need to learn forgiveness, her other sister Sophie had suggested. Amy bristled at the thought.

She finished her shift, smiling at tourists and ignoring early morning rudeness with a practiced disconnect that came from being too tired to care and headed home. Her cell rang just before she pulled into the driveway of Tim's sister's house a block from Magazine Street where Amy and Timothy lived over the garage in a tiny pied-à-terre that Amanda and Ricky usually rented out to strangers. When they'd offered it to her, Amy had insisted on paying rent, but her sister-in-law had given her the lowest possible rate. Thankful, she had pushed the memory of Tim's death and the grief that followed out of her mind. She had to stay strong for Timothy and provide for him. He missed his daddy so much.

Amy pressed the call button and answered. "Hello," she said, silently wishing Sophie and her two other sisters wouldn't keep badgering her about coming to Kentucky for Christmas.

"Listen, I know you don't want to hear any of this, but we really need to talk."

Amy climbed out of her rattletrap car and slammed the groaning door. "Make it quick. I have thirty minutes before I have to head out on my bus route. Middle-schoolers don't like to wait to get home."

Sophie sighed and Amy pictured her sister pushing at her thick auburn hair, her steely-blue eyes flashing an unseen message over the phone lines. "We have someone very interested in buying the ranch, remember?"

Amy stopped halfway up the stairs, a rush of so many emotions spilling over inside her brain that she had to grab the hand railing. Her sister had mentioned a large real estate company wanting to buy them out, but Sophie hadn't been too thrilled about it. Amy hadn't pushed the matter, but she was so ready to be done with the place.

"Go on."

"He's from Lexington but has an office in Bluegrass Crossing—Dan Wentworth with Wentworth Properties. He wants to develop our land into some sort of fancy subdivision. At first, I was against it, but now

I'm not sure. Jo-Jo and Bella are sure they don't want to sell. We want to make a final decision, but we need your input."

"How much is he offering?"

Sophie named a hefty price. "We don't want to move on this until—"

"Move," Amy said, wondering after hearing the number why Sophie would hesitate. "Convince Jo-Jo and Bella to change their minds. We could all use that money. I'd finally be able to finish my business degree and maybe buy a house for Timothy and me." Amy felt a glimmer of hope thinking about her share of the money.

"Amy?"

Amy pulled out of her daydreams. "What?"

"Jo-Jo and Jed are set in stone, and Bella has fallen in love with David all over again. They both seem pretty sure they're going to stay here. And . . . Matt and I . . . we've grown very close."

Amy closed her eyes and touched two fingers to her pounding head. "Define very close."

"He's asked me to marry him. And I accepted."

"Can't get any closer than that. I thought you said he wanted to reenlist in the Marines."

"He's decided to stay here with me. As an RN now, he can find work anywhere."

Amy wanted to scream, "Traitor!" But she couldn't call her sister that, no matter her own pain. She'd found love once and lost it. Why should she deny any of her sisters the same?

"Sounds like I'm outnumbered."

"No, don't look at it that way," Sophie said. "But you need to come home and . . . at least see the place before we make a decision. We've done a lot of work, but we still need to do more. We won't feel right going any further on this without you. And we don't want to do anything until after Christmas anyway."

Amy stopped on the tiny landing where she'd placed a lacy wrought-iron bistro set so she could enjoy morning coffee amid the tall palms and the ancient banana tree fronds shooting up in Amanda's courtyard. She and Timothy had decorated it with white sparkling lights for the holidays. "I have to work, Soph."

"You won't be driving that bus during the Christmas break, right?"

"No, but I still have the café to consider, and I have pastry orders to fill."

Her third job involved baking and selling her own luscious desserts. The diner had been showcasing her work, so she had a pretty steady following and a lot of Christmas orders.

"Think about it, Sis," Sophie said. "One last Christmas at the ranch for old time's sake. For Mama's sake."

Her sister was using *the Mom card?*

Amy made it inside and collapsed against the old marble-topped table that also served as the kitchen counter, the phone still pressed to her ear.

"For old time's sake," she mumbled, her mind in turmoil, her stomach in knots. Swallowing, she stared at her car keys. "Mama always did love Christmas."

"Yes, she did," Sophie replied. "Look, this isn't easy for any of us, but things are changing around here. You should be a part of that. Call me back when we can talk more."

Amy ended the call, wishing her sister hadn't been so insistent. But if going home would help get the place sold, she'd gladly head back to Kentucky. She didn't want to remember that old horse farm. But for some strange reason, her stomach churned when she thought about selling.

"So not fair," she shouted to the empty little apartment. None of them could afford the upkeep. It involved a lot of land and a big operation that accrued heavy expenses.

She wasn't sure what to do.

Seeing the worn Bible her mother had given Amy on her sixteenth birthday, she grabbed it and sank down on a barstool.

Forgiveness.

She'd turn to the Scriptures. Mama had always done that, even on her darkest days.

But all of her mother's fervent prayers hadn't saved her own marriage. When Amy was twenty-five, Marlena Tucker had been killed on the interstate by a drunk driver. She'd left her four daughters to struggle with the horse farm while their unyielding father was off serving his country in a war zone. Amy didn't want to return to the place where she had so many bad memories.

No way. She did not plan to go through that kind of pain ever again. So she rested a hand on the unopened Bible and closed her eyes.

"I need help, Lord. I need to find a way to get over all of this and let go of the past . . . and the farm."

Then she hurried out the door to her second job.

CHAPTER TWO

"Mommy, why do we live over the garage?"

Amy turned from the tiny two-burner stove and stared at her seven-year-old son. He had his daddy's blue eyes and dark blonde hair, but he had her curious nature and fiery temper.

"Well, because Aunt Amanda and Uncle Ricky asked us to move in here. They needed a renter, and we were looking for a new place to live."

She turned back to the beef-and-vegetable soup she was heating, images of their former Garden District cottage moving through her mind. A lovely little house in a sought-after area, but a home she could no longer afford. She'd sold it with a heavy heart and used what little equity she'd received to pay off some bills.

"Cause Daddy went to heaven," Timothy said on a solemn note.

Bracing herself, Amy turned with a soft smile and faced her son. He sat at the counter doing his homework, his eyes centered on her. He wanted to talk about his daddy, something she'd never felt the need to do regarding her own father. Maybe that's why she had a hard time talking about Tim after he died. Her husband had been a great father.

"Yes, Daddy went to heaven, but we are blessed because we get to see Aunt Amanda and Uncle Ricky every day. You visit with them when I'm working late shifts or when I'm busy filling orders so you won't be so lonely. They love having you around."

"And you, too, cause you're a good baker."

"Well, thank you for that," she said, glad she'd distracted him. "Are you ready for your soup and grilled cheese?"

Timothy bobbed his head. "I love your homemade soup."

"And my grilled-cheese sandwiches?"

Another head bob. And then, "Where did you meet Daddy?"

So it was gonna be one of those nights. She plugged in the colored lights strung across the tiny blue spruce they'd picked out together at a local nursery. The tree came to life with blinking brilliance that showed off the homemade ornaments she treasured.

Amy wished she could shine so brightly.

"Well, we met in high school, but we got married in Nashville, Tennessee," she said, knowing her son had heard the story countless times. "I was working as a waitress while I went to college and your daddy was trying to become a famous country music star." She went on, willing herself not to tear up. "One night after he'd sung at the restaurant, we ordered coffee and pie and . . . then he asked me to marry him."

"Coconut pie." Timothy made a face. "It was love."

A little shiver moved down her backbone. "Yes, it sure was."

"He liked to play his guitar."

"Yes, he did," she said, bringing Timothy a bowl of soup and his sandwich. Tim had sold his first guitar in order to buy a baby bed for their son. Once they were doing better, she'd bought him another guitar—used, but still a nice replacement. "But . . . he heard about the job at the shipyard, and since his sister lived here in New Orleans, we came here, and then you were born."

"And we were happy for a while," Timothy finished, his voice going soft.

Things had been normal, good, steady. Tim had still played the guitar now and then at a local café, but for the sake of his family he'd given up on his big dreams.

"We were, indeed." Blinking, Amy sat beside him and stared at her own bowl of soup. "You and I are still happy, right?"

He shrugged and nibbled a carrot. "Sometimes. But sometimes, I get sad."

"Me, too," she admitted, her heart breaking. "What would make you feel better?" *Other than having your daddy here.*

Timothy got up and went to the old cabinet where she kept a few books and photo albums. Pulling out a beat-up, fabric-covered album she'd had since high school, he opened it and pointed to a picture she'd forgotten. Or maybe, tried not to remember.

"I want to go there," he said, his chubby little finger pointing to the house. "I know you used to live there, and Daddy told me about it some." He gave her that blue-eyed puppy dog look Tim used to give her. "Aunt Joanna says I should see where you grew up."

"Really, and when did Aunt Joanna tell you that?"

"That night she called, and you didn't hear your phone ringing 'cause you were in the shower. Remember? I talked to her before you and then you argued and told her bye."

"Oh, yeah, that night," Amy replied. So her sneaky sister was trying to influence her son. She'd probably set Jed up to calling, too, since he'd tried to talk Amy into coming home. Now Jo-Jo had enlisted Bella, Sophie, and Amy's own son to convince her.

"It sure looks cool," Timothy said. "And pretty."

Shocked, Amy stared at the wrinkled black-and-white photo. It was a full-on shot of the Kentucky farmhouse, with horses roaming in the pasture beyond the sprawling, wraparound porch and a mountain vista in the background.

She didn't speak. Instead, she glanced to the other side of the counter where she'd placed her Bible earlier that day.

Amazed at the things that flowed through her son's brain, Amy nodded. "Let's eat our supper and get you ready for bed, and then I'll call Aunt Sophie."

Timothy's blue eyes lit up in a way she hadn't seen in a while . . . in a way that she'd missed. "Are we going?"

"How would you like to go there for Christmas?" she said, unable to form more words.

Timothy hugged her close. "That'd be so cool, Mommy."

"Yeah, wouldn't it though."

Amy held her son tightly and willed the tears away. She couldn't keep making excuses. It was time to face the past and meet it head-on. For old time's sake, for her mother's sake, and now for her son's sake.

Forgive, Amy. Forgive and forget.

Two weeks later, Amy loaded up her old car and turned to wave to Amanda and Ricky. "Thank you for helping me finish up my Christmas orders," she said to Amanda.

Amanda laughed, her brown eyes the shade of fresh pecans. "Are you kidding? Ricky was so thrilled to be head sampler, I don't think he'll ever be the same."

Ricky, a brawny heavy-machinery operator, nodded and rubbed his stomach. "I think I gained ten pounds, but it was worth it."

Amanda motioned to Timothy. He ran to her and hugged her close. "You take care of your mama," she said, her gaze meeting Amy's. "And come back soon."

After they said their good-byes, Amy buckled Timothy into the back amid overnight bags and a trip bag full of books to read and coloring books and an electronic game to occupy him during the eleven-hour drive.

"You're coming. Really?"

Sophie's words came back to Amy as she headed toward the on-ramp to Interstate 10. Her sister sounded both relieved and choked up.

"Yes, really. You can thank Timothy. Apparently, he has a hankering to see the old homestead. He found a picture in one of my photo albums after Jo-Jo sweet-talked him."

"You used to love taking pictures," Sophie remarked, laughing. "I'm sure you have a lot of them."

"Yes, and God has a sense of timing that amazes me."

She'd cleared things with the café, promised to work double-time during Mardi Gras, and she'd finished up her pastry and pie orders in record time, setting a cut-off date for having to turn down any orders two weeks before Christmas.

Her three sisters had not only returned home, but they were all involved in new relationships. Old flames and new developments. Amy didn't get how finding love would help their situations when they all had to leave again. But then, she didn't know the whole story either.

"There's something about this place," Sophie said. "It's home. We all tried to get away from it, but it's drawing us back. *Daddy* is drawing us back."

"And you're actually thinking of staying in Bluegrass Crossing?" she asked, surprised and feeling a bit betrayed.

"I think so," Sophie said. "Matt's willing to stay here so . . . we might."

The farm couldn't be home to Amy ever again. If she could remind her sisters of the albatross that had hung around their necks for most of their lives, they could all finally get on with their futures.

"We have two weeks, kiddo," she said to Timothy. "I hope you get your fill of the place by then."

"But Santa will find us, right?"

"Of course," she said, making a face in the rearview mirror. "Bluegrass Crossing is right on Santa's route. No way he'd miss you there."

"Is the grass really blue?" Timothy asked with a curious squint.

"No, but it does have some grass that has a bluish tint to it, so that's how it got its name."

"Are there still horses there?"

"Yes," she replied. "A few retired racehorses and rescue horses—they need some tender care—that city slickers come out to ride. You'll see when we get there."

"I don't know my other aunts very well."

"No you don't," she said. Something else she needed to remedy. "I think you'll like them."

And she really wanted to meet this hotshot developer and pick his brain about what he planned to do with the vast acreage. Building houses was good, but she wondered what kind of houses. Big? Little? Stacked together? Far apart? It seemed foreign to imagine the main house and the stable . . . gone.

She told herself she should feel a sense of relief. But somehow, she only felt that old weight of regret.

Before the day ended, they'd had their fill of gas station snacks and burgers and fries, and Timothy had grown bored with the whole adventure. Amy pulled the groaning car into the long lane leading up to the house with a mixture of relief and dread churning inside her. Timothy had fallen asleep an hour earlier, and Amy had used the silence to relive every moment of her life in Bluegrass Crossing.

Dusk gathered in shades of gold and amber across the pastures where fences needed mending. The soft sun shimmered over the old house like a halo and hit the rambling front porch with all the flare of a welcoming beacon.

The house, which frankly didn't need too much light shining on it, looked the same . . . but more aged and wrinkled. An evergreen wreath swathed in red velvet ribbons hung on the front door like a shiny after-thought, and the twinkle of colorful strung lights winked at her from the railings and rafters. The once cream-colored house with the red shutters and cedar porch posts and railings came back to her in full focus, like that old black-and-white picture, but with peeling, faded colors now.

And then she noticed the man standing in the yard looking up at the house. He was clean and polished . . . in a Kentucky kind of way. Nice boots and jeans, a tweed sports coat with suede patches at the elbows, and a head full of tawny strands of thick, unruly hair.

When he heard her car rattling up the drive, he turned and waited for her to park.

Amy shut down the creaking, sputtering motor and thanked the Lord that her car had made it there in one piece. Then she got out and glanced at the stranger who stood watching her with eyes as golden as the setting sun.

And while he watched her, something happened to Amy. She turned warm and cold at the same time, and a new awareness flowed over her like honey on a biscuit.

She was *home*. But what had she come back to?

CHAPTER THREE

Dan Wentworth knew this woman, even though he'd never laid eyes on her before.

The oldest sister, Amy. The three other Tucker beauties had seemingly changed their tune on unloading this amazing family horse farm. Now they wanted to stay and make the place shine again. Dan had it on good authority that this one might still be anxious to sell. If he couldn't get the whole three-hundred acres, maybe he could buy a fourth of it at least. But seventy-five acres wouldn't allow for much of a subdivision. Not the kind he needed to build anyway. Dan always went big. He needed the whole parcel.

He'd need to put on his best face for this one and hope she had some sway with her sisters. But right now, he could see the attitude in her every movement. She stood with one hand on the car door in what looked like an attempt to turn around and leave. Her gaze moved over him with a keen awareness that held a bit of panic.

Like the other Tucker women, she was pretty. Not as tall as Sophie . . . probably a lot more complicated than the composed Bella . . . and surely not as forthcoming and open as organized Joanna—Jo-Jo to her sisters. But they all came from a batch of pure stubborn, according to the housekeeper, Sarah Weatherly.

Amy wasn't too tall and her hair was a bright, shimmering golden blonde with a hint of red that the setting sun seemed to cling to for a while longer. She wore an old pair of jeans with a faded blue sweater and chunky, brown boots. No nonsense.

"Hi," he said, walking toward her. "I'm—"

"Dan," she said, her blue-green eyes widening. "Dan the Developer, right?"

"How'd you know?"

She didn't miss a beat. "I saw that gleam in your eyes."

He laughed and extended his hand, hoping the gesture didn't seem cheesy. "I see my reputation has preceded me."

She almost smiled. "I'm Amy Tucker Brosseau. My *sisters* have preceded you. They keep me up-to-date on everything around here, and since you're the only prospective buyer we've had, it's easy to figure out who you are and why you're here."

Was that a warning? A challenge? A brush-off? Not a hint of *boy-am-I-happy-to-see-you.*

Dan decided to jump right in with both feet. "Then you probably know that I *really* want to buy this place."

"So I hear." She turned toward the car. "But since I just got here and I'm kind of tired, can we table this pitch until I feel more human?"

Calling himself all kinds of stupid, Dan nodded. "I'm sorry. Absolutely, this can wait. I talked to Sophie, and she told me you were on your way." He shrugged. "I was taking a look at the house. It sure looks pretty in this sunset."

"Yeah, until you wake up the next morning."

Surprised at the tinge of bitterness in that comment, he turned back to her. "It's rough around the edges, but it's got good bones."

She brushed past him and went around to the other side of the car. "Is that why you're in such an all-fire hurry to tear it down?"

Whoa. Her sisters claimed Amy wanted to sell and sell fast, but she didn't sound all gung ho to him. Maybe she'd had second thoughts on that long drive there.

"We can talk about that another time," he said, his tone gentle but firm. "It was good to meet you."

She didn't really respond. Instead, she opened the door and leaned in. Dan heard her talking to someone and stopped to listen. When he saw her struggling to lift someone out of the car, Dan immediately hurried to help her.

That's when he saw the little boy curled up in the back seat, sleeping away.

Amy tried again. "C'mon, buddy. We're here."

Hearing the catch in her words, Dan touched her arm. "Let me."

She didn't even look up. "Thanks, but I've got this."

"I don't mind," he said, maneuvering her out of the way with a gentle hand on her arm. Then he leaned in and lifted the sleeping boy and his blanket out of the cramped back seat.

She tried to take the child into her arms.

"I'll carry him," Dan said, holding tight to the dead weight of a tiny person. "Lead the way."

She didn't move, but the look on her face said it all. She was weary. The kind of world-weary that ripped through a person and left them so tired they just gave up on a lot of things in life. Dan knew what weary looked like. He'd been that way at times and, having suffered and survived, he could understand her attitude.

"I'm used to carrying him," she said, her tone low and full of a huskiness that slipped inside his soul and burrowed deep.

"I can see that," Dan said. "C'mon. It's cold. Let's get you both inside."

She nodded, grabbed a few things out of the front seat, and followed him up to the house. Before they made it to the porch, the front door swung open and Sophie rushed out.

"Amy!"

When she saw the boy in Dan's arms, her blue eyes went wide. "Dan? I thought you'd left. Is that Timothy? Amy, is he okay?"

"He's asleep," Amy said on a winded whisper. "He sleeps like a log. I . . . I couldn't get him up."

"Where to?" Dan asked when Bella came into the hallway, her sneakers squeaking on the old wooden floors.

Bella took one look at everyone and pointed to the back of the house. "Second bedroom on the left."

Then she rubbed a hand over the kid's dark-blond hair. "He's grown so much."

"Is she here?" That would be Jo-Jo. Always bright and cheery, and a tad bossy. "Oh Amy. You're here. We're all here. At last."

He listened to the feminine chatter and figured hugs were taking place all around. He wondered about the shredded tear in the fabric of this interesting, conflicted family as he laid the little boy on the big bed. Dan reached for the old action-figure embossed blanket the child clung to and wrapped it around him. The kid moaned softly and rolled over.

Dan ran a hand over his head and smiled. "Out like a light."

When he turned around, Amy stood at the door with a shell-shocked expression etching her pretty face. "Thank you," she said. "You can go now."

Amy finished unloading the car and took the last bag, filled with her meager presents for her sisters and placed it in the room she'd be sharing with Timothy. For that night, at least.

"Once he's rested, we can show him the loft," Sophie said when Amy came back into the great room. "I figured he'd love camping out up there the way we used to."

"Good idea," Amy said, heading to the refrigerator for water. The essence of the house settled over her, as worn and familiar as her son's tattered blanket, and it brought out all the memories she'd shoved into a dark corner. The scent of lavender merged with traces of leather and cherry tobacco, as if both of her parents had walked through the room. She remembered long nights of giggling up in the loft, or watching old movies and dancing to their favorite pop stars' songs . . . Mama calling up that they needed to quiet down so a person could get some sleep . . . then sneaking up the stairs to scare them silly, and singing and dancing with them until they all tumbled onto their sleeping bags in elated exhaustion.

And then… Mama sitting on the stairs to the loft, crying softly when she thought no one was listening.

Amy finally made herself look toward the corner by the fireplace. Tuck's old leather chair still sat where it had been for as long as she could remember. If she went and touched the aged leather, she'd probably feel his imprint still embedded in the buttery-soft grain.

He'd returned after retiring, and he'd died right there in that chair. But they had all been gone by then. Even Mama. She'd thought he might have died sad and lonely, but, amazingly, Tuck had found faith late in life and he'd apparently embraced it.

Thank you for that, Lord.

Why didn't I reach out to him?

"Are you hungry?" her sister asked, jarring Amy out of her regret.

She hadn't taken the time to cry, and she didn't have time for it now, either. After catching up for a few minutes, Jo-Jo and Bella went with Jed to check on the horses and shut things down for the night, leaving Amy and Sophie alone.

"We ate on the road."

"We have cookies," Sophie said, grinning. "Sarah made them. You remember Jed's mom, right?"

Amy nodded. "Yes, of course. She still lives around here?"

"Yes, here," Sophie said, pointing to the floor. "Here in this house. But she's visiting a friend in town tonight. She'll be back tomorrow. She moved in here after . . . we all left. To help out with feeding the few hands we have, and later to help with Daddy when he was so sick. Jed lives in the manager's house now where he grew up when his dad ran the place. Jed's cousin Matt Weatherly was Tuck's nurse, but Sarah cooked and cleaned for both of them. We told her she didn't have to leave, and since Joanna and Jed have gotten close again . . ."

Amy let that hang in the air for a minute. "Is there something in the water here now? Everyone so cozy and coupling up? Jo-Jo and Jed, finally. Bella and David getting close here when they've been together-but-not-together in Chicago for so long. And you and Matt the Marine nurse. Really? Love all around?"

"It's catching," Sophie said. "And it's complicated. We'll tell you all about it once you're rested and not so ornery."

"I'm not ornery," Amy snapped.

Sophie sent her a steely-eyed glare. "You sure were rude to Dan."

"I wasn't rude," Amy retorted. "I was tired and not ready to hear his spiel."

"But isn't he the nicest man? Loves horses but good at his job. We keep telling him we're pretty sure we don't want to sell."

"If he's loves horses, why is he in real estate?"

"His daddy owned Wentworth Properties and started grooming Dan and his sister Rachel to take over before he was a toddler, according to Dan's mother, Bettye. Mr. Wentworth finally passed the crown to Dan about five years ago. Rachel works more on interior design, but Dan's the man when it comes to the overall architectural details and subdivision designs. His first love, however, seems to be horses. And he's been great about giving us advice."

"Right." Amy couldn't imagine why since he wanted to tear all of this down.

After a dramatic pause, Sophie shrugged and pushed at her hair. "He volunteers here a lot, helping with the children who come for therapy, and he gives free lessons when he has the time. He's good with kids."

Amy thought about how gentle Dan had been with Timothy. Gentle but sure. Confident and in control. After he'd tucked in her son, he'd quietly left.

Yeah, and he did have that whole dressed-up cowboy thing going on.

Amy went in search of one of Sarah's cookies. "I reckon he's been great about things since he wants to win y'all over. If he plans to tear this place down and build swank-o houses, why is he volunteering so much?"

"He likes to help kids in need," Sophie replied. "And he's smart about renovating and staging and making things look better for buyers. The man knows his stuff." Then she added, "And we think he's lonely. He likes all the guys, so they hang out together a lot."

She opened the refrigerator, then whirled back to Amy. "I didn't like Dan when I first met him. I wanted to buy the place myself but . . . I had to give up on that notion. The farm is a big investment. One I can't afford . . . on my own anyway."

Amy didn't miss the implications of that comment. Sophie couldn't buy out her sisters, and she couldn't manage the ranch without a large staff and a larger bank account. And since she worked as a veterinarian for someone else, taking on this place was almost impossible.

So in had stepped Dan the Developer. Amy noted he hadn't been wearing a white hat.

"Again, if he's the one buying, what does he care if we have fake flowers on the tables and candles burning when he comes to snoop around?"

Sophie stared at Amy with a new determination and a too-keen interest. "And why are you so worried about what he's doing? I thought you were all geared up on selling."

"I am." She snagged a cookie off the plate sitting on the black-marble island. The rich butter cookie in the shape of a tiny green Christmas tree melted in her mouth. "These taste just like Mama's."

"I know! Jo-Jo and Bella found Mama's Christmas cookie cookbook."

She popped another cookie into her mouth. "Anyway, I'm still trying to wrap my brain around being back here. It didn't help, seeing Dan the Developer first thing, but . . . I'll get over it."

"Good to hear," her sister said with a dash of sarcasm.

Ignoring Sophie's grin, Amy turned toward the great room where a huge Virginia pine stood loaded down with familiar ornaments. "Wow. That's beautiful."

"Jed and Jo-Jo did it," Sophie replied. "When we found out you and Timothy were coming after all, we pulled a few decorations off the tree for you guys to place. Maybe tomorrow night? We could make pizza. Remember how Mama used to do that when we decorated?"

"Yeah."

She didn't want to remember, but the memories seemed to ooze out of the woodwork around here.

"Okay. I'll run to the store in the morning and buy what we'll need." Sophie popped a K-cup in the Keurig coffeemaker, hit the button on top, and grabbed a cookie. "After I doctor my coffee with creamer, let's go sit by the fire and you can tell me what you really thought of Dan."

Amy frowned and rolled her eyes. "I'll go into town with you. I'd like to see if anything's changed."

But she couldn't ignore Sophie's comment. She had a good idea that something *did* happen between her and Dan Wentworth. Something that made her both uncomfortable and . . . *elated*. Not ready to call those feelings an attraction, Amy instead decided her heightened awareness about Dan Wentworth stemmed from him holding her future in his hands. Or because she held his future in hers. More confusion to add to the pile growing in her head.

But that awareness wasn't going to keep her from finding out everything she could about his grand intentions and his big wallet. She was there to work with her sisters on getting this place sold, and then she planned to get on with her life.

No matter how sweet he'd been in helping her with Timothy.

CHAPTER FOUR

D an checked the messages on his phone first thing in the morning. Still nothing from the Tucker sisters.

His dad was pressuring him to finalize the deal on their horse farm. It would be a big feather in his cap, but Dan had mixed feelings regarding the vast property he'd had his eye on for months.

Part of those mixed feelings now involved Amy Tucker Brosseau. Sophie, who'd been hesitant to sell anyway, had warned him they couldn't talk business until they heard from Amy. She wanted her older sister there in person for that discussion, good or bad.

Well, now that sister had arrived... with a big chip on her pretty shoulder. A firecracker in a nice, feminine package.

He'd hoped she'd be the determining factor in all of this. That she'd greet him with open arms, accept the generous offer he had extended, and convince her sisters to do the same, all in one fell swoop.

That had not happened yet. But . . . it was early. She needed to settle in and discuss things with everyone. The woman seemed like a prickly pear, colorful but dangerous. Untouchable. But then, she was right to talk to her sisters first. Maybe she'd already convinced them. He needed to quit worrying and put her out of his mind.

Then why had he thought about her all night?

Had to be because of the boy.

Dan had always wanted children, but that hadn't quite worked out for him. After one failed marriage, he planned on staying on the bachelor list for a long time to come. He'd put having a family out of his mind and focused all of his energy on building Wentworth Properties into a statewide development company. That left little time for any kind of serious relationship, much to his dear mother's dismay.

Great, except for the going-home-alone-each-night part. Last night, when he'd watched Amy trying to lift her son out of that car, her expression filled with love and toughness, something inside Dan had flared up and hit him right in his gut. Afraid to analyze what that something might be, he chose to ignore it. He'd been so heavily buried in real estate that maybe coming up for air seemed a lot like an attraction. This keen awareness of her, he'd decided, stemmed only from nerves and the need to win. Nothing more.

Dan had dated since his nasty divorce, but he didn't have anyone special in his life. He wouldn't mind getting to know Amy a little better while she was here though. Like a bad penny, he had to keep showing up or he'd lose this deal. Amy's fourth of the Tucker land could be his back-up plan. His daddy had taught him to always have a Plan B.

Sophie had come close to trying to buy the place, and though she had good intentions, she didn't have the capital to pull that off. Even in bad shape, the place was still a gem. Three-hundred acres of rolling hills and farmland with enough property to build vast estates that included stables and at least ten acres per lot.

Dan wanted that gem. He could see the curving streets lined with mushrooming live oaks and lush azaleas along the sidewalks, the big farmhouse- and craftsman-style homes with sloping graceful yards, the rolling hills and flowing stream that would make a lovely community park centered among the estates. He could envision all of it because he'd designed it.

The holidays were coming up and that meant his mom and dad would expect him out at their house for the annual Sunday open house right before Christmas . . . and then again for Christmas dinner. Not that he minded, but he was tired and he longed to go up to the old hunting cabin on the far side of the Wentworth spread north of Lexington, a place where he could rest and hunt or walk along the creek bed.

"No rest for the weary." That's what his daddy always said. No whining allowed in the Wentworth household.

Dan poured himself another cup of coffee and sat down to return calls and read emails. But a sharp *tap-tap* on his office door brought his head up.

"I didn't see anyone at the desk outside, so I came on in."

Amy Tucker Brosseau stood there in jeans and a worn leather jacket, her hair down around her shoulders in a burst of what looked like scattered sunrays.

Surprised and wary, Dan stood up, his pulse pounding a tad too fast. "Hi. How are you?"

She stared him down and then took her time looking at the pictures and plaques on his wall. "Wow, you've won a lot of awards."

Embarrassed, Dan tried to regain his footing. "Yeah, well, the *business* has won awards. The Chamber of Commerce appreciates that we've stayed in Bluegrass Crossing when we could have moved our main offices to Lexington."

"Yeah, this building is impressive," she said, her arms crossed in a definite stance of resistance. "Looks like y'all take up the whole block."

He nodded and felt defensive. "We rent out offices in the back to other businesses, too."

"Smart."

He came around the desk. "Have a seat and tell me why you're here."

"Right down to business," she said, slipping past him to settle into one of the high-back, red-leather chairs across from his desk. "Honestly, I'm not sure why I'm here. I came into town to pick up some groceries, and . . . I saw the Wentworth name on the building. This used to be a grand antebellum mansion on the local historic registry, and now it's a real-estate office. Decided I'd like to see the place."

"And now that you're here?"

Her vivid blue-green eyes reminded him of a deep mountain lake. "Now I understand a lot more about you and why you want our land so much."

"What's to understand?" he said, leaning back against the desk. "I see potential. I buy land. I build on that land. Everybody wins." He motioned his hand around the room. "I saved this place and got tax credits for doing it. It's still registered as a historical property."

"Not everybody wins though," she replied. "I'm not sure what will become of my sisters and me. And even though I want to sell the horse farm, I have to be sure my family will actually benefit."

"But you're the one who's ready to get this over with, according to your sisters."

"I am ready. I was ready the day I left Kentucky."

Dan hated to be blunt, but she seemed the type who could take it. "It seems to me that you and your sisters kind of gave up on the old homestead."

"We didn't give up," she retorted, her eyes fire-tipped with anger. She crossed one leg over the other and started swinging a booted foot back and forth, a sure sign that the woman wasn't happy. "We *had* to let go. Big difference."

He tried again. "And now you're all back. You might think you're home to end things, but . . . it could be a new beginning."

"I don't see it like that," she said. "I really came here today to talk to you alone. I've heard it all second hand, and I like to hear things straight from—"

"The horse's mouth," he finished with a grin.

She tossed some of that waterfall hair. "Or maybe in this case, the mule's mouth."

Dan shrugged off the insult. He liked the fire in her eyes, even if it scared him. "What do you want to know?"

"Everything," she said. "I have a little while since Timothy is following Jed around this morning."

"Are you hungry?" Dan asked, suddenly starving—suddenly nervous.

"I might be," she said. "I nibbled something at breakfast, but I could eat again."

"We have a good café in the back of the building. Used to be the kitchen and formal dining room. Now it's the Bluegrass Bistro."

"Do they have coffee?"

"Yes. The best, in my opinion."

"Let's go."

He lifted away from the desk. "Let me clear up a few things and alert my wayward secretary, and we can be on our way."

She stood and tugged at her jacket. "I'll wait out in the reception area."

Dan watched her walk out, his heart doing funny little flutters. It wasn't every day a pretty woman waltzed into his office demanding a full explanation regarding his intentions.

He couldn't stop smiling, but he had to proceed cautiously. She might look like a delicate flower, but Dan saw steel in those eyes. She'd sell . . . but she'd demand every penny she could wring out of him.

He'd have to do some convincing over breakfast. He said a quick prayer, asking God for guidance. He'd need some divine help with this one.

Amy didn't know what had come over her. One minute she was headed to the grocery store, and the next she'd turned her old jalopy into the parking lot of Wentworth Properties.

The big three-story brick building with the white columns and long tiled front porch had caught her attention since it had been rezoned from private to commercial and was now a business—with the Wentworth name on the sign in front of it. Then she'd decided she wanted to question Dan Wentworth on her own and get a feel for the man without her overbearing sisters adding their opinions, observations, and comments.

Now she sat in this cute little bistro lined with pictures of Kentucky Derby winners. Along with those interesting photos, colorful local artwork hung on the walls, available for sale.

Sitting with a man who both mystified and confused her, Amy fought back the urge to get up and leave. Dan was nice. No doubt about that. And a gentleman. Anyone could see that. But this was a bad idea. Something about him set her on edge and made her doubt all the bad things she'd tried to forget about her own home. Maybe because he'd obviously grown up in an upscale, high-end world where people like her didn't belong. Maybe he just brought out all of her insecurities.

"Here you go," the waitress said with a perky smile. "Here's your biscuits and gravy, Mr. Wentworth. And a waffle and fruit for your friend."

"Thanks, Candy," Dan said, his smile making the young woman blush. "We'll take it from here."

Code for "Don't bother us anymore unless I raise my hand."

The girl nodded and trotted off to her next table.

"That's a mighty small waffle," he said, his tiger-like eyes glancing at her plate. "You need some bacon and eggs with that."

"I waitress at a diner almost every day," she replied. "I see plenty of bacon and eggs, and I usually *smell* like bacon and eggs. I like waffles and fruit. But you go right ahead and clog your arteries with that gravy. Which looks wonderful by the way."

"Made from scratch by Miss Berta Barton. She's been cooking here for thirty years. She was the cook for the former owners who were descendants of the original owners. She kind of came with the property."

When a gray-haired woman with a jolly laugh peeked out from the swinging door, he waved to the little sprite. "Hey, Miss Berta."

"Hey, Dan!" The woman's silvery-blue eyes ignited. "Eat up now!" The woman grinned at Amy and then went back into the kitchen.

"Thirty years. That's a lot of biscuits," Amy replied between bites, impressed that he seemed to love historical buildings *and* dedicated cooks. "This waffle is amazing."

"Never had a bad thing here." His smile radiated a quiet confidence. "Our employees are friendly and loyal."

She could see that in the way everyone had greeted him when they'd walked in. "You seem to respect them in return."

"I do. I value them and appreciate their hard work. Good, church-going people."

Was he trying to pander to her, or was that sincerity in his words? She'd go with sincerity for now. "So . . . why do you want to buy our farm?"

His eyes turned a burnished gold. "I want to build homes there. Estate homes with acreage and stables."

He went on to describe the master plan involving stately homes with enough property to house horses and allow a family to thrive in a country setting near the big city. It sounded amazing and beautiful and exclusive.

"It'll be a nice subdivision," he said.

"For all those daddy's girls out there who want a pony or two?"

"Maybe. Is there something wrong with a father wanting the best for his children?"

Amy got that sinking feeling she'd tried so hard to keep at bay. "Sometimes a father only wants what's best for himself and his career."

"Your father," he remarked. "Bad memories."

She put down her coffee cup, and Candy materialized to give her a refill. "I have some good memories," she admitted. "But a lot more bad ones." She shook her head. "They both died too young, but Tuck passed away on the land he claimed to love, even though he was never really home enough to work that land, to train the horses, to talk to the hands, or to help raise his four daughters."

"I'm sorry." Dan leaned in. "But he left you his legacy. Surely that counts for something."

Her head came up at that statement, anger sparking in her heart. "He left us a rundown horse farm."

"Do you really want to sell the place?"

His quiet question held her there, suspended between then and now. "Yes," she finally said. Then she stood up. "I have to go. I don't even know why I came here."

"I'll walk you out." Dan threw some money on the table and followed her toward the door.

"I can find the way to my car."

He kept walking with her, even when she nearly ran. When she reached her car, he touched a hand to her arm. "Amy, you're bound to have mixed emotions about this, but selling the property is a sound decision. You can all benefit from the profits and let go of the past. It'll give you a solid foundation for Timothy."

She knew all of that, yet it sounded so cliché and practiced. And invasive. "Do you tell all of your potential sellers that?"

"No," he said, his eyes centered on her. "I don't pressure people. I see the big picture, but sometimes it's not about the big picture. It's more about all the little things that make up a life, a home, a family. It's like a puzzle that's missing some of its pieces."

She nodded. "That's how my heart feels right now. As if some of the pieces are missing. And honestly, now that I'm here, I'm not so sure what I should do."

"I'll help you figure it out," Dan said, "if you'll let me."

She didn't respond, but she did look him in the eye with a stormy directness that belied the rattling of her heart. "Thank you for breakfast. I'm sure we'll see each other again soon enough."

But she hoped not too soon. She needed some time to absorb the push and pull of being around a man who might change her life forever. She needed some time to pray and get her soul aligned with what her head told her.

CHAPTER FIVE

"What took you so long?"

Amy whirled from the refrigerator to find Bella staring at her from the kitchen door, her brown hair caught up in a ponytail. "I drove around, checking things out," she said. Then because she felt guilty for not being truthful, she added, "And I stopped by the Wentworth building."

"Oh," Bella said, advancing into the room with enough curiosity to help her put away the cheese, pepperoni, and vegetables she'd bought for their pizza-making event. "And what did you think of the *Wentworth building?*"

Amy didn't want to talk about her feelings. "It's lovely."

Bella's eyes brightened. "And did you talk to any of the Wentworths who work in that building?"

"Yes, I did," Amy finally blurted. "I talked to Dan. We got off to a bad start last night, so I wanted him to explain his grand plan for turning this place into something worthwhile."

"I think it's worthwhile the way it is," Bella replied, a daring lilt in her words. "I didn't like Dan when I first met him."

Amy put away the milk, eggs, and butter she planned to use to make some cupcakes. "I'm getting that none of you liked him at first. What changed?"

"Our attitudes," Bella said. "He's a good man who's a successful businessman, but he's not pushy. And until we sign on the dotted line, he can hang around all he wants. But we can't put this off much longer. We all have lives to get back to—*or not*—and decisions to make."

Amy hoped Dan didn't plan on hanging around a lot. That would be way too distracting. "But none of you are sure about selling now, right?"

Bella nodded, grabbed a can of mixed nuts, and started nibbling. "True. Once I came back with David and he and I'd had some quiet time together away from Chicago, he started pointing out what a jewel this place could be. I have to admit, the more David and I discussed it, the more viable it sounded to stay and make things work. Then Dan showed up, and now the idea of selling to him is gnawing at me."

"What's his story?" Amy asked after opening a bottle of water. When Bella's right eyebrow quirked and her expression turned smug, she wished she'd kept that question to herself.

"He was married," Bella said. "Bad divorce." She shrugged. "His family is fairly wealthy. He has a younger sister who's married with two children. She and her executive husband live in a big house inside the family compound near Lexington."

"Family compound?" Amy couldn't imagine someone living in a *family compound*. "I could tell from the building and his office that he's successful, but he's not snobbish at all."

"No, but his family has roots in this area that date back before the Civil War," Bella said. When her phone buzzed, she held up a finger and checked it. "It's David. I have to take this."

Amy watched her younger sister rushing off to talk to her fiancé. A native Kentuckian, David wanted to settle down in his home state. Bella and David had met in Chicago and dated in a long distance sort of way since they both traveled a lot for work, but Bella, who worked as a high-powered executive, had never planned to return to Kentucky. When David suggested that they both head home for Christmas, she'd agreed since she had some vacation time. After returning and rekindling their somewhat stale relationship, Bella and David were now figuring out where to live once they married. So Bella was siding with Sophie and Jo-Jo on possibly not selling. Amy knew what finding someone to share your life with could do that to a person, but all three of her sisters? And right now at such a crucial time?

Where did that leave Amy?

Before she could even form a disgruntled pout, the kitchen door burst open, and Timothy rushed in sporting a big grin and a tousled head of hair.

"Mom, this place is great. There's a creek and Jed took me fishing and I caught a bluegill. That's a fish."

He spaced his hands apart to show her the estimated length. "Jed says I caught a good-sized one, but we threw him back so he can grow."

Amy's heart lifted, seeing her son so excited. "I used to catch bluegill from that very creek. Your granddad taught me."

She stopped, a distant memory surrounding her like mist on a mountaintop. She could hear Tuck's bold laughter as he urged her on. "Hold the line, Amy. Gotta give him time to grab the hook along with the worm."

"Mom!"

Amy blinked, her eyes burning with unshed tears. She saw her son pointing at the cookie jar. "What, honey?"

"Can I have a cookie?"

"Only one," she replied, her tone husky with raw-edged pain. "We're making the famous Tucker family pizza for dinner."

"I get to help," Timothy said. "Aunt Jo-Jo said I could."

"We all get to help," she replied. "It's a tradition. But you smell fishy, so go wash up."

Timothy hurried off toward the back of the house as Jo-Jo and Jed walked into the kitchen.

"I have a great idea," Jo-Jo said, grinning at Timothy's departing back. "We're gonna pull out all the old photo albums and show them to Timothy."

Amy frowned but nodded. "I guess that might be fun."

Jo-Jo shrugged. "It's Christmas, Amy. Later, after dinner, we need to sit down and discuss what we should do. Dan's offer is tempting, but it's looking now like it's three against one on selling."

Bella waltzed in from the front. "And we know who that one is."

Jed stepped forward. "We could invite Dan over tonight and go over the details one last time, now that you're all here together."

"She's frowning again," Bella said, her gaze on Amy.

Amy didn't know why Dan Wentworth had gotten under her skin so quickly. It had to be because she had something he wanted, and she wasn't sure what to do about that. She didn't want to like the man, but she couldn't find a reason not to. He was good-looking and sure-footed, and he had a confidence that made her feel good when she was with him. But that same confidence scared her, too.

Dear Lord, help me to make the right decision.

Why couldn't she make a decision and then persuade her sisters to accept Dan's offer? Unloading this place was what she'd wanted since the day the letter from Tuck had arrived. No, since the day she'd left. She wanted to be done with this old horse farm. But now that she was back, she was starting to see it wasn't the farm she wanted to leave behind, but the painful memories.

Her sisters were depending on her and, as the oldest, her opinion carried a lot of weight. But she hadn't done her part to help them. She'd abandoned the place and them. And while she didn't regret leaving and getting married, she did regret the selfish way she'd never looked back. Didn't she owe them her full support now?

But if they did sell the place, what would she do? Go back to New Orleans?

"Amy?"

Jo-Jo stood beside her. "I know you aren't sure what to do. I don't know what to do either. But Jed can tell you all you need to know about the cost of the upkeep on this place. And Dan can explain how the sale would work."

"And David," Bella offered. "He's already helped us clean the place up, and he has experience in real estate."

Finally, Amy nodded. "If Sophie agrees, we'll have the meeting tonight. I guess Matt will want to come, too."

"I'll call her right now," Bella said.

Soon, everyone had dispersed, leaving Amy alone in the kitchen, memories of her daddy's laughter echoing around her with a sweetness that penetrated the barrier she'd put up around her heart.

Dan hadn't expected to be back out at the farm so soon after the not-so-successful impromptu breakfast he'd had with Amy. Wondering if the sisters had made a decision, he pulled his Cadillac Escalade into the sprawling front yard and parked underneath a towering live oak near a line of several other cars.

Not one to get nervous, he hopped out of his SUV and tugged his leather jacket closed. The wind whipped against him, icy on his skin. He glanced out toward the stable where Jed Weatherly had explained to him when they'd first met that they housed five working ranch horses along with rescue horses and retired racehorses that would eventually be adopted out. Jed and a few hands took care of the place and made extra income by opening the stable to school groups and people who wanted to experience horseback rides on the weekends. Some of the horses served as therapy animals.

Dan knew most of the horses by name since he volunteered as often as possible out here, giving riding lessons to kids. He hadn't planned to do that, but the first time he'd come out to tour the place, Jed had shown him Big Red, a grandson of a mare named Maranatha . . . and Stanley, a gelding in rehab . . . and Lucinda, the gray mare with arthritic knees.

He'd been hooked, and since he rarely made it back to the fancy stable at his family home at Wentworth Hills, he immediately asked Jed how he could help, thinking he'd make a donation.

"We need volunteers," Jed had replied.

If you buy this place, all that will be gone.

Before Dan could ponder that thought, the front door of the house burst open, and the little boy he'd put to bed last night ran out onto the porch.

When the kid looked up and spotted Dan, he stopped in his tracks. "Hey."

"Hey, yourself," Dan said. "Where you going in such an all-fire rush?"

"We found an old sleigh in the barn, and I get to help clean it up and put lights all over it and—"

"And you're talking mighty fast," his mother said from behind him. "Timothy, slow down and let Mr. Wentworth come inside. It's cold out here."

Dan grinned up at her. "But this one is ready to get that sleigh up and running."

"It don't run," Timothy said on a pragmatic note. "It's pretend."

"It doesn't run," Amy corrected, her no-nonsense eyes moving over her son.

"I said that," Timothy retorted. "Can I go look at it again, Mom?"

"Why don't we wait till morning? It's late and the horses are getting settled for the night."

"I'm gonna learn to ride a horse," Timothy told Dan.

"That's great," Dan replied. "I teach horseback riding. Maybe I can help you."

Timothy did a fist pump and turned to head back inside while his mother stood there with her arms crossed, a doubtful expression on her face. "Do you really teach lessons?"

"Yes, I really do," Dan replied, taking in her pretty green sweater and worn, rolled-up jeans over puffy, suede boots. "Right here, every other Saturday. I've been around horses all my life. My sister is an award-winning horsewoman."

The look of surprise on her face was worth the trip. "Interesting."

Then she waved a hand toward the door. "Come on in. We're making pizza, and we could use your help chopping vegetables."

Dan stepped closer. "Vegetables on pizza? Isn't that a crime?"

She flipped her hair away from her chin. "No, that's every woman's excuse to eat pizza."

"Got any sausage or pepperoni?" he asked with a whine.

"Of course. We're not completely helpless in the kitchen. Our mama taught us the way to a man's heart."

As if she'd realized what she'd said, Amy shook her head. "That hasn't always paid off though."

Dan met her gaze and saw the hint of sadness in her eyes. "Your mama sounds like a wonderful woman."

"She was," Amy said, "even if her husband somehow forgot."

And just like that, her good mood seemed to disappear. Catching up with her, he said, "Hey, why exactly was I summoned here tonight?"

Amy kept walking. "For pizza, of course." Then she glanced back over her shoulder. "And . . . we all have questions about your proposal."

"That's fine," he said. But when he walked into the spacious great room and saw Jed, David, and Matt sitting there, he wondered if the Tucker girls had brought in reinforcements to make him see that they weren't going to sell the horse farm after all.

Chapter Six

Sarah sidestepped Amy as she poured drinks and tasked Timothy with setting out paper plates. "Okay, we have four large pizzas baking," the white-haired woman announced. "Ready in about twenty minutes."

"We'll help," Jo-Jo said, hurrying to wipe the long counter so Timothy could place the plates.

"No." Sarah had a no-nonsense attitude and a steel-magnolia backbone. "You all go and get to talking. You'll be good and hungry by the time the pizza is done."

Jo-Jo took Amy by the arm. "You can't avoid this by staying in the kitchen. Jed knew what he was doing when he asked his mom to come on back. He needed her to herd us like we're stray cats."

Amy smiled at that. With her feisty attitude, Sarah Weatherly reminded her of a human hurricane. But she was one of the kindest, most loving women Amy had ever known. Miss Sarah had always been loyal to the Tucker family. Amy respected her in the same way she'd respected her own mother.

She followed her sisters into the great room where all the men had gathered around the fireplace, talking football and NASCAR. The scene looked so natural that Amy had to stop and catch her breath. She only wished there could have been happy family scenes like this one here before.

Dan stood laughing with Jed, his smile brighter than the crackling fire. Why did her heart betray her each time this man came around? It had only been a little over twenty-four hours since he'd turned toward her there in the yard, the house silhouetted behind him. She'd been determined to get to the bottom of his motives that morning, and he'd somehow turned that confrontation into a breakfast in the quaint café. Now it seemed as if the house and Dan belonged together. With her.

Shaking her head to get rid of that crazy notion, Amy moved into the spacious room crowded with oversized worn furniture. When Bella motioned to the men to quiet down, all eyes turned toward Amy. She didn't know she was the spokesperson here, but Sarah had Timothy busy in the kitchen, so Amy couldn't use him as an excuse to exit the room.

"I guess Dan's wondering why we invited him to our pizza party," she said, her gaze flitting around the room before she made herself glance at him.

His eyes held a warmth that filled her with that funny feeling again. That feeling of belonging there with him. That feeling of wanting to stay and fight for the things she'd left behind long ago.

He filled the void with a quip. "Because I love pizza?"

"We all came for that reason," David retorted with a grin.

Dan didn't wait for an explanation. "Let me guess. You're trying to decide what to do with this place, and you want to have a final sit-down to ask me some questions."

"Wow," Jo-Jo said. "Just wow."

Bella looked a bit skeptical, but she smiled and sank down on the arm of the sofa. "We do have some concerns."

Dan held Amy in his sights, which caused her to want to get this over with. He went on, smooth as a windless lake. "I'm used to that. I buy land that's been in families for generations. It's to be expected that a lot of emotions are tied up in things." His steady gaze stayed on Amy. "Your sisters have been waiting for you so you can make this decision together. I don't mind, especially if it involves homemade pizza."

David nodded. "The Tucker sisters just need to know that their parents' land will be in good hands."

Amy finally spoke. "You've made us a generous offer, and we've talked about it, but we'd still like to wait until after the holidays to make the final decision. After we eat, we'll gather back here and get down to business. My sisters invited Jed, David, and Matt here because Jed and Matt knew my father and David has real estate and investment experience." She shrugged. "And because their futures depend on what we decide, too."

"Or maybe because the three of them can toss me out on my ear if I don't say what you want to hear?"

Everyone laughed, but Amy saw the concern behind his banter. He had a lot at stake here. What would happen if he didn't get this deal? And was he being nice to her because he needed the land?

"Pizza is ready," Timothy called from the kitchen, a proud grin on his face. "I helped make the man ones."

"We have *man* ones?" Matt asked.

Timothy bobbed his head. "Yeah. They have tons of meat. Fully loaded, Miss Sarah said."

"Well, let's get to it," David replied, giving Timothy a high-five.

"We need to say grace," Timothy informed them. "Miss Sarah said so."

Dan met Amy at the edge of the counter. "You okay with this?"

"I want this," she reminded him. "My sisters might have been swayed by three handsome, capable men, but I'm going to make up my own mind."

"I don't see any more handsome men here," he said. "But if I have my way, we'll be working together to give us both what we want. And . . . I don't mind that one bit either."

She didn't tell him that he ranked right up there with the other three. But she did remind herself not to get distracted by all his Kentucky confidence and charm. Amy needed money, and fast. But she also needed to know she was making the right decision without any added pressure from a suave, real-estate developer who made her heart lift and expand like a hot-air balloon. Because Dan Wentworth, as nice as he seemed, only had one goal here—to build fancy estates on their land.

Two hours later, only two slices of pizza remained on the baking stone and the official part of their meeting was over. Jo-Jo had walked to the stable with Jed to check on the horses, and Sophie and Matt helped

Timothy decorate with a few felt Christmas ornaments for the tree. Bella and David had insisted on helping Sarah clean the kitchen.

That left Amy sitting with Dan in the great room.

"I guess I should mosey on home," he said, getting up to rub his stomach. "The pizza was good. I've never had actual homemade pizza before."

Amy stood and put her hands in the back pockets of her worn jeans. They'd talked shop for well over an hour, and Dan had done his best to stay honest and sure. Did Amy trust him yet?

She stared at the embers in the fireplace. "Mama loved to cook from scratch. She believed a good home-cooked meal was much better than any kind of take-out food."

"Having eaten a lot of take-out, I can vouch for that," Dan replied.

She slanted her head, causing her hair to tumble down onto her sweater. Dan envied that sweater right then. "Even though we grilled you about everything from drainage to acreage to erosion to the size of each estate house?"

"All good questions," he replied, hoping he'd made a good impression. Hoping she'd walk him to his truck.

"I'll walk you out," she said, grabbing a coat from a wall hook near the door. "Thanks again for coming. We're going to finish decorating the house tonight and tomorrow."

"Any pizza involved in that?"

She gave him a thoughtful stare. "No. I promised the clan I'd make red-velvet cupcakes and gumbo tomorrow night."

Dan caught a hand against his heart. "You're killing me."

She only hesitated a moment. "You can always come back and bring those comps you mentioned. That, and anything else we might need."

He opened the door and a blast of frigid air greeted them. "I think we'll have snow for Christmas."

"Oh, so you predict the weather, too."

"I'm pretty good at guessing. We've already had a massive blizzard this year. That little extra nip in the air makes me want to bundle up and stay by the fire."

She snuggled into her jacket. "Yes, winter is here."

Dan wanted to keep the conversation going, but he didn't want her to freeze to death. "Well, I guess I'm off then. I might take you up on that offer for gumbo. And a cupcake."

"We'll have plenty," she replied. "But where do *you* live?"

That question turned him back to her. "In a condo in the Wentworth building."

"Let me guess. The penthouse?"

"Well, it is on the top floor but it's nothing special. Just a two-bed-room industrial type loft."

"Oh, I see. So you can watch over your domain?"

He needed to set her straight. "It's not my domain. It's my family business. I like being close to the office."

"Interesting."

"You say that a lot. I'm not sure it's a compliment."

"Well, you're an interesting man. I think *that's* a compliment."

He took the bold step of staring her down. "But you're wondering why I'm delaying getting out of here. Am I stalling because I want to sweet-talk you into this deal, or am I stalling to see if there's something real between us?"

She stared right back without blinking. "You talk in riddles and crazy sentences. I want the truth. I've only known you for about five minutes, so I'm wondering about way more than anything that has to do with you, Dan Wentworth. Like how I'm gonna spend my part of that big check you keep mentioning."

"Oh, so you're the one using me?"

"And why would I be using you?"

"To get that big check."

"That wouldn't take much since you seem ready to roll."

"*I've* made *my* decision," he said, leaning close. "But I can tell you this. No matter what this family decides, you and me, Mrs. Tucker-Brosseau, we have some unfinished business."

Her eyes widened in surprise. "Oh, and what would that be?"

"We need to get to know each other, away from your sisters and our well-meaning friends and this place that seems to hold a lot of angst and memories for you."

"I never said I wanted to get to know you."

"You didn't have to."

With that, he turned to leave. But Dan knew he'd be back. Again and again. Because now he wasn't just after this land.

No, he'd found something even more valuable.

A woman who could go toe-to-toe with him.

CHAPTER SEVEN

"Than looks good."

Amy turned from straightening the wreath made from magnolia leaves, holly berry cuttings, and evergreen branches. Dan stood looking up at the house. He'd called to say he was bringing more paperwork and pictures of comparison subdivisions he'd helped design and build. And he timed his trip with the gumbo and cupcakes she'd planned for dinner.

That made her smile. She wanted him around, and she didn't want him around. She hadn't felt this way since . . . since she'd fallen in love with Tim. That memory sobered her and made her feel guilty for even looking at another man.

"Thanks," she said, pivoting to meet him at the bottom of the porch steps. "It's for the sleigh we found in the barn."

"The decorations add that festive touch," he added with another smile. "I can see y'all have been busy today."

"Being here with not much to do makes all of us get creative. Sophie is helping Jed and Jo-Jo with the horses, and David and Bella are off doing something highly romantic. Matt is probably on his way here. He can't seem to stay away from Sophie these days."

"Love is in the air," Dan said, his gaze moving over the bright, colorful lights strung across the porch railings and the roofline. "But Christmas brings out the good feelings in everyone."

"Even someone as ornery as me?" she asked.

"I hadn't noticed."

They both burst out laughing at that.

"From what I hear, you've had a lot to deal with," he said, the big envelope he'd brought held tightly in front of him. "I meant to tell you . . . I'm sorry about your husband's accident."

"It was a shock," she admitted, able to talk about it more now than in months past. "He kissed me good-bye one morning, and then, a few hours later, I got the call."

"I can't imagine going through that," Dan said. "I had a hard time after my divorce, but losing your spouse that way must be devastating."

She wanted to ask him about his marriage, but she didn't feel she knew him well enough yet. "I'm sure a divorce is just as hard in its own way," she said, hoping she sounded sympathetic.

Dan motioned to the chairs on the porch. "Mind if we sit a minute. I've been running all day long."

Amy figured that was a ruse to get *her* to sit down since she was tired from sprucing up the house. "I can take a load off. The gumbo is simmering, and the cupcakes just need icing. You timed your arrival perfectly."

"Is that pathetic?" he asked, his golden-brown eyes sparkling. "That I'd make sure I'm here at mealtime?"

"No, that's smart. A bachelor who talks about too much take-out needs a good, hot meal now and then."

"And you did invite me, right?"

"Right." But she'd hoped he wouldn't show up. And she'd hoped he would. Maybe she was just as pathetic as he thought he was.

"You did mean it when you said I should come on back?"

"Of course." She pushed back her windblown hair. "But I need to freshen up."

Dan stared over at her. "You have a leaf." He reached up to swipe at her overgrown bangs. "Right there."

His touch confused her almost as much as the way his golden eyes held her. She stood so fast, she almost tripped. "I should get inside."

"I should go in with you then."

"Okay, if you don't mind visiting with Sarah and Timothy while I go and get cleaned up."

And put on makeup and lose ten pounds and find something clean to wear.

He followed her inside. Amy watched for signs of gloating, since he still thought they were going to sell to him. But instead of gloating, Dan looked around and nodded his head. "Nice."

They'd scrubbed the place down from ceiling to floor, sweeping, polishing, and even painting here and there. They'd freshened curtains and taken down mini-blinds to let the light inside. Sarah had her sisters working on it before Amy got there, but that morning they'd all made a final push to get the house in order for their big Christmas reunion.

"One last Christmas," she said, not even realizing she'd said it out loud. "Mama would love this."

Dan didn't speak. Instead, he gazed at the Christmas tree that almost grazed the vaulted ceiling. "I'm sure she'd approve," he said finally in a quiet tone.

"Hey, Mr. Dan!"

Timothy plowed into the room and immediately launched into a discussion about the horses and the stable and the hayloft and the loft upstairs that had become his domain. Before Amy could speak, he'd dragged Dan upstairs to see what he'd done with the place.

Amy stood in the center of the great room, her brittle and battered heart softening as she heard her son's animated chatter echoing out over the house. She and Timothy had been doing okay. But she missed Tim with an ache that felt like a deep wound, and she hadn't realized how much her son missed his daddy. What must her little boy have felt? Just seeing how he'd taken up with Jed and the others, especially Dan, made Amy want to hug him close and tell him how sorry she was that she'd ignored his grief.

Dear Lord, how could I have been so blind?

She'd been so caught up in trying to survive, she'd forgotten how to live. When was the last time she'd taken Timothy to the zoo or to the Riverwalk or to a movie? When was the last time she'd just sat and read a book with him or gone to one of his Little League games? No, she'd left those things to Amanda and Ricky while she worked and fretted and pushed her grief away.

"Honey, are you all right?"

Amy felt Sarah's hand on her arm. Blinking, she nodded. "Yes, for the first time in a long time, I'm okay. It's just that I've been kind of sleepwalking my way through life since—"

"Since Tim died?"

"Yes," Amy answered, her throat clogged with emotions that ran so deep she wasn't sure she could stand to bring them to the surface. "Yes."

Sarah nodded and kept her hand on Amy's arm. She must have had such moments after her husband, Mr. Dewayne had died. The understanding in her eyes clarified that. "Suga', go get a nice shower. I'll finish up with supper."

Amy couldn't speak, but when she glanced up at the loft area, she saw Dan standing there watching her. And she also saw empathy in his eyes.

"What's he doing back here?"

Amy turned from the kitchen window, coffee in her hand. It was the Saturday before Christmas and several kids had shown up for their horseback-riding lessons. Sophie stood behind her, her blue eyes bright with questions.

Amy shrugged. "Well, my very persuasive son asked Dan to give him riding lessons. And Dan agreed. I guess he's trying hard to sweeten the pot on this deal."

"So he's using your son to get to you? Maybe we need to tell him we're all in this thing. Are you leading him on, Amy?"

"Excuse me?"

"I mean about selling," Sophie replied. "Maybe we should tell him we're leaning toward keeping the place."

Amy would have disagreed on keeping the farm a few days ago. Now she didn't know. "Right." Then she smiled. "No, I think he genuinely loves horses. But his family's place is north of Lexington, and he apparently works all the time so he can't get up there to ride, so he volunteers here."

"He wants to ride here?"

Hearing the sarcasm and disbelief in Sophie's voice, Amy giggled. "He's slumming, okay?"

Sophie let out a derisive unladylike snort. "That man is after one of two things—this place or you. Or maybe both."

Amy almost spit out her coffee. "What?"

"We've all noticed it," Sophie said, her auburn ponytail bouncing as she slanted her head. "Dan looks at you in a way that's got nothing to do with land and houses, darlin'."

"He's not here for me," Amy replied, hoping the heat radiating from her face wasn't a blush. "I mean, if he is here for me, it's only because he's trying so hard to persuade me."

"Does he understand that the rest of us have pretty much decided to keep the place?"

"I don't know if he's quite gotten that," Amy admitted. "It's not over until the last sister agrees." And that sister needed some serious alone time to pray and contemplate what to do.

Sophie, a good six inches taller than Amy, stared down at her with a defiant fire in her eyes. "You were the one who wanted to get this over with. Are you going to hold out on us now?"

"I don't know what to do," Amy said. "I can't sleep and I don't have an appetite. Timothy is having the time of his life and . . . the other night I realized I'd been neglecting him and . . ."

She stopped and glanced at Tuck's old leather chair, that well of torment bubbling over again. She wouldn't have a meltdown in front of Sophie.

"I don't know what I want anymore."

"Do you like him?"

Sophie had always been able to see right through her. They'd shared a bedroom for most of their childhood, which meant they'd also shared all the intimate details of their adolescent angst. No, Amy couldn't hide the truth. Not from Sophie.

"I like him. He's nice. He's polite. He's successful. And he's giving my son free horseback-riding lessons."

"Any one of us could have done that," Sophie pointed out with a soft smirk. "Even if we're not as polite and successful as Dan Wentworth."

"But Timothy asked Dan," Amy said, that admission gnawing at her. "They've bonded somehow."

"Well, Dan Wentworth has a way of bonding with people when he wants something."

"And you know this how?"

"I just get that feeling is all."

Amy finished her coffee. "I'm walking down to the stable to watch, if that's okay with you."

Sophie finally smiled. "You have my permission. You might even try flirting with him while you're there." Then she pressed her hands against the kitchen island. "After all, two can play at that getting-what-they-want game. You understand what I'm saying?"

"Sophie! Are you suggesting I make that man forget all about this property and focus on *me*?"

"Oh, he's already doing that. But if you keep this up, he just might decide to join the rest of us here and make a go of this place."

Amy pursed her lips and shook her head. "Dan Wentworth would never do that. He's got a life."

Her sister patted her on the shoulder, a knowing look in her eyes. "Then what is he doing messing in ours?"

CHAPTER EIGHT

Amy watched as Dan patiently showed Timothy how to mount the docile, auburn mare with the same name as her sister Sophie. Dan was amazing with kids, she had to admit. He methodically explained how to use the mounting block and how to land gently on the saddle so the horse wouldn't startle. Then he showed Timothy how to use both legs to squeeze the horse right beneath the girth to walk forward.

Amy's fists knotted in fear since she remembered falling off a pony once, but Timothy did as he was told, and the horse Sophie, obviously used to these lessons, took him on a slow circular walk. It helped that Dan held her halter at times and guided the ride.

Timothy enjoyed being able to give a low holler of "Whoa!" after Dan showed him how to stop the horse. After that, they worked on turns and trotting, with Dan right there guiding both of them, and Timothy giggling and glancing toward where she stood to make sure she'd seen every step.

Dan answered a hundred rapid-fire questions before instructing Timothy on what to do. Each time Timothy accomplished a task, Dan praised him. He showed Timothy how to get acclimated to the horse and how to win her over by gently coaxing her. If Timothy made a mistake or misunderstood, Dan grinned and explained all over again. By the time the lesson had ended, Amy's heart overflowed with gratitude and joy, and her feelings for Dan and this old homestead had collided into one big wind of change.

The kind of change that scared her and enticed her all at the same time.

"What'd you think?" Dan asked Amy after the lesson ended and the bitter chill of dusk took over. Off in the distance, the sun moved toward the horizon in a lazy, yellow-orange descent that hovered over the tree line in a shimmering half-circle.

Before Amy could find the words to tell him the light version of her reaction to watching him with her son, Timothy rushed up and high-fived Dan and then latched onto Amy. "Did you see me, Mom? I can ride real good. Mr. Dan said so."

Amy didn't even try to correct his grammar. "You sure can, honey. I'm glad you're learning."

"Maybe we can ride together," Timothy said. "You, me, and Mr. Dan."

Dan's golden-brown eyes lifted to meet Amy's gaze straight on. "I like that idea."

"Can we, Mom?"

"We'll have to see," Amy said. "You and I have to get back to New Orleans before the New Year."

Timothy's blue eyes dulled. "I like it here. I wish we could stay forever."

He took off toward the stable. Amy almost went after him, but Dan held her arm. "He's a boy. Let him do some soul-searching on his own. He'll be fine."

"And how do you know that?" she asked, thinking he'd never been a parent.

"In case you haven't noticed, I'm also a boy."

"I've noticed," she admitted. Then she smiled. "It's so hard, trying to be a good parent."

"You *are* a good parent. And even if you go back to New Orleans, you've shown him a part of yourself. He won't forget that."

"How did you get so smart?" she asked on a teasing note.

"I was born this way," he deadpanned with a shrug.

Amy shook her head at that. But she thought about what it would do to Timothy if she convinced her sisters to sell the place. Which, from the looks of it, wasn't going to happen anyway. Each time she broached the subject, they all seemed to run in the other direction. Amy figured they'd called her home only as a gesture of goodwill and to convince her to fall in line with them. Now she was caught in the middle, her head and her heart at war with each other.

And Dan Wentworth wasn't helping matters.

She took one last glance toward the stable. When she heard Timothy talking to Sophie and Jo-Jo, Amy kept walking toward the house with Dan. "Thanks for helping him. When we get home, I'm going to find the nearest stable and continue his lessons. I can give him that much at least."

"Good idea," Dan said. "Hey, I was wondering if you'd like to get away from here this weekend."

Amy's heart tripped on itself, and she almost did the same with her boots. "What do you mean?"

He actually laughed. "Don't worry. I'm not gonna kidnap you. It's just that there's this thing Sunday afternoon."

A thing. He wanted her to go to *a thing* with him. "What kind of thing?"

"A Christmas open house at my parents' place."

Her heart bumped like an old wagon on a rutted dirt road. "A thing at your parents' place. You mean the estate where you grew up?"

His sheepish look said it all. "Yeah. They do still live there and that's where they have the open house every year. I'm always forced to bring a *plus-one*, as my mom and sister like to call it."

Amy thought she might hyperventilate. "So you feel forced to ask *me* to be that plus-one?"

He lifted his hands, palms out. "No. Oh no. No force here. I *want* you to be my plus-one. I'm asking you to go with me . . . as my date."

She couldn't breathe for a moment. "You want me to go with you to this thing . . . on a date?"

"Yes, I want you to go with me to the open house as my date. No plus-one, no force, no *thing*. Just you and me, one-on-one, together."

"In your parents' home with lots of other important people milling around."

"It's a big place. And we don't have to stay long. I can show you where I grew up. And on the way, I can show you some of the subdivisions we've built."

Amy stopped so fast that he skidded toward her, his hands grabbing her arms. "Are you asking me on this so-called date so you can sway me a bit more by showing me some fancy neighborhoods?"

Dan dropped his hands as if she'd caught fire. "Uh . . . no. I just thought—"

"I know what you thought. I think I'm busy Sunday."

"Amy."

"Dan."

He looked so flustered, she almost laughed. But Sophie's warnings flashed code red in her head. "My sisters think you're trying to sweet-talk me into selling, but I don't want to believe that."

"Then don't believe it." The confusion left his face as he advanced toward her again. Leaning close, he said, "If I really wanted to sweet-talk you, I'd be doing a better job than this. I just want to go out with you."

She didn't know what to believe, but the way he looked at her with those tiger eyes gave her hope and sent a warm shiver down her backbone. She should tell him to get in his expensive SUV and hit the road. But before she could utter that brush-off, her heart got in front of her good sense.

"What time Sunday?"

"You're going?"

Well, he did seem genuinely surprised. "I said, what time?"

"I'll pick you up after church. We'll take our time. We don't have to be the first ones there."

"Dress?" she asked.

"Dress?" He looked so cute when he got confused.

"What should I wear? Dressy or casual?"

He squinted. "My sister wears cocktail-type stuff."

She didn't have cocktail-type stuff with her. Not that she'd ever been one to dress up much anyway. "Okay," she said, wondering what she would wear. With three sisters to help her, that shouldn't be *too* difficult.

"You're going with me?"

"Yes. But if I ever find out you're doing this as a ploy to sway me, Dan Wentworth, I will not be a happy woman."

He did that leaning-in thing again. "Oh, it's a ploy, all right. A ploy to get you alone."

And with that, he turned and headed to his vehicle, a big grin plastered on his face. When Amy turned back toward the house, she saw Bella and Sarah standing on the porch, both of them grinning.

Dan didn't know what had come over him. He hadn't planned on asking Amy to go to the Wentworth open house, but somehow his mouth had popped the question before his brain could catch up.

His mother and sister would demand explanations since, in spite of their pointed invitations, he rarely brought a date to any of the social events they put together. But bringing a woman he'd just met to this particular event would make their eyes bug right out of their heads. They'd corner him, demanding details, and they'd probably scare Amy right back to the car.

No, that wouldn't happen. Amy could hold her own with anyone, and she'd do it with boots on.

She's a client, he practiced on the way back to town. *Just thought she'd enjoy seeing some of our properties. She's a friend. We're working on a possible contract for the land that's been in her family for generations.*

"She's a Tucker."

That would shut them all up. They'd know what that meant since his dad really wanted this sale to go through. But he couldn't tell his family that Amy was the only Tucker who still wanted to sell. They'd take it the wrong way.

Just as Amy had earlier.

To Dan's way of thinking, however, this wasn't about land anymore. This was about an interesting, pretty woman who'd captured his attention the minute she'd stepped out of her beat-up old car. And his heart soon after.

He couldn't tell his family *that* either.

CHAPTER NINE

"I can't believe I'm doing this." Amy stared at herself in the mirror. "I can't do this."

She tried to brush past her three sisters, but Bella grabbed her arm and spun her back around. "Amy, you look great. Mom's dress fits you perfectly since Sarah took it in a bit."

Sophie's gaze moved over the red satin dress with the black portrait collar. A fifties-style that they were pretty sure their mother had made from an old pattern she'd found in the attic; the dress had been one of her mother's favorites. A lush, black velvet collar, flared skirt of shimmering satin, and a matching black bow sashed at the waist that made Amy look even slimmer than she already was.

She blinked away the tears threatening to ruin the makeup her sisters had slapped on her earlier. "I can't wear Mama's dress. It doesn't feel right."

"You look so much like her," Jo-Jo said. "She'd want you to wear it. This is a fancy event. You need to look the part."

"And what part is that?" she asked, suddenly scared. Afraid of the feelings she'd *developed* for Dan the Developer. "I shouldn't even be going. I don't know him that well."

"You know what you need to know," Sophie replied. "You yourself said he's a good man."

"But he's trying to buy us out," Amy reminded her sisters.

"Not if you tell him no," Jo-Jo said, hope shining in her eyes. "We want to keep this place. You know that."

"So you can refuse to sell, and I'll be outvoted," she told them. Turning serious, she added, "I'll be okay if you do that. Y'all know *that*, right?"

Sophie picked up the black shawl someone had found in their mother's closet. "We understand we have that right, but it would be nice to have your blessing since you're our big sister."

Bella reached for Amy's hand. "What's holding you back, Amy? Do you hate the farm so much that you'd really sell it just to make yourself feel better?"

Amy looked from one to the other. "I don't know. I thought I hated it. But . . . I remember the good times, too. This dress, like everything else around here, has brought it all back. Mama wore this to a Christmas party not long before Tuck left for the last time."

Bella touched Amy's upswept hair and tugged a few curls loose to cascade down her neck. "Don't let the memories from the past ruin the dreams of the future. Mom wants us to be happy. Go and be happy with Dan, even if it's just for a couple of hours. Let this dress be your beacon, not your albatross."

Amy plopped down on the bed, the full skirt cascading out around her like a big red heart. "I'm scared. Dan . . . *does things* to me."

"Makes your heart beat faster?" Bella asked with a knowing smile.

"Makes you smile a lot," Jo-Jo added, her gaze dreamy.

"Makes you want to settle down and cuddle up," Sophie supplied to finish things off. "We all know the feeling."

"Yes," she finally admitted. "But I loved Tim. I'm not sure I'm ready to take a risk like that again. It's crazy."

"Not so crazy," Jo-Jo said. "I think this Christmas together is meant to be. God brought us together here where we grew up for a reason."

"For four hunky reasons," Bella said, the levity of her comment making them all laugh.

"For all the *best* reasons," Jo-Jo added. "We belong here."

"I don't know," Amy said. "But . . . I do know I want to see Dan today and get to know him better. Timothy—"

"Will be fine," Sophie said. "He's with the guys, having the time of his life. He won't even miss you."

Amy stood and straightened her shiny skirt. "Thank you. All of you."

"Group hug," Bella called.

They all huddled around Amy, making her feel warm and loved, protecting her in a way she'd long ago forgotten possible while they whispered a prayer asking God to guide all of them.

When her sisters broke free, she looked in the mirror one more time. "Okay. Today, I decide one way or another. Just to get you all off my back, if nothing else."

"And then we celebrate Christmas together," Joanna whispered. "No matter what."

"No matter what," she replied.

No matter how I feel about Dan Wentworth.

Dan couldn't stop staring at her.

"You look amazing," he said after he helped Amy into his Escalade. He'd practically had to lift her, but in typical Amy fashion, she'd brushed him off and held tight to the convenient handle over the passenger-side window, hopping right up onto the big leather seat.

She'd smiled at him, her hair trying to escape the intricate clamp holding it in a luscious pile on top of her head.

"I don't wear dresses much," she admitted after they were on the road.

Outside, snow clouds gathered to the west, but the SUV's heater blasted soft, warm air all around them.

"You should," he said, still in awe, not sure what was going on with his heart.

They talked about a lot of things on the way to the open house, but Dan purposely didn't mention the horse farm or how much he hoped she'd talked her sisters into selling. Today was not about that. Unusual for him to not talk about work, but then being around Amy and her family had changed him. He enjoyed the chance to get to know her while they chatted, and he tried to be honest with her about the life he'd had, growing up a Wentworth.

When they pulled up to his parents' house, Dan turned toward Amy. "Don't let them intimidate you, okay? They're really nice people."

She giggled at that. "This coming from their son. Are you always this polite?"

"No," he admitted. "I'm nervous, but only because my mom and sister are going to flip when they see you."

She touched her hair, panic in her eyes. "Why? Do I look frumpy? Old-fashioned?"

Dan fell for her in that instant, completely. He took her hand and leaned across the seat. "No, darlin'. You look so beautiful, they're gonna want to keep you." Then he gave her a quick kiss on the cheek. "Just be you, Amy."

"I hadn't planned on being anyone else," she said, relief in her eyes. "And . . . I can't wait to see this place."

The estate was huge. Made of aged bricks and arched stone and wood entryways, the house shone with discreet decorations. The rounded front door, made of dark, heavy wood, was topped by an elegant stone balustrade. Inside, similar arched, wooden doorways graced the open foyer, and a curved staircase laced with intricate, black wrought iron held a garland of fresh evergreens and red ribbons. An enormous Christmas tree decorated with exotic ornaments and Kentucky charm stood in the marble entryway and shot up toward the stair railing. In the den, floor-to-ceiling windows gave a stunning view of the rolling hills and pastures.

Amy couldn't stop gawking. "Dan, this place is the real deal."

Dan grinned at her. "It's home. It's been updated and fancied up over the years, but the bones are solid. Underneath all this, it's just home."

Amy thought about the farm and wondered how someone like Dan went from this to what he'd seen at their place. No wonder he wanted to level it. Before she could fret too much about that, Dan's family swooped in and made her feel completely welcome. His mother, Bettye, petite and blonde, and his sister, Rachel, with brown hair highlighted in gold like Dan's and hazel eyes like their father's, handed her food and drink.

Then Mr. Wentworth, gray-haired and debonair, smiled and talked politely to her. "Dan rarely brings home a date," he said. "It's so nice to see him with such a lovely woman."

"We'll talk later," Rachel said before taking off to corral one of her preschoolers.

"Your dad asked me about our land," Amy told Dan later when they decided to go for a walk around the property. He'd supplied her with a heavy coat borrowed—or stolen—from his sister and said he wanted her to see something.

"And what did you tell him?"

"I didn't know what to tell him," she admitted. "I said my sisters and I are going to decide after Christmas. I got the impression he doesn't know they've done a one-eighty on this."

"I haven't discussed it with him," Dan said, holding her elbow to keep her steady on the rocky trail that worked its way between two fenced horse pastures. "He'll know when I do."

Deciding to let that go since Dan had hinted at some contention between him and his father, Amy enjoyed the chilly, fresh air.

They walked to the massive barn, and Dan showed her his gelding, Rudolph. "Because of his red nose," he explained while she offered a treat to the big roan with the distinctive red marking.

As they rounded a curve, Dan stopped her and tugged her close. "I wanted you to see this."

Amy took in the site of an old, hand-hewed, two-storied cabin set along a flowing creek, its deep front porch complete with two aged, wooden rocking chairs. A simple evergreen wreath hung on the heavy door, and a small cedar tree standing between the two rockers was decorated with what looked like hand-carved, wooden ornaments. A giant live oak stood near the cabin, its massive branches lifting out like a canopy over the house.

"This has been in my family for generations," he said. "It was my first renovation. I had to hire some experts to find matching logs to get it back to its original glory, but it's perfect now. It has modern conveniences but historical essence."

"It's beautiful," Amy said, her heart opening when she heard the pride in his words. He might build opulent homes for other people, but his heart was clearly right here. Simple and timeless and steeped in history. "It's so . . . *Dan*."

"I've never brought a woman here," he said. "Buddies, friends and family, but never . . . someone special. My ex-wife didn't like me working on this on weekends."

Amy stared at the cabin and then looked at him, the tears she'd so long fought off coming to the surface. "I didn't know I was special."

"And that's what makes you special," he said.

Then he leaned down and kissed her on the cheek. Amy loved the way his lips felt on her skin. Dan was gentle and sure, and he made her feel safe. As his strength and confidence merged with her stubborn, steely resolve, Amy realized that she trusted Dan. She trusted him without any more doubt. She trusted him enough to cry in his arms and tell him how much she missed her daddy. And she trusted him enough to wonder out loud what she should do next.

"For now, come inside out of the cold," Dan said, leading her to the cabin door.

CHAPTER TEN

They entered the cabin and Dan gave Amy a quick tour. Everything from the old-fashioned kitchen with lacy, white curtains to the quaint bathroom to the iron headboards on the quilt-laden beds made this place a peaceful getaway.

"My mom and sister helped me decorate it for Christmas," he said. "For you, really."

"You decorated this for me?" Amy asked, touched to her core.

"They didn't know that, but yes. I wanted to impress you. I learned how to make real hot chocolate, too."

"Why?"

"Why wouldn't I?"

He'd started a fire and now it crackled to life. Coming to sit beside her on the tufted sofa, he put down his mug and touched her hair. "You and me, we've got this thing going on."

"This thing?" She smiled. "Is this *thing* kind of like the thing you invited me to today so you could get me here alone? Is that the thing you're talking about?"

"You know it." He kissed her forehead.

"And this has nothing to do with you hoping I'll talk my entire family into selling you our land?"

He pulled back. "Is that what you think?"

"It crossed my mind."

Dan straightened and placed his hands together. "Before you got here, I hoped you'd convince your sisters. Maybe even a little bit after you got here. But . . . Amy, I don't care about that anymore."

Amy wondered if it even mattered whether he was using her or not. He was a man trying to do what he was good at—create amazing places for people to live and raise their families. Places with roots, like this cabin, like the horse farm where she and her sisters had grown up.

"Look, I lost my first wife because I was so busy trying to prove myself to my old man," he said. "I won't go through that again. Building houses is one thing. Living in a solid home is another. Having you in my life is so much more important than having the Tucker land. And that's where I'm at right now. Here with you."

Amy accepted that as the truth. She could see the sincerity in his eyes.

When they started back to the main house, snow as light as spun silk began to fall.

"I'd better get you back home or you'll be forced to spend the night here with my family."

"I could handle that," she said. "I'm not so sure you could, however."

"My mom and sister are dying to get you alone and quiz you about our relationship," he admitted. "It's terrifying."

When they got back to the house, Dan left her to put away the borrowed coat. Most of the guests were gone, so Dan's father came to stand with her by the fireplace. "So I hear you're willing to sell my son *your* acreage. Did you two seal the deal on that walk?"

"Not yet," she said, wishing he hadn't put her on the spot. "We'll let that rest until after Christmas."

Mr. Wentworth leaned close. "Dan did mention the possibility of buying just one share if all of you aren't on board. After all, one sister with seventy-five acres is better than no acreage at all." Then he took her hand. "It was a pleasure meeting you, Amy."

The heat of a burning blush, coupled with the fireplace behind her, made Amy feel a little ill. She'd misunderstood what Mr. Wentworth was implying. Seventy-five acres? If she decided to sell her part—something that had never entered her mind—she could take the money and run.

And Dan would have something he'd set out to get. Enough land to build at least five estate houses.

One sister was all he needed.

And she'd played right into his hands.

She'd been quiet all the way home. Dan wondered if he'd gone too far, taking Amy to see the cabin, telling her he cared about her. Maybe she wasn't ready, being a widow and all.

"Did I blow it today?" he finally asked when they were almost to the turnoff to their old horse farm. The snow fell in hushed flakes, but the roads remained clear.

"I don't know," she finally said. "You tell me. Do you want my seventy-five acres so badly that you're willing to act like I'm special to you?"

"What?" Dan pulled off onto the long drive to her house but stopped the SUV. "What are you talking about?"

She opened the door to get out. "You planned this all along, didn't you? You decided if you can't convince all four sisters, go for the one who needs this more than the others. The pathetic widow who doesn't care about this place anyway, right?"

Dan's heart fell like a chunk of plaster and seemed to shatter at that moment. "Amy, I told you how I feel. Why would you think I'm lying to you?"

"I want to know the truth. Your father seems to think you cut a deal with me for my share today. Where would he get that notion?"

Dan closed his eyes. He'd mentioned that to his dad long before he'd met Amy. But before he could explain, she hopped out and started walking.

Dan cranked the Escalade and followed her. "Amy, get back in here so we can talk!"

"No. You can leave now. I'm not selling."

Frustrated, Dan finally ditched his vehicle and got out. By the time they'd made it to the front yard, snow covered both of them, and she shivered in her light wrap.

He took off his jacket and tugged it around her. "Your pretty dress will be ruined."

She pushed the jacket away. "It won't be the first time something I love gets ruined."

And then she burst into tears and ran into the house.

Amy cried most of the night. All the angst she'd held so tightly inside came pouring out. Her sisters and Sarah tried to console her, tried to understand what had happened, but she couldn't talk about it. So she held an old Bible tightly to her chest, hoping to absorb some peace.

She sobbed for her parents and the time they'd wasted . . . and then she cried for Tim and the love they'd shared. The others kept Timothy occupied, but late in the night, she heard a timid knock on her door.

"Go away."

"Mommy, it's me. I need to talk to you."

He opened the bedroom door before she could pull herself together. Amy sat up in bed and tried to smile. "What are you doing up so late?"

"I know you've been sad, and I wanted to sit with you the way you sit with me when I'm sad."

Amy couldn't speak, but she willed herself to try. "That's so nice. C'mon then." She patted the bedspread and he hopped up to stare over at her. "What do you want to talk about?"

"My grandpa," Timothy replied. "The one you never mention."

On Christmas Eve, all was quiet at the farm and no one had seen Dan Wentworth all week.

Amy told her sisters what had happened. "I think he wanted my share all along. He was so smart about things. He never once mentioned that he'd be willing to buy one share. But I know now that's what he was trying to do."

"Then why didn't he just come out and say that?" Sophie asked. "He had you right there, all cozy in that cabin."

"I don't know," she admitted. "I think he was waiting until the very last minute."

Until he had me hooked.

"Do you love the man?" Miss Sarah asked, sympathy in her eyes.

"I thought I was falling for him," Amy replied. "But—"

Bella ran into the great room from the kitchen. "Dan's here."

Everyone scattered, leaving Amy to stomp toward the door, flinging it open before he could knock.

"I'm not selling," she said, about to close the door in his good-looking, sad, hopeful face.

But his hand on the door and his boot on the jamb stopped her. "I have a plan, and you need to hear me out," he said. "Because I'm not leaving until you do."

Amy stepped outside and closed the door behind her. "What are you trying to do?"

"Keep you," he said, his eyes bright with humility and hope. "But I need everyone here, so I can explain this. Please, Amy."

Amy wanted to send him away, but her traitorous heart told her to listen.

Just listen.

She hadn't listened when her daddy needed her, and she regretted that. Dan had taken her to the cabin, and he'd made her feel so wonderful. Surely, there had to be more between them than just this expensive dirt underneath their feet.

Be still and know.

"You have about fifteen minutes," she said, opening the door.

"I only need ten," Dan said from behind her.

"I'll get everybody together."

⌒

Dan prayed this would work. He didn't want to lose Amy. And he couldn't help feeling like his plan was more than a little brilliant. Now to convince the family.

Amy gathered her sisters and their men in the great room and turned toward Dan.

It looks like I'm on.

"You'd better state your case before Timothy and Miss Sarah get back from the stable," Amy warned.

Dan swallowed. "I think y'all might like what I've come up with."

"We're not selling," Amy replied, her boot tapping on wood.

"You don't have to, but . . . just consider this. How would y'all feel about keeping the main house and ten acres, and—"

"That's selling," Jo-Jo interjected.

"Let me finish." Sweat sizzled underneath Dan's cotton shirt, but he kept right on talking. "You keep the main house as a lodge where guests could come and stay . . . and the additional thirty-five acres to use for your riding academy and rehab center. Then each sister gets ten acres surrounding the central area of the house and the stable to build whatever you each want."

The room went quiet for several moments that seemed frozen in time.

"What about the rest?" Amy asked. "That's just the seventy-five acres you wanted from me. So you'd get two-hundred and twenty-five?"

"Could we take a vote?" Sophie asked, turning to stare at the others.

"Are you serious?" Amy cried, deciding they were all intent on betraying her.

"Listen to the man," Jed said, apparently another traitor in the room. "Together, you'd all have seventy-five acres to do what you want with."

"What *we* want," Jo-Jo clarified.

"What *we* want," Jed repeated with a grin. "Each sister would have plenty of land to build, and the money to do it."

"In the shape of a horseshoe around the back of the property," Dan interjected. "I have it all planned out. The subdivision can start beyond the creek and the tree line to the south. There's another pretty stream located down there, and I can reroute it through all the properties. You won't even know there are any houses around you."

Amy glared at her sisters. "What do I care? I'll be gone."

Dan's heart crumples at her remark. Dejected, he was oh-so weary from staying up all night devising this plan.

The sisters huddled with their men, Amy the odd one out, but she listened and finally nodded before turning back to Dan, bringing his hope back to life.

"We split it—half and half," she said. "We keep a hundred and fifty acres, and you can buy the rest of the property located on the other side of the creek bed near the stream. That means we'd have thirty acres for the main house and stable, and thirty acres each to build on or . . . do whatever we choose."

He let out a sigh and wiped at his brow. This next part was why he was really here, and he steeled himself for her reaction.

"I can only agree to that under one condition."

Amy marched toward him. "Take it or leave it, Dan Wentworth. I just want you out of my hair."

"You don't mean that," Dan said, opening his heart for all to see. "And I can't do that . . . unless you stay here with your thirty acres. I want *you*, Amy. I'm doing this for you. And for Timothy. And for the house I want to build for us on that ten . . . I mean . . . *thirty* acres."

Bella stood. "So you'd buy half our land, and we'd get the rest. I like the idea of a lodge here that we could all run together."

Jo-Jo beamed, turning to Jed as she thought aloud. "Each of us has something to offer a venture like that, don't we? I mean, Sarah and Amy can run the nuts and bolts of the lodge, like a big B&B. Bella can do the PR and promotion to let the world know we're here. And while Jed continues to manage the place on a grand scale, I could work with him to run the rescue and rehab end of the stable." After a moment's thought, she gasped. "Oh! And Soph, you can start that equine vet practice you've been dreaming about and run it right out of a new clinic and paddock and still build a house for you. It's like a bunch of puzzle pieces that suddenly fit together. Like it's all just . . . *meant to be!*"

Dan fought off the inappropriate urge to hug the stuffing straight out of Jo-Jo. Her innocent, baby-of-the-group sensibilities thrilled him to no end. If only Amy could catch her creative vision.

"I do like the idea of each of us having our own acreage around the lodge," Bella said. "I think I can live with that."

They all nodded in agreement and turned toward Amy in unison.

"What do you think?" Dan asked, reaching for her hand. "I'm guessing you're thinking about . . . building a house with me and Timothy . . . and how you'd be near your sisters, but not in this house where all the memories still live. And you're thinking we'll make new, happy memories. We'll be a family, *surrounded* by family."

"Wow," Bella exclaimed, beaming at Amy. "Sis?"

Amy stared at Dan with misty eyes. "I . . . uh . . . I don't know."

"Amy," Sophie said. "Take the deal. It works for everyone. We can use the money to fix up this place. At last, it will come alive again."

"You can call the place *Leatherneck Farms*," Jed said with a grin. "Your daddy would like that. He used to say this place was just an old leatherneck, same as him. Tough and solid, but in desperate need of some tender-loving care."

Silent tears streamed down Amy's face. "I can't fight all of you."

She reached for Dan's hand, but he scooped her into his arms and kissed her tears, and then he held her head with both hands. "Best deal I've ever brokered. I'm not letting you get away."

Later that night, Amy stood by her daddy's old leather chair, one hand touching the soft grain. "I'm home, Daddy," she murmured. "I'm finally home."

Dan stepped next to her and kissed her on the cheek. "We've got a lot of unfinished business, you and me."

"I know," Amy said. "I know."

Outside, snow covered the land in a white blanket that made Amy feel warm and safe and cozy.

And loved. *So loved.*

The front door whooshed open and Jo-Jo appeared, a broad grin plastered across her face. "Jed will drive the sleigh up the hill in just a few minutes. Is Timothy ready? He's going to love this."

Before Amy could reply, the long-familiar *jing-jing-jing* of the sleigh bells of their childhood sounded from the front of the house. Her heart soared as she rushed toward the open door and placed an arm around Jo-Jo's shoulder.

"Remember what Tuck used to say?" she asked her younger sister.

"Every time the sleigh bells ring—" Jo-Jo began, and Amy chimed in to finish it with her. "—one of my girls gets their wish."

The two of them laughed at the memory.

"I guess it works. All my wishes are coming true," Jo-Jo said.

Meet the authors online!

Sandra D. Bricker

    Website: sandradbricker.com

    Facebook: facebook.com/SandraDBricker

    Twitter: twitter.com/SandieBricker

    Pinterest: pinterest.com/sandradbricker

Lynette Sowell

    Website: lynettesowell.blogspot.com

    Facebook: facebook.com/lynettesowellauthor

    Twitter: twitter.com/LynetteSowell

    Pinterest: pinterest.com/lynettesowell

Barbara J. Scott

    Website: www.barbarajscott.com

    Facebook: facebook.com/BarbaraJScott01

    Twitter: twitter.com/BarbaraScott01

    Pinterest: pinterest.com/barbarajscott01

Lenora Worth

    Website: lenoraworth.com

    Facebook: facebook.com/lenoraworthbooks

    Twitter: twitter.com/elnoraw

    Pinterest: pinterest.com/lenoraworth

    Blogs: Inspiredbylifeandfiction.com

    craftieladiesofromance.blogspot.com

FOUR HISTORICAL
NOVELLAS

Cowboy Christmas Homecoming

Mary Connealy,
Ruth Logan Herne,
Julie Lessman,
Anna Schmidt

Glad tidings, hearts binding.

To curl up with your own copy,
order from fine retailers today.